WINTER TURNS TO SPRING

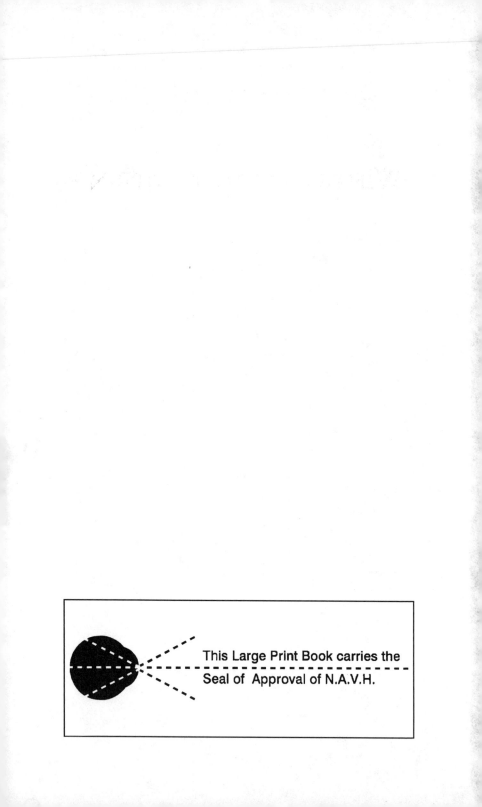

This Large Print Book carries the
Seal of Approval of N.A.V.H.

FOUR SEASONS

WINTER TURNS
TO SPRING

CATHERINE PALMER &
GARY CHAPMAN

THORNDIKE PRESS
A part of Gale, Cengage Learning

GALE
CENGAGE Learning

Detroit • New York • San Francisco • New Haven, Conn • Waterville, Maine • London

GALE
CENGAGE Learning

Thorndike Press® Large Print Christian Fiction.
The text of this Large Print edition is unabridged.
Other aspects of the book may vary from the original edition.
Set in 16 pt. Plantin.
Printed on permanent paper.

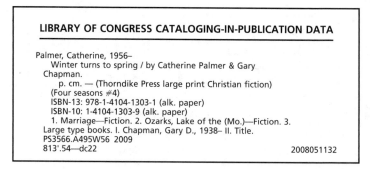

LIBRARY OF CONGRESS CATALOGING-IN-PUBLICATION DATA

Palmer, Catherine, 1956–
    Winter turns to spring / by Catherine Palmer & Gary
Chapman.
        p. cm. — (Thorndike Press large print Christian fiction)
    (Four seasons #4)
    ISBN-13: 978-1-4104-1303-1 (alk. paper)
    ISBN-10: 1-4104-1303-9 (alk. paper)
    1. Marriage—Fiction. 2. Ozarks, Lake of the (Mo.)—Fiction. 3.
Large type books. I. Chapman, Gary D., 1938– II. Title.
PS3566.A495W56 2009
813'.54—dc22   2008051132

Published in 2009 by arrangement with Tyndale House Publishers, Inc.

Printed in the United States of America
1 2 3 4 5 6 7 13 12 11 10 09

FOR TIM, WITH LOVE
C.P.

New love is the brightest,
and long love is the greatest;
but revived love is
the tenderest thing known upon earth.

THOMAS HARDY

NOTE TO READERS

There's nothing like a good story! I'm excited to be working with Catherine Palmer on a fiction series based on the concepts in my book *The Four Seasons of Marriage.* You hold in your hands the fourth and final book in this series.

My experience, both in my own marriage and in counseling couples for more than thirty years, suggests that marriages are always moving from one season to another. Sometimes we find ourselves in winter — discouraged, detached, and dissatisfied; other times we experience springtime, with its openness, hope, and anticipation. On still other occasions we bask in the warmth of summer — comfortable, relaxed, enjoying life. And then comes fall with its uncertainty, negligence, and apprehension. The cycle repeats itself many times throughout the life of a marriage, just as the seasons repeat themselves in nature. These concepts are described in *The Four Seasons of Marriage,* along with seven proven strategies to help couples move away from the unsettledness of fall or the alienation and coldness of winter toward the hopefulness of spring or the warmth and closeness of summer.

Combining what I've learned in my counseling practice with Catherine's excellent writing skills has led to this series of four novels. In the lives of the characters you'll meet in these pages, you will see the choices I have observed people making over and over again through the years, the value of caring friends and neighbors, and the hope of marriages moving to a new and more pleasant season.

In *Winter Turns to Spring* and the other stories in the Four Seasons fiction series, you will meet newlyweds, blended families, couples who are deep in the throes of empty-nest adjustment, and senior couples. Our hope is that you will see yourself or someone you know in these characters. If you are hurting, this book can give you hope — and some ideas for making things better. Be sure to check out the discussion questions at the end of the book for further ideas.

And whatever season you're in, I know you'll enjoy the people and the stories in

Deepwater Cove.

Gary D. Chapman, PhD

ACKNOWLEDGMENTS

So many people affect the writing and publication of a novel. I wish to publicly express my deep appreciation for Dr. Gary Chapman. His God-given wisdom and his amazing books have enriched both my writing and my personal life beyond measure. I'm so grateful to have been given this opportunity to partner with a true gentleman, a man who reveals his commitment to God in all he does.

For sharing both laughter and tears, my longtime friends are treasures I cherish. Janice, Mary, Sharon, Roxie, Kristie, BB, and Lucia, I love you. My prayer support team holds me up before God, and I can't thank you enough, Mary, Andrew, Nina, and Marilyn.

I also thank my Tyndale family for all you have meant to me during these past ten years. Ron Beers and Karen Watson, bless you for making this series a reality. Kathy

Olson, I can't imagine having the courage to write a single word without you. Your careful editing and precious friendship are truly gifts from the Lord. Thanks from the bottom of my heart to Andrea and Babette in marketing, along with the public relations department, the amazing sales team, and the wonderful design department.

Though I often leave them for last, first on my list of supporters, encouragers, and loved ones are my family. Tim, Geoffrey, and Andrei, I love you so much.

Catherine Palmer

CHAPTER ONE

Brad Hanes walked across the parking lot toward Larry's Lake Lounge with one goal in mind — and she would be sitting at the far end of the bar. Yvonne Ratcliff, the tavern's entertainer, had a rich, earthy voice that welled out, filled the crowded, smoky room, and strummed every sinew of Brad's body.

Aware that his wife wasn't fond of Yvonne — or the other regulars at Larry's — he had debated letting his coworkers from the construction site go on without him. In December, the water's surface at Lake of the Ozarks reflected the ice-gray sky. The wind whipping across the town of Tranquility bit right through his denim jacket. It wouldn't be a good night to stay out late, Brad knew. Still, nothing sounded better than a few brews, some laughs with his friends, and a couple of hours shooting pool while listening to music.

"You sure Ashley won't mind us hanging out at Larry's for a while?" Mack Lang, another member of the construction crew, ambled alongside Brad. "My number-two ex wanted me home for dinner at six every night on the dot. She about suffocated me with all her rules and regulations."

"Nah." Brad shook his head. "Ashley's probably not even at the house. She started that sideline business selling necklaces, remember?"

"Them homemade beads?"

"Yeah, and with Christmas just around the corner, she's working day and night to fill orders."

"Still clocking in at the country club, too?"

"Sure. Ashley's not giving up that job." As he and his friend neared the tavern, Brad reflected on his wife — her black-and-white waitress outfit clean and pressed, her long red hair wound up in a bun, and her pale neck stacked with beaded necklaces she'd made.

Ashley would know her husband planned to go to Larry's this evening, though she'd asked him a hundred times to steer clear of the place. She complained that Brad drank too much, came home smelling like a dirty ashtray, and always went off to work the next day with a headache. Some of what

16

she said was true, though he argued that he didn't see anything wrong with having a few beers with his friends.

"She probably wouldn't even notice if I did come home," Brad said, a surge of frustration filling his chest. "I'm a plain guy, you know. I don't ask much of a wife — a clean house, the laundry done, and three squares. With the necklace production going full steam, Ashley can hardly stay focused enough to tie her own shoes. She never fixes my supper anymore. I have to scrounge up a can of soup or a box of macaroni. Pretty pitiful after a long day building condos in the middle of a Missouri winter."

"Welcome to the club," Mack said. "I hated marriage, but I hate being a bachelor, too. I guess you'll have to find your fun wherever you can. Speaking of which . . . sounds like Yvonne is on stage."

Brad tried not to react to the comment, undoubtedly a reference to the growing attraction between himself and the singer. He hadn't realized it was so obvious.

Yvonne — or *Why-vonne,* as she pronounced it — had a beautiful voice, and she was easy on the eyes, too. She had a kid, she'd told Brad, but childbearing hadn't hurt her figure any. With her long brown hair, black-rimmed green eyes, and skintight jeans, she could do things with her voice that kept every male eye in the place riveted.

But Yvonne's focus was always on Brad. Every song she belted out was aimed straight at him, and when she took her usual place at the end of the bar, he couldn't do anything but amble over and buy her a drink or two.

Reaching for the door, Brad heard Yvonne launch into a familiar song about the joys of being a redneck woman. But as he pulled on the handle, another sound sent shivers up his back. The high-pitched wail began as a sharp *"Yow!"* and then ebbed into a pathetic *"wow, wow, wow."* Brad turned toward the noise, and it started again.

"Yow! Wow, wow, wow." After a moment, the sequence ended with a softly muttered *"ow."*

"What in the — ?" Brad took off his ball cap and scratched his forehead as he studied the rapidly filling parking lot.

"Sounds like a baby crying," Mack said as the two men took tentative steps in the direction of the wails.

"No way. Who would leave a kid out in this cold? Things like that happen in big cities, not here."

"Yi! Why, why, why, why?" the voice howled.

"Nee-ow-rah. Boo-rah-rah."

"Hey!" Brad called out. "Who's there?"

Though it was only a little after five in the afternoon, the light was so dim he could hardly see. He dropped his cap onto his head again and adjusted the brim.

"Lookit." Mack elbowed him. "Over there."

At the corner of the brick wall that edged Larry's Lake Lounge sat a cardboard box. And it was moving.

Colder than the evening breeze, a chill zipped down Brad's spine. He and Mack neared the box. Brad noted blue and red lettering that indicated it once had held beer cans. As he peered inside, a pair of large brown eyes looked up at him.

"Wow!" The tiny mouth displayed two rows of sharp white teeth as it cut the air with a piercing *"Woe, woe, woe!"*

"Holy moley," Mack said. "It's some kind of critter."

Relief flooding his chest, Brad hunkered down beside the box. "What are you any-how?" he asked the lump of dusty gray fur. "You a raccoon? Or a kitten? You're putting up a mighty big fuss; that's for sure."

"Don't touch it," Mack warned. "You could get bit and die of rabies."

"Yi! Yi! Yi!" The creature tried to turn

19

around, bumped into the side of the box, and then lifted its head to howl. *"A-woo! Oooo! Yow, yow, yow."*

"Rabies," Brad muttered. He reached into the box and slipped his hand under the soft, downy belly. Cupping the animal, he made a cursory examination. Ears, eyes, tail, snout, fuzzy legs, and four paws.

"It's a puppy," he pronounced. "And the talkingest one I've ever met."

"Yawp." The little head darted forward and a small pink tongue licked Brad's nose.

"Agh, not that!" Brad wiped away the moisture with the back of his hand. He flipped the puppy over and determined he was holding a male. "Who left you here, fella? You must be freezing."

"Brother," Mack said in disgust. "You gotta be some kind of jerk to dump a puppy in weather like this."

Brad knew that Missouri country folks often didn't have the means to get their pets fixed. That meant thousands of mixed-breed, unwanted puppies and kittens were abandoned on the roadside each year. Animal shelters and city pounds usually picked them up, but many starved, were killed by larger predators, or got hit by cars.

"At least they put him near a public place," Brad observed. "I guess they figured he'd find a home."

"He ain't finding a home with me."

"Me neither."

The jukebox started up inside the tavern. Yvonne must have finished her song set and would be taking her usual place at the bar. Married nearly a year now, Brad knew he shouldn't give the woman a second thought. The sultry songbird was older than Brad by several years, and she had been around the block a few times. She told him she had tried to make it in the Nashville music scene but found the going too rough. She had sung backup at one of the big shows in Branson for a while too. But eventually she came home to the lake area — single, sexy, and looking for a good time. That siren call was getting harder to resist by the day.

"Wow!" The sharp yelp startled Brad. The pup had curled up in the crook of his elbow. *"Ick, ick, ick."*

"What are you talking about now, you little yapper?" Brad murmured as he stroked the matted fur. Pressing his small head against the man's palm, the dog expressed his delight in human touch. Brad grinned. "What do you want, boy? Huh?"

"Uh-oh," Mack said. "You're starting to sound like a sucker."

"I'm not taking him home. But still . . . he

21

can't be more than a couple of months old."

"I bet he's barely off his mama's milk. We had dogs when I was growing up. You shouldn't take 'em from the mother too soon."

"I always wanted a dog. My dad ran off strays with a shotgun."

Though the puppy appealed to some tender place inside him, Brad knew things were going so badly with Ashley that it would be a mistake to arrive home with a puppy. She'd probably pack up her beads and run back to mama and daddy. Which might be a good idea after all.

Brad wasn't looking for a relationship with Yvonne or any of the other attractive young women who made Larry's their regular watering hole. He didn't want Ashley to leave him, either. But how long could two people go on this way? Chilly silence interspersed with arguments. Blame. Name-calling. Accusations.

Sex was a rare occurrence in the marriage too, and that didn't sit well with Brad. Before their wedding, Ashley couldn't get enough of him — and vice versa. Lately, they hardly had time for a kiss. With him working days and her working nights, they were rarely even in bed at the same time. You couldn't expect a twenty-two-year-old

22

man in the prime of life to forgo that kind of pleasure. Pleasure? No, it was a *need.*

"Brrrp . . . brrrp . . ."

Brad glanced down to find that the puppy was snoring softly. "Great. He went to sleep."

"What did you expect? Probably been out here freezing most of the day." Mack gave a snort. "Might as well take him home. You know you want to."

"I don't want a dog. But how can I put him back in that cardboard box? We'll walk out of Larry's in a couple of hours and find him frozen stiff."

Brad couldn't imagine abandoning the dog to the ice-cold air and stepping into the warmth of the bar without wearing guilt like a chain around his neck. He wanted to head inside, settle down next to Yvonne, and smell that perfume she wore. She'd start flirting with him, and he'd buy her a few drinks. Then she would saunter back onto the stage and sing to him until he was so woozy with beer and temptation he could hardly stumble to his car.

He had a feeling it wouldn't be long before he gave in. *Why-vonne the Con,* most of the men called the sensuous songstress. It was no secret that Yvonne used her looks and her wiles to get what she wanted out of a man. But at this point, Brad hardly cared. He wanted the same thing. A little fun. No strings. No expectations. No responsibilities. It all sounded good to him.

"Brrrp . . . brrrp . . . brrrp."

His hand on the puppy's head, Brad studied the front of Larry's. Three or four couples had gone inside since he first picked up the pup.

"Someone else will find the dog and take it home," Brad told his friend. "We're not responsible for the mangy little mutt. Come on."

Without allowing himself time to think, he set the puppy back inside the box and yanked open Larry's front door.

"Yow!" The terrified shriek tore through Brad's brain and went straight to his heart. *"Yow-wow, yow-wow! Owoooooo!"*

With a muttered curse, Brad bent over, scooped up the dog, tucked it under his jacket, and headed for his car. He could hear Mack laughing behind him.

"Sucker!" his friend called. "I'll tell Yvonne hi for you!"

Gritting his teeth, Brad opened his car door. This was a mistake. A big, big mistake. He and Ashley didn't have room for a dog in their small house. They didn't have a fenced yard. No one could look after the puppy while they were at work. The whole thing was a very bad idea.

He plopped the puppy onto the passenger's seat. Maybe someone in the neighborhood would take the animal. He slid in and started the motor. Jaw tight, he drove out of the parking lot and onto the short stretch of road that led down to Deepwater Cove. This was not what he wanted to be doing. Maybe Ashley was right and he shouldn't spend so much time around Yvonne and the other bar patrons, but why should he have to go home and watch TV alone all night?

The pressure of four paws warmed his thigh, and Brad looked down to find the puppy settling comfortably on his lap. *No,* he thought. He didn't want a dog. Or a wife, a home, a job, a steady paycheck.

At one time, those things had seemed like impossibly lofty goals. His chaotic childhood had made such dreams seem unattainable. But he had found Ashley, won her heart, bought a house, married the woman he loved, and settled into his work and a life he had expected to be wonderful.

It wasn't.

Now things were coming apart fast, and he shouldn't be taking home a dog. The mutt would require a long-term commit-

25

ment, and that was exactly what Brad had been wanting to escape.

"Brrrp . . . brrrp . . . brrrp . . ."

The puppy's gentle snoring calmed Brad's nerves as he pulled into the driveway. Leafless branches widened the view during the winter months, and Brad saw moonlight glitter on the lake like dancing fireflies.

The dog barely stirred as Brad climbed out of the car and carried him toward the house. Ashley had left every light on, as usual. The girl blamed him for their money troubles, but the real fault lay at her feet. All those beads. And plastic bags. And boxes. And postage. Did she have any idea how much cash she ran through every month on her little necklace business?

Once inside, Brad saw that the house was pretty much the way he had left it early that morning. Ashley hadn't washed a dish, swept, vacuumed, or even put away the groceries she must have bought during the day. He studied the array of canned vegetables, cake mixes, and jars of spaghetti sauce on the kitchen counter.

Ashley's parents ran a hot dog and ice cream shop in Camdenton, and that was about the only food she knew how to fix. Her friend Esther Moore had been teaching her to cook real food, but Mrs. Moore had passed away at Thanksgiving. Now Brad couldn't even mention the old woman's name without Ashley dissolving into a puddle of tears. And his wife had abandoned all efforts to learn to prepare tasty, hearty meals from scratch.

Still cradling the exhausted puppy, he rooted around in the freezer until he found some turkey casserole left over from who knew when. He heated it in the microwave, placed a small helping on a saucer, filled a bowl with fresh water, and set everything down on the floor.

Without pause, the little critter stepped onto the saucer, waded right into the warm casserole, and began to wolf it down. Unable to keep from laughing, Brad grabbed a fork, seated himself beside the dog, and dug into what was left in the container. Now and then, the dog would look up and wag his tail before returning to his dinner.

That's what's missing around this house, Brad thought. *A little appreciation. A few kind words of affirmation.* The least Ashley could do was thank him for the hours of work he put in every day on the construction site. Besides that, many afternoons he *did* avoid the bar to come home and work with Esther's husband. Charlie Moore and Brad were finishing a new addition to the house and spiffing up the rest of the place. They'd been painting, repairing cracks in the ceiling where the roof had leaked, caulking the bathtub and sinks, and weatherproofing the windows and doors.

At least the puppy noticed what he had been given and was grateful. After a long drink of water, the mutt clambered into Brad's lap and joined him in polishing off the rest of the turkey casserole. Oddly enough, Brad didn't mind the little black snout rooting around the corners of the glass dish.

"We're two of a kind, huh, pal?" he told the dog. "Someone dumped you into a box in the parking lot. And I'm left here night after night in an empty house by the lake. We both got abandoned by people we thought loved us. Stinks, doesn't it?"

The puppy sat down in the empty baking dish and leaned against Brad's chest. "You planning to take another nap? Well, I guess I'll join you. Might as well. Nothing else to do around here."

Brad picked up the dog and set the pan in the sink along with the other empty plates, glasses, and pots. Then he dropped down onto the sofa. After unlacing his work boots, he kicked them off and stretched out on the saggy cushions. The remote control was out of reach, and he considered rising to get it. But the puppy had already made a nest in the crook of Brad's arm.

"Brrrp . . . brrrp . . . brrrp . . ."

Chuckling, Brad wrapped his hands around the filthy little fur ball and closed his eyes. Ashley would have a fit when she walked into the house sometime after midnight. But at least he wasn't at Larry's. He hadn't even popped open a beer. And he certainly wasn't gazing at Yvonne Ratcliff with thoughts that embarrassed even himself.

Ashley struggled to stay awake as she steered her old, battered Honda along the curving tree-lined highway toward Deepwater Cove. Borrow ditches bordered the two narrow lanes, and she knew how easy it would be to drop a wheel off the pavement and flip the vehicle. Names of three of her classmates from Camdenton High School marked homemade crosses perched on a slope along this path. She didn't want her parents to weep as they decorated a cross with roses and ivy at the place where she had perished.

The thought of death brought Esther Moore to the forefront of Ashley's mind, and she couldn't prevent the tears that spilled down her cheeks. Though two weeks had passed since the stroke that took her friend's life, Ashley still couldn't believe Esther was gone. Oddly, it comforted her to cry inside the warm, silent car where no one could see.

Brad hated his wife's emotional outbursts — of any kind. And rather than comforting her or cuddling her in his arms, as he had at the start of their relationship, he now told her to shake it off. Get over it. Snap out of it. As though recovering from death could ever be that easy.

Sniffling, Ashley turned the car into the Deepwater Cove neighborhood. She'd once been so eager to get home she could hardly keep her foot from pressing too hard on the gas pedal. In her imagination, the little house she and Brad had chosen seemed to sit like a cozy cottage by the lake just waiting for their loving touch. The rooms would wear coats of softly glowing paint. Quaint antiques and pretty curtains would dress them up. Outside, gardens of foxgloves, petunias, and geraniums would welcome guests.

"Piece of junk," she muttered as she parked beside Brad's car in what was once the graveled driveway — now a patch of shriveled weeds. "I hate this house. Leaky windows. Stupid wall heater. Freezing floors. Termites."

The sight of the burrowing pests had been their first indication of trouble. Neither had thought to ask for an inspection before they bought the place. Ridding the house of termites had cost an arm and a leg, and Ashley still got a crawly feeling when she was home alone.

Which she usually was.

Pushing open the front door, she spotted her husband stretched out on the sofa. He'd probably been drinking, as usual. He usually fell asleep on their couch, the TV on and his smelly work boots lying haphazardly on the stained carpet.

Ashley set her purse on the floor near the door and shrugged out of her coat. Tonight her darling husband hadn't even managed to turn on the television. She swallowed, wondering who Brad had been sitting with at Larry's. The few times they went to the bar together, she noted jealous looks from several of the women who frequented the place. The very idea that her husband might take up with one of them nauseated her.

After stepping out of her black work shoes, Ashley padded across the floor toward the kitchen. Though she worked at a restaurant, she was always hungry when she got home. Seeing the pile of dishes in the sink, her heart fell. Didn't Brad understand how busy she was — working like a maniac to get all her necklace orders filled before Christmas as well as laboring nearly forty hours a week at the country club? Couldn't the man lift a finger in the kitchen?

"Brrrp . . . brrrp . . . brrrp . . ."

Ashley paused at the counter bar dividing the kitchen from the living room. That didn't sound like Brad's usual snore. This was deeper and stuffy with congestion. Despite her irritation, she felt an instant stab of worry. What if her husband was sick? In some strange way, she almost wished he would be. Then she could make him some chicken noodle soup and cuddle up with him on the couch. He wouldn't be able to go to Larry's, and they'd be together like in the old days before things turned lousy.

"Brrrp . . . brrrp . . . brrrp . . ."

Concerned, she tiptoed back across the room to where he lay. It was hard to see in the faint moonlight that filtered through the window. Ashley usually left on one light — or more — when she went out. She hated coming home to a dark house. Brad's snoring disturbed her, though it came regularly with each breath.

Kneeling beside the sofa, she leaned over

and turned her ear to his chest.

"Barp?"

At the yelp, something damp, furry, and ratlike moved against her cheek. With a shriek, she tumbled backward onto her heels and hit the floor with a thud.

Brad shot up off the couch.

"What?" he blurted out, his eyes bleary. "What is it?"

"It's *me.*" Ashley reached over and switched on a lamp. "Who did you think it was? What's wrong with you?"

"What's wrong with me? You're the one who's screaming."

"What was that thing?" She shuddered. "There was something lying on you, Brad. I felt it."

"Oh no." He leaped up and began throwing pillows off the couch. "Where'd he go? Come here, boy!"

Ashley got to her feet as Brad worked his way around the living room, looking behind the sofa and lifting the curtain hems off the floor.

"What are you *doing?*" She felt a familiar choking sensation rise in her chest. "Bradley Hanes, how much did you drink tonight?"

Straightening, he looked her in the eye. "I did not drink a single beer. And for your

33

information, there is a puppy hiding some-where in this house, and you had better help me find him."

"A *puppy?*"

"Wow!" The sharp, high-pitched yelp sounded from the kitchen. *"Wow, wow, wow!"*

Spinning around, Ashley barely beat her husband past the bar. As she came to a halt, she spotted a small, shapeless mound of matted, dirty fur seated beside a puddle on the floor. From somewhere beneath the fur, a tail began to wag.

"Aw, man!" Brad pushed past her and scooped up the creature. His voice softened as he stroked the puppy's head. "That's a great way to introduce yourself, you little yapper. What's she gonna think now, huh? She'll boot you right out the front door, and then what will happen to you?"

Ashley stared at her cooing husband, a state of mild shock numbing her senses as he cradled the puppy in one hand and ripped off a length of paper towel with the other. A few quick swipes, a spray of disin-fectant, and that spot of linoleum floor was cleaner than it had been in weeks.

Who is this man?

"You planning to be nice now?" Brad asked the wad of tangled hair. He held it up and pointed its wet black nose toward his face. "You can't mess on the floor, pooch, you hear me? You have to let us know when you want to go outside. Like this."

In his stocking feet, Brad strode into the living room, knelt on the floor, and lifted the puppy's paw to the door. First he demonstrated by scratching the wood himself. Then he put the dog's nails against the door and they practiced a few times.

"See?" he murmured, his cheek pressed against the gray fluff. "That's how you do it. No puddling, piddling, or anything else inside the house. If you can't figure out the rules pretty fast, kiddo, you'll have to go back to the box in the parking lot. You don't want that, do you? I didn't think so. You be a good boy."

So exhausted she felt as if she were dreaming, Ashley watched her husband — muscle-bound former football jock, deeply tanned construction worker, beer-guzzling good-time man — kiss a dog right on the nose.

Looking up at his wife, Brad gave her a lopsided grin.

"What do you think?" he asked, holding out the puppy. "Pretty cute, huh? Is he a keeper?"

Ashley studied the man she had married, the man who had disappointed and failed her in nearly every way possible. Blue eyes soft, he rubbed his hand over the puppy's matted fur.

Was there anything left between them? Anything worth saving?

The dog sighed and settled into the crook of Brad's arm. In a moment, its eyes closed.

"Brrrp . . . brrrp . . . brrrp . . ."

The gentle snore brought the hint of a smile to Ashley's lips. She nodded as she gazed at her husband. "He's a keeper."

CHAPTER TWO

Brad dipped a spoon into the box of chocolate ice cream tucked under his arm like a football. Ashley was undressing — always a favorite activity for him to observe — only now the puppy kept nipping at the legs of her black slacks or snatching a sock and racing around the bedroom with it.

"Stop him!" she said finally, turning on her husband. "I'm too tired for this. You have to lock him in another room. And put down some newspapers, too."

"Lock him up? Are you kidding?" The image of the dog crouched alone in a corner brought back memories of Brad's own childhood punishments — dark closets, his father's belt, a slap across the face. "He doesn't mean anything by it, Ash. He's just playing with you."

"I don't want to play, Brad. I want to go to sleep."

"Yeah, you never want to play anymore. I

37

figured that out months ago."

She shot him a dark look as he set the ice cream box on the dresser and picked up the puppy. "And don't let him lick your spoon like that," she added. "Chocolate is poisonous to dogs."

"You don't think I know how to take care of him, do you?" He put the dog on the floor and sank down onto the edge of their bed. "Admit it."

"Brad, all I'm saying is dogs can die from eating chocolate."

"But you said we could keep him, right?"

"I don't care what you do with him. Just don't let him chew on me. And you'd better give him a bath. Tonight. He's probably got fleas and ticks and worms and who knows what else. You'll need to get him neutered, too, or he'll run all over the neighborhood looking for females. If he digs in someone's yard, they'll be furious. I guess you're planning to foot the vet bill out of your paycheck."

Brad stared at his wife. She was letting down her hair, a cascade of thick red-gold waves that tumbled to her waist. Any other time, he would have been unable to resist throwing his arms around her and easing her onto the bed. . . . But now Ashley wadded up her slacks and hurled them into a plastic basket in the bottom of the closet. Boy, she was in a fine mood.

"If he's *our* dog," Brad said, "we'll pay for him together. That's what married people do, remember?"

"*I'm* not the one who has forgotten he's married. I don't hang out at a bar with my high school buddies all night, staring at girls. I work two jobs so I can pay the bills we owe. The bank already repossessed your truck. What do you want me to do next — sell the junker I've owned since my sophomore year in high school?"

She balled up her shirt and threw it into the closet.

Uncertain how to respond to this tirade against him, Brad studied the puppy. The dog had sunk his tiny teeth into the toe of Brad's sock and was backing up in a mighty effort to tug it off. Though he wanted to grin at the little rascal, Brad knew there was nothing amusing about Ashley's accusations.

After nearly a year of marriage, they still hadn't figured out how to blend their incomes. When they were getting along, they agreed to put everything into one account and pay bills from it. But when they got angry, both decided their own paychecks were private. Money flowed and ebbed at the bank. Mostly ebbed. Credit card charges gradually mounted, and the company kept upping the interest rate while requiring timely payments to avoid hefty late fees. Worst of all, the mortgage check often failed to make it into the mail on time.

"Listen, Ashley, you're the one who's always ordering supplies for your bead business." Brad gave in and let the puppy have his sock. "I don't know why you blame me for all our problems. You've run the credit card up so high we'll never get it down. And you don't give a rip about our utility bills. I came home tonight and found every light in the house blazing like it was Christmas."

"Christmas?"

At that, she bit her lower lip and jerked on her favorite blue-flowered flannel nightgown — a garment he hated with a passion. Without speaking, she turned on her heel and headed for the living room. With a *yawp!* of delight, the puppy scampered after her.

Brad looked down at his one bare foot.

He had no idea what to do. What could a man even say to a woman like this? Ashley was so emotional. If she wasn't laughing, she was crying or angry. Usually he couldn't even begin to figure out why.

"These are the papers you'll need to put down whenever you leave the house," his wife said, reentering the room with a stack of advertising tabloids in one hand and a bowl of water in the other. "And don't you dare let him into the new room. That's the only good thing we have. I don't want that dog chewing it up."

"*That dog?* What are you so mad about, Ashley?" Brad stood and followed her into the bathroom. "You should be happy. I didn't go to Larry's tonight. I didn't look at any woman except my wife — who put on her dumpiest gown just in case I might be feeling a tiny bit of what's left of my desire for her. In fact, I came into an empty house with nothing to eat but some kind of leftover junk out of the freezer. I don't see what I've done that's so awful."

"You *exist,* Bradley Hanes!"

She paused, her back to him, and stiffened. A sob echoed off the tiled walls. With a loud sniffle, she dropped to her knees and set the bowl of water by the sink. Then she began spreading the papers across the floor.

Fighting the anger that roared through his chest at her declaration of disgust for him, Brad saw a tear fall from Ashley's cheek onto the ad sheet. Then another. She leaned her back against the bathroom wall, curled her knees to her chest, and buried her head in her arms. As her shoulders shook, Brad hooked his thumbs into the belt loops of his jeans and stared at her. How had he managed to be so stupid as to *marry* that huddled mass of hair, tears, and ratty old nightgown?

"I'm sorry." The muffled words emerged from Ashley and gradually began to seep into Brad's consciousness. She inhaled deeply. "I'm so sorry, Brad. I shouldn't have said that. I just can't believe our marriage is . . . I can't believe we . . . Oh no! A flea!"

She bolted up off the floor, her index finger and thumb squeezed together. Covering her eyes with her free hand, she held the other out in his direction. "It's a flea! It was on my arm. I don't know what to do with it! Oh, yuck. This is disgusting. Here, take it. Take it, take it!"

He reached for the miniscule pest. The moment Ashley opened her fingers, the flea vanished. Brad looked down to find the puppy staring up at him, tongue hanging out as he panted happily.

"We have to wash the dog," Ashley announced. She bent over the tub and began running warm water. "Pick it up and put it in here. We'll use your shampoo. Ugh, this creeps me out. What if the fleas get everywhere in the house? Pick it up, Brad!"

"*It?*" He looked into her red-rimmed brown eyes. "The dog is a male. And I'm going to bed."

"No, you're not!" She grabbed his shirtsleeve. "Put that puppy in the bathtub, Brad, and I mean it. I hate fleas. I can't stand bugs. I'm going to ask Jay which exterminator they use."

"Who's Jay?" Brad demanded as he lifted the puppy and set him in the tub. "You never mentioned Jay."

"He works at the club. He's in charge of customer relations."

"How old is this guy?" Dread dropped like a stone into the pit of Brad's stomach as he pushed the puppy toward the stream of water running from the faucet. In the time he'd known Ashley, she had never mentioned any men at the country club other than the bartender, the chef, and the busboys — all of whom were too old or too young to attract her interest. Knowing how hard he was fighting his attraction to Yvonne Ratcliff, Brad suddenly realized he ought to keep his eye on his own wife. If he could feel so strongly about —

"Yow!" As the puppy slid under the warm cascade, he let out an ear-shattering yelp, spun around, and began trying to run in the other direction. Tiny claws clattering on the tub's porcelain surface, he made no

progress whatsoever to get away from the water.

"Yow! Wow-wow-wow!" Wailing piteously, he slipped and fell belly-first into the puddle that had collected around the plug. Trying to stagger to his feet again, he clunked his head on the side of the tub.

"Oh, my goodness!" Ashley lifted him out of the water with both hands and gathered him in her arms. "Are you okay? That was a bad bump. Let me see."

Dumbfounded by his wife for the umpteenth time that night, Brad watched as she carefully examined the puppy's furry little head. Finding nothing wrong, she pressed her lips to one floppy ear. The dog licked her cheek, and she giggled.

"Stop that, you silly goober," she murmured. "Now you've got to get into this tub and have a bath. No ifs, ands, or buts. Oh, Brad, I'll bet he's never been washed. Isn't that awful? He looks like he crawled out from under a barn somewhere. I bet he misses his mama and his brothers and sisters. Poor little guy."

Brad knelt beside Ashley as she placed the puppy in the tub again, held him firmly with one hand, and ladled warm water over him with the other. Knowing instinctively what she would want next, Brad squirted a trail of shampoo down the dog's back.

"Help me hold him," Ashley instructed. "He's not going to like this."

Both grasping the squirming pup, they worked the shampoo into a lather. Instantly the foam turned brown as the dirt turned to sludge and began dripping into the tub. Ashley fussed and clucked over the dog while working shampoo through the long hair on his ears and body and down to the end of his tail. Just as she leaned back to take a breath, he gave a mighty shake, splattering the bathroom and its two human inhabitants with muddy suds.

"Oh no!" Ashley squealed, bursting into laughter. "Grab him, Brad. He's getting away."

The muck in the tub giving him traction, the dog was doing his best to leap out. Brad could hardly keep a grip on the slippery ball of bubbles.

"Yarp! Yarp! Yarp!"

"Run some clean water on him," he told Ashley. "I can't hold him."

"He's getting away!" she shrieked as the puppy shook himself again.

She cupped her hands under the running tap water and threw it over the dog.

Brad managed to wrap both hands around the animal's tummy, spreading his fingers as if holding a football. Despite the howling and yowling, he shoved the puppy back into the warm stream and helped Ashley rinse him down.

"He's brown!" she exclaimed. "And here's a white spot on his head. Look at his legs — they're white too. I thought he was gray, didn't you? Let's shampoo him again."

"Again?"

Though Brad considered this a very iffy idea, he cooperated as his wife lathered the puppy one more time. Now the soap foamed up white, and the defeated dog submitted mournfully to his final rinse.

Grabbing a towel, Ashley wrapped the wet puppy and nestled him in her arms. "He's so sweet," she murmured. "Look at his big brown eyes, Brad. Isn't he adorable? And now he smells good too. Poor boy. You're lonely, aren't you? Yes, you are. Just a lonely little baby boy."

Brad perched on the toilet lid. It had to be one or two in the morning. In a few hours, he'd need to shower, drink some coffee, and head off to the condominium complex his employer was building near Sunrise Beach. Bill Walters didn't like the men showing up late, and he had little tolerance for nonsense. The work was steady, it paid well, and he had made some good friends. But other than that, Brad couldn't find much to like about his job. The last thing he needed to be doing was washing a puppy in the middle of the night.

"He's really cute," Ashley said, her own brown eyes turning on her husband. "You found him in a parking lot?"

"Larry's. I was on my way in with Mack when we heard this racket coming out of a cardboard box. The little guy was inside. I couldn't let him freeze."

"Aww." She leaned up and kissed her husband's cheek. "I didn't know you had such a soft spot."

"Hmm." He rested his elbows on his knees.

"What?" she asked.

"Sometimes I'm not sure you know much about me at all, Ash. Seems like we fight most of the time these days. It's as though we're enemies instead of two people who are supposed to be in love. A few minutes ago you said you were mad at me because I exist."

"Don't bring that up, Brad. I said I was sorry. I didn't mean it." She shook her head. "I'm so tired, and the house is a wreck, and we work all the time, and nothing is ever fun anymore. *We* aren't fun. I don't know what happened to us."

"Brrrp . . . brrrp . . . brrrp . . ."

Ashley glanced down at the puppy in her arms and then smiled at Brad. "He's asleep," she whispered. "He must be exhausted. And look at this bathroom. And us."

It was a sight to be seen, Brad had to admit. The white tile walls wore polka dots of brown mud. His shirt was sopping, and he was wearing only one sock. Ashley had the dog bundled up against her chin, but Brad had no doubt her nightgown would be dripping wet.

"I'll rinse the tub," he suggested, "and you find some kind of box for him to sleep in. How's that?"

"I love you, Bradley Hanes," she said, kissing him again. "I love you, and I want everything to be wonderful again for us."

As he swirled clean water around in the tub, Brad shook his head. He did *not* understand his wife. Were all women so emotional, or was it just Ashley? How could she be hateful one minute and then turn lovey-dovey the next? Did she adore her husband for rescuing the puppy? Or did she simply adore the puppy?

Marriage was one big guessing game, Brad had decided. He never knew what he might find when he encountered his wife. She could be weeping over Esther Moore's death, exulting about a large order for necklaces, angry with him for an offense he hadn't realized he'd committed, or laughing because something funny had happened at the country club. And whatever mood she was in spilled right over onto Brad. How could a man ever win?

He knew he shouldn't have brought home the dog. In the long run, the puppy would be trouble. But he had enjoyed seeing Ashley smile again. She was right about one thing. They rarely had fun anymore. All things considered, marriage was the pits.

Standing, he stretched his arms. Every muscle ached. He'd been lifting studs into place all day at the condo site, and his neck and biceps felt as though they'd been hit with a sledgehammer. Too tired to think straight, he brushed his teeth and tugged off his wet shirt. Ashley would be mad at him for not putting it into the dirty clothes pile in their closet, but at this point, he would be lucky to make it to the bed. He dropped his shirt on the bathroom floor along with his jeans and the single sock.

As he pushed open the door to their bedroom, he spotted his wife silhouetted in the moonlight streaming through the window. The damp blue flannel nightgown was gone. She was brushing her long hair, and he could see the outline of her every curve.

"Ash?" His exhaustion suddenly vanishing, Brad stepped up behind his wife and slipped his arms around her waist.

"Thank you for not going to Larry's," she whispered as he brushed his mouth across her lips. "Thank you for saving the puppy from freezing."

"Thank you for taking off that gown."

"I love you, Brad." Turning in his embrace, she ran her hands over his shoulders and began to massage the taut muscles. "I miss you."

"I'm right here, pretty girl," he murmured. "All yours."

With a sigh of pleasure, she slipped onto the bed. Brad stretched out beside her, hardly able to believe that things were transforming so quickly from a nightmare into a dream. As their lips met, he felt something bump against his shoulder.

"Barp?"

At the sound, Brad's breath hung in his chest. But Ashley laughed and curled closer into him.

"I couldn't get the puppy to stay in his box," she said. "You don't mind, do you?"

"Well, I —"

As she began to kiss his neck, Brad re-

50

alized that of course he didn't mind. Not at all.

"I heard Brad and Ashley Hanes got themselves a puppy," Patsy Pringle commented as she began trimming Miranda Finley's short blonde hair. "Some people are saying it's a mutt, but others think it might be a purebred. You're living next door — have you seen it?"

"Oh, all the time. Yappy, they've named him. Appropriate — the dog talks nonstop. I've never heard anything like it. Based on the ears and the vocalizations, I suspect he is part Cavalier King Charles spaniel. There's evidence of a Blenheim spot on his head, which could be significant, but I think I see a trace of border collie and maybe some golden retriever, too. No, I'm sure Yappy has no pedigree. Trust me on that, Patsy. I used to be a regular at the dog shows in St. Louis."

Since moving to the lake area the previous spring, Miranda had become a regular client at Patsy's beauty salon, Just As I Am. After Esther Moore's death, she had thoughtfully requested the weekly Friday afternoon appointment Esther had kept for years. Patsy was grateful. Somehow having a friend in the chair and the assurance of

51

interesting conversation made the hour pass a little easier.

"You've been to dog shows? For fun?" Patsy couldn't imagine such an activity being interesting. Recently she had learned to enjoy attending stock car races with her fiancé. Pete Roberts, owner of the tackle shop next door, was a serious NASCAR fan. Dog shows and car races. To each his own, she supposed.

"I have dear friends who own an adorable bichon frise," Miranda explained. "She won several blue ribbons, and her pups are in high demand. Can you take a little more off the back, Patsy? I'm wearing turtlenecks so often these days. You know how easy it is for the hair to sit in just the wrong place with a high collar like that? I wouldn't wear a turtleneck normally, but I have to spend so much time in and out of the new house that I've started layering. Turtlenecks, sweaters, jackets, coats. It makes everything easier. I can peel them off one at a time when I start to feel warm."

"How are you getting along over there?" Patsy asked. A few weeks back, Miranda had purchased the long-vacant home next to the Haneses' little place. The house had a wonderful view of the lake but not much square footage. Also — though Patsy hated to bring this up — rumor had it the wood framing was riddled with termites, just as Ashley and Brad's house had been. She sincerely hoped Miranda had ordered an inspection.

"To tell you the truth," the older woman said, "the move from St. Louis has been overwhelming. If I didn't have Charlie Moore helping me, I don't know what I'd do. The pest company found termites, you know."

Patsy sucked in a breath. "Really?"

"Of course that dropped the price considerably, but the kitchen and spare.bedroom are nothing but matchsticks. Thank goodness Charlie is such a sweet man. I had asked him earlier if he would mind helping me move furniture. But as it turns out, he's actually rebuilding a large part of the structure of my house. We're adding a bay window to the kitchen so I can put a table there to look out on the lake in the morning. The bedroom is getting a new closet and window frames. I ended up putting all my furnishings and decor in storage until I can safely move in without falling through the floor."

"Gracious sakes." Patsy rubbed some gel on her hands and began to work it through Miranda's hair. "I had no idea the house was that bad. Well, I'm sure it doesn't hurt Charlie to stay busy these days. He must be missing Esther something awful. I can't imagine losing a loved one right in the middle of the holidays. He looked devastated at Thanksgiving, like he was in a daze. I guess he must have been, too. I think we all were."

"I'm not as upset about Esther's death as most, I imagine." Miranda studied herself in the mirror as Patsy manipulated the short strands into place. "I know my beliefs aren't popular around here, but I'm convinced that Esther Moore's beautiful soul has already found a new home. The cycle of life goes on, and as humans we join the rest of the world in the eternal rotation of regeneration and renewal."

It was hard for Patsy to hold back a snort of derision. She understood how important it was to respect the faiths of others. Still, Miranda's crazy idea that Esther might have been reincarnated was a little too much. One of the strongest, most righteous churchgoing women Patsy had ever met, Esther lived out her faith on a daily basis.

"I do agree that Esther has gone on to a better place," Patsy said. "An eternal place. I call it heaven."

Miranda took Patsy's hand and beckoned

her closer. As Patsy bent down, Miranda whispered, "Esther is the puppy."

"What?" Patsy exclaimed, stiffening.

"The dog Brad found the other day. Yappy. I'm convinced Esther's timeless essence has returned to help Ashley."

"Esther is a *dog?*" Stricken by Miranda's words, Patsy couldn't keep her voice as low as she usually did. In the salon, the strains of her favorite music covered the whir of blow-dryers, the chatter of women in black vinyl chairs, and the clink of cups and saucers in the tea area. But Miranda's comment was just too much.

"That puppy is a *male,*" Patsy declared, hand on her hip. "He's just a mutt Brad found in a cardboard box at Larry's Lake Lounge and took home to keep him from freezing to death. Now, come on, Miranda. You can't tell me you really believe Esther Moore came back as a dog."

"Not Esther herself. Her *soul.* And why not? We both believe in the eternal spirit of life. You think the soul begins at birth and passes through death into some sort of reward-based heaven."

"Or hell," Patsy couldn't resist adding. "And you don't go to either place as a reward. According to the Bible, you can't get into heaven because of the way you

55

acted on earth. It all has to do with your faith."

"Well, yes . . . I know your views, Patsy. It seems like every time I turn around here at the lake, someone is preaching at me. But I believe the spirit has no beginning and no end. It simply *is*. Divine energy indwells each of us, and Esther's soul — if that's what you want to call it — has gone into a being that will help someone who is in need. Her friend Ashley."

Patsy gave Miranda's hair a final shot of spray and clamped the lid back onto the can with more vigor than was necessary. This was taking things too far, and she couldn't simply stand there and listen to such nonsense. Client or not, Miranda had no right to say such things about Patsy's dear friend.

"If Esther Moore had a choice in what she was to become," Patsy informed Miranda, "it wouldn't be a dog. Sure, she loved Boofer, their old pooch who rides around in Charlie's golf cart. But why on earth would she want to turn into a half-frozen muddy little puppy?"

"To rescue her friend, of course." Miranda stood up, making no effort to speak quietly. "Ashley and Brad are obviously having marital problems. I'm right next door, but anyone can see it. That puppy might just be their salvation, Patsy. If Esther could bring that about, I have no doubt she would do it."

With that, she strode toward the cash register. Patsy had a feeling she wouldn't be getting her usual generous tip, and she didn't care. Miranda was an attractive woman, a good friend, and a kind grandmother, and she had done her best to become a part of the Deepwater Cove community. But her big city ways and her ideas about religion regularly caught folks off guard.

Evidently there were plenty of people out in the world who believed in spiritual essences, reincarnation, soul regeneration, and things like that. They thought morality and virtuous values would reap eternal rewards. But how anyone could think that Esther Moore — sweet, kind, genuinely fun, and a good Christian to boot — might have turned into a tangle-haired mutt was beyond Patsy.

Miranda left the salon, her hair lovely but her nose a little out of joint. She didn't leave a tip, either. That was all right with Patsy. The chance to sit down in the tea area and sip a cup of Earl Grey sounded like the perfect tonic for her bleak humor at the end of a long, trying day.

On her way to the hot water urn, Patsy greeted several regular clients who were conversing over steaming cups and nibbling sweets from the dessert counter in the tea alcove. The large plate glass windows fronting the street let in a warm late-afternoon light that gilded the round tables and chairs.

Ever since the Tea Lovers' Club had formed that spring, so many lovely memories had been created in the cozy space. Most of them included Esther Moore. But other loved ones, too, filled the room in Patsy's imagination, including Miranda Finley with her serene daughter-in-law. Pregnant with a second set of twins, Kim Finley looked happier and more rosy than Patsy had ever seen her. Brenda Hansen and her beautiful daughters, Jennifer and Jessica, would be discussing the upcoming wedding —

"Hey, Patsy, I was thinking about borrowing your car and driving it around the parking lot to see if maybe I won't bump into something this time. What do you say about that idea?"

Slipping out of her reverie and straight back into reality, Patsy noted the handsome, curly-haired young man who had taken a chair beside her.

"Cody Goss, you are not about to take my car or anyone else's for a joyride," Patsy replied. "I could not believe Jennifer let you borrow her car in the first place. Just be glad all you dented was her license plate when you hit that lamppost. You know good and well that you have to study the driving manual, pass the test, and earn your learner's permit before you're allowed to get behind a steering wheel. And even then, you have to have a licensed driver in the car with you. At this rate, you'll be lucky to find anyone brave enough for the job."

"That driving book is the most boring thing I have ever read, Patsy. It's not about impressionist art or parliamentary procedure or living on a mountainside or anything interesting. It's mostly numbers."

"Yes, it is, because numbers are part of driving." Trying to calm herself, Patsy took a sip of tea. Poor Cody never intended to upset anyone with his awkward questions and strange comments. In fact, he was probably the most good-hearted and sincere human being she had ever met. But there were times when he just about drove Patsy to drink.

"I don't like numbers," Cody said. "They don't stay inside my head."

"I realize this is difficult, honey. But if you

want to get your driver's license, you have to memorize speed limits and how many feet to stay away from another car and all that. You've made it through a lot worse in your life. I know you can do this. Just keep trying."

Cody looked down at the table. He had been eating chocolate cake a little earlier, and crumbs were stuck to the part of his mustache he'd missed while shaving that morning. Patsy's heart softened as she reached out and brushed off the crumbs. The young man did try so hard at everything.

"I have an idea," she said, laying her hand over his. "How about if we ask someone to work with you on memorizing the numbers in your driving book?"

"If that someone is Jennifer, I already tried. She won't. She's on vacation from her missionary school, but she stays in her room and doesn't come out. When she does, she tells me she's in there *thinking*. I tell her that I'm thinking too, and I'm thinking that she needs to get out of her bedroom."

"She will when she's ready, Cody."

"I really love Jennifer, Patsy. I love her with my whole heart. But sometimes I don't understand her even one little bit."

"Welcome to the world of men, buddy."

Pete Roberts clapped a hand on Cody's back, gave Patsy's cheek a kiss, and settled into a chair at their table. The second male to join the Tea Lovers' Club after Cody, Pete had made a habit of visiting the alcove in Patsy's salon about this time every afternoon.

"Women are a mystery," he informed Cody. "Just when you're sure you know what they're thinking, you find out you are dead wrong. You'd better give Jennifer a little more space, Cody. She had a hard time in Mexico. Those thugs that roughed up her missionary group ought to be taken out and horsewhipped."

"Nothing bad would have happened if I'd been with her," Cody insisted. "I would never let anyone knock down Jennifer and her friends and steal their purses and their watches and rings. I could protect Jennifer. I would rather let somebody kill me than hurt her."

"Aw, Cody," Patsy said, rumpling his curly brown hair. "You're too good."

He scowled. "I could be bad if I had to, Patsy. 'Greater love hath no man than this, that a man lay down his life for his friends.' That's John 15:13, and 'lay down your life' means to die."

"But no one could bear for you to be

61

killed," Patsy protested.

"I would lay down my life for Jennifer, and if I did get killed by thugs, I would not turn into a dog, that's for sure, which is exactly what I have told Miranda Finley."

Patsy glanced at Pete. He was looking at her as if he'd just had his brains scrambled like a batch of raw eggs. She slipped her arm around her future husband's beefy biceps and leaned against his large, comforting shoulder.

"Cody, were you eavesdropping on Miranda and me?" she asked.

"No, I was listening to you talk."

"That's the same as eavesdropping. Miranda and I were having a private conversation."

"Yeah, a conversation about Mrs. Moore dying and turning into Brad and Ashley's dog. What if Mr. Moore ever finds out that the lady whose house he is working on thinks Yappy is his wife? He will either get angry or drop over of a heart attack."

"Well, you shouldn't eavesdrop in the first place. It's bad social skills."

"Okay." Cody looked away for a moment. But his remorse was quickly replaced by determination. "There are worse things than bad social skills, Patsy."

He held up his hand and began to tick off

the points with his fingers. "The number-one bad thing is telling people that Mrs. Moore might be a dog. Number two is being a thug and scaring Jennifer, who won't talk to me anymore. Three is telling the salon ladies that Brad and Ashley are having trouble in their marriage, even if everyone already knows. And four is writing a driver's license book full of numbers that some people can't memorize because their brains don't work that way."

"Wait, now." Pete gave Patsy a worried look. "Someone thinks Esther Moore turned into a dog? The Hanes kids are having marriage problems? Am I the only one around here who doesn't have a clue?"

"I'll explain later," Patsy told him.

Cody stood. "I'm going to start mopping," he told her. "And in case Mrs. Finley doesn't know, Mrs. Moore never had fleas."

CHAPTER THREE

Ashley slid a plastic tray across the table toward her work area. As she sorted through the collection of beads it held, she swallowed hard against the flood of sorrow that surged up inside her. Only a month ago, she realized as she fingered them gently, Esther Moore had arranged these beads in their little compartments. Before Esther's stroke, the Moores had volunteered to help out with Ashley's wildly growing jewelry business. Each afternoon the couple sat together on their porch and picked through the sacks of beads she had given them.

When Charlie returned the plastic trays one morning after his wife's death, he told Ashley that some of the beads might be in the wrong compartments. Esther had gotten more and more confused in her final days, he recalled. Charlie also blamed himself for not trying harder to persuade his wife to have a medical procedure that might have prolonged her life. Ashley reminded him that the doctor had insisted nothing could have saved Esther, and Charlie shouldn't feel guilty.

Sniffling, Ashley noted that Charlie had been right about the bead trays. This one was something of a disaster. Blue beads had gotten mixed with purple ones, and red beads were in the pink beads' compartment. But the inconvenience hardly bothered Ashley. She was so sick of stringing necklaces and bracelets that she hardly cared what colors she used.

"Are you all right?" The soft voice came from the stairway that led up from the walkout basement. "I thought I heard someone crying."

Ashley brushed at her cheek as she turned to find Jennifer Hansen standing on the last step. The two had known each other for years. Ashley had been in the same grade in school as Jennifer's younger sister, Jessica. The three girls were friendly in high school, but as they got older, Ashley started working at her parents' snack shop in the afternoons. Jessica usually made the social rounds, while Jennifer buried herself in homework. It had been difficult to spend time together, and the three had grown apart.

"I'm okay," Ashley told the lovely young blonde. "Just tired, I guess."

"Do you still work at your parents' place near the school?"

"Not unless there's an emergency. I waitress at the country club now."

Ashley noted that Jennifer was drifting toward the worktable, and she desperately wanted to be left alone. She regretted having to work on her beads in the Hansens' basement craft room. Her own home was far too small to accommodate the thriving enterprise, and that meant spending hours feeling as though she had invaded the family's privacy.

Ashley wished Jennifer would go back upstairs. The two young women had nothing in common anymore. Ashley wouldn't even know how to begin talking to someone who had decided to be a missionary. Frankly, that sounded like the weirdest thing in the world.

"My parents go to the country club fairly often," Jennifer remarked. "They like the food. Dad told me they meet his real estate clients or Mom's interior design customers for dinner there."

"Yeah, I see them a lot." Ashley returned to threading a length of clear monofilament through a set of red beads that a customer in St. Louis had ordered for Christmas.

"So, essentially you're holding down two jobs." Jennifer slipped onto the stool across from Ashley and leaned her elbows on the worktable. "My mom says you've been working on the beads day and night since you set up your Web site."

"Miranda Finley set it up. She made my business cards, too."

"She designed some for Cody — for his faux painting business. I guess she wants to encourage everyone." Jennifer fell silent for a moment, watching Ashley string beads. "But maybe not everyone wants so much encouragement."

Ashley pushed a thick strand of red hair behind one ear and didn't look up. "Well, this takes a lot of time, but I'm glad to be bringing in some money. At least . . . I'll be glad once people start paying me. So far, it's been me mailing beads and invoices and hardly anyone sending back a check."

"Maybe you should make people pay first."

Glancing up, Ashley fought the irritation that comment provoked. What did Jennifer Hansen know about business anyway? She had never been forced to do a lick of work in her life. Her father owned one of the most successful real estate agencies at the lake. Her mother had just opened a decor and gift boutique in Tranquility. Jennifer drove a new car and had graduated from college. Now she was attending a religious seminary and planning to go off into the jungle and preach to the natives.

Focusing on the necklace again, Ashley admitted she might be feeling a little too critical. Jennifer's trip to Mexico hadn't gone well, but did that give her the right to hide in her room and pout? If such a thing had happened to Ashley, she would be expected to clock in at the country club that same night. She'd have several dozen necklace orders to fill too.

"I don't know anything about business," Jennifer said, echoing Ashley's thoughts. "I majored in anthropology. I'm sure you were right to send the beads first and then trust that the money would come in. I know I couldn't run a company."

"If you had Miranda Finley pushing you from behind, you could. The woman never lets up."

Jennifer smiled. "I heard she got all her St. Louis friends to place orders."

"And they told all their Kansas City friends, their New York friends, their Los Angeles friends. . . ." She huffed out a breath. "It's crazy. I mean, these are just *beads.* What's the big deal? I never wanted to run a business anyway. I used to think I'd be a kindergarten teacher, you know? Any five-year-old could make these stupid things."

With that, Ashley threw a bead onto the table. It ricocheted past Jennifer and hit the wall. Dropping her head into her hands, Ashley gave up trying to hold in her grief. What was the point in acting so self-assured? she wondered, as tears spilled down her cheeks. Her life was in tatters anyway. None of it fit together or worked the way it was supposed to. The whole thing was a big joke.

"Your beads are beautiful," Jennifer said gently. "They're works of art. Everyone loves them — especially Mrs. Moore. She was always talking about your beads and so proud of you for starting to sell them. The two of you had gotten really close, hadn't you? I know you helped her a lot after her accident."

"She helped *me*," Ashley sobbed. "Mrs. Moore sorted beads for me, and she was teaching me how to cook. But she also . . . well, she was my friend. We talked about things. She used to say, *'I'm so silly,'* and it was true. I never thought an old lady could be interesting and fun to hang around with, but she was. I miss her so much. I can't believe . . . I can't believe she's dead."

Ashley couldn't keep from glaring at Jennifer, as if somehow she and her precious religion were to blame for everything. Though Jennifer obviously had nothing to do with Esther Moore's death, still the grief and anger poured out.

"If God is so wonderful that you want to go off to the jungle and tell people about Him," Ashley ground out, "then why did He let Mrs. Moore die? She was a good person. She was never mean to anyone. How come murderers and thieves and . . . and *drunks* . . . how come they get to go on living and making other people miserable? Is that fair? Is that right? No way. If anyone deserved a long, happy life, it was Mrs. Moore. But she had to have that stupid stroke, which left Mr. Moore . . . and me . . . and Boofer and everyone . . . alone. I hate that."

Jennifer had been examining the delicate painted and etched beads in the tray while Ashley blurted her thoughts. But as Ashley finished ranting, Jennifer pushed the tray aside and wiped at her own cheeks.

"I don't know, Ash," she mumbled tearfully. "I don't get it either. I mean, it's almost the same with me. Our mission team was in that hot, filthy little town in Oaxaca

70

doing a good thing. We weren't hurting anyone. We were passing out Spanish Bibles. Free, too. We'd been with the people for a couple of days, sleeping in their houses and eating their food and trying so hard to show how much we love them. How much *God* loves them. And then one night out of the dark came this gang. They had clubs and sticks, and I think there was even a gun. I knew they were going to kill us all — I really did. I thought, *I'm going to die, and I never got to be a missionary or a wife or a mom or anything.*"

"Wow, Jen," Ashley said. "I didn't know it was so bad."

"Oh yeah, it was. When I came to, I was lying in the mud with a big lump on the back of my head, and my friends were crying, and everyone was scared to death, even our team leader. No one in the town helped us, either. Not at first. We all just held on to each other and prayed, and then the police got there and a few people came out of their houses to watch. An old Land Rover took us to the clinic. *That* place was a total joke. No beds or sterilized needles or stethoscopes or anything you would expect. They had alcohol swabs and codeine — that's it. The whole thing was awful, and I don't know what I'm doing anymore. I thought

71

God wanted our team to be down there and He would protect us, but then all of that happened. It's so confusing."

Ashley set down the necklace she had been beading. "Are you okay now?"

"No!" Jennifer lifted her head, her face red and her eyelids puffy. "I'm not okay. I used to feel confident about everything. I thought I knew what God wanted me to do. But now . . ."

The two young women looked into each other's eyes. Ashley didn't know whether she felt worse for Jennifer or for herself. How could things get so terrible when you were this young? You'd think it would take a lifetime to mess up your whole world this bad. But she and Jennifer Hansen had managed it before they reached twenty-five.

"I'm really scared all of a sudden," Jennifer said.

"I can't imagine living out in the middle of nowhere all by myself. The mission organization I've signed up with — they do put us in teams, and we would have a communications radio, and a plane could come if something went really bad. But the married couples and their children would be together in their own little houses. At night, I'd be alone, Ash. Completely alone."

"You'd have God."

"God . . . ," Jennifer whispered, her eyes filling again. She shook her head as the words choked out. "I feel like He betrayed me. I know Christians aren't always protected from bad things. But why me? Why our group? I'm so confused."

"Maybe your brain was injured when the thugs hit you on the head."

Finally the hint of a grin appeared on Jennifer's face. "I had all kinds of scans when I got back to Missouri. My brain is fine. The problem is with my heart."

"Come on, Jen. Your heart hasn't changed. You still believe all those things you told us at the TLC meetings. Think how many times you've scolded Miranda Finley and preached at everyone. You're like Joan of Arc in that movie — crusading around and challenging people to repent. You just got the stuffing scared out of you in Mexico, that's all."

"That's for sure. But it did change me, Ash. It made me think about so many things — questions and worries and dreams I'd been keeping on the back burner."

"Like getting married? Ha. Trust me, it's not all it's cracked up to be."

Ashley could feel Jennifer's eyes trained on her. Picking up the necklace again, she searched for red beads in the compartments of her tray. Considering Jen's misery over living life as a single woman, it might not be a bad idea to let her know the other side.

"You imagine everything will be wonderful when you're married," she murmured, her focus on the necklace. "It's like — wow, if dating is this great, then marriage has got to be even better. I used to feel like I was the center of Brad's universe. He spent tons of time with me, and he couldn't keep his hands off me."

Catching herself, Ashley glanced at Jennifer. "You probably don't believe in sleeping with a guy before marriage, do you?"

"I've never found a rule God made that was *bad* for people." Jennifer rolled a few red beads in Ashley's direction. "So, yeah, I believe in waiting. I suspect things work out better for couples who do."

Ashley had to think about that for a moment. None of her single friends were virgins. Except Jessica and Jennifer Hansen — both winners in the Miss Religious competition. These days, people hardly thought twice about it. On the other hand, things with Brad weren't working out very well for Ashley. But that wasn't because they'd had sex before marriage. Was it?

"Anyway," Ashley went on, "nowadays Brad and I hardly see each other — and there's definitely no cuddling. He works days building condos for a construction company. I work nights waitressing."

"But that can only be eight hours for each of you," Jennifer pointed out. "There are twenty-four hours in a day. That should still give you at least eight hours together."

Considering whether to tell the truth, Ashley threaded a few more beads and then tied off the monofilament. Jennifer had been honest with her, so why not just spill the beans?

"We could spend time together," she said. "But Brad goes to Larry's after he gets off work around three in the afternoon. I don't have to be at the country club until five, but I hate that bar — women staring at Brad and flirting with him. He's *my* husband, but it's like I'm not even there."

"What does Brad do?"

"Plays pool mostly. The bar has a new singer he thinks is awesome. I haven't seen her, but I wouldn't trust any barfly as far as I could spit. I've asked Brad not to go to Larry's, but he does it anyway unless he's planning to work on our house with Mr. Moore. They're trying to repair some of the damage from the termites and rain. With Brad always busy, I come over here and work on the beads. Besides, there's no point in trying to carve out a couple of hours together. We usually end up in a fight anyway."

"But you could go out to dinner. Or snuggle on the couch. And what about when you get home from work?"

"Brad's totally zonked by then. I usually find him crashed out somewhere snoring."

"Is there some way you could find a job with hours that matched Brad's a little better?" Jennifer asked. "There's a lunch shift at the country club, isn't there?"

"The tips are twice as good at night. I need the money. My parents are always on the brink of going under, and I've helped support them for years. Brad doesn't know it, but I still give them money every month. If I didn't, they probably wouldn't make it."

"You keep secrets from your husband? Is that a good idea?"

"I'm sure not going to tell him. He goes ballistic all the time about money anyway. Brad thinks my bead business is a total waste. He's always on my case about having to pay for envelopes, packing tape, clay, enamels — the things I need to keep filling orders. I wish I'd never started this."

"I'll help you."

The offer was impulsive. Was it insincere? Ashley studied Jennifer for a moment.

"You don't want to string necklaces, Jen," she said. "It's boring."

"I need boring." Jennifer reached over and began to sort beads in the tray. "I've just been through the least-boring experience of my life. I'm so freaked out I can't even decide whether to go back to school next semester. It's as though that gang of thieves in Mexico robbed me of a lot more than my purse and watch. They stole my courage. These days, the idea of flying halfway around the world and living by myself in a hut almost makes me panicky."

"You could always take Cody Goss."

At that, Jennifer looked up, startled. But when she saw the grin on Ashley's face, she relaxed. "Cody *could* protect me, you know."

"He sure could." Ashley shook her head. "He survived on his own after his dad kicked him out. And he made it from Kansas to Deepwater Cove without even knowing how to read a map."

Jennifer giggled. "Cody seems to be able to do almost anything he sets his mind to."

"Yeah, he's okay — but he drives me crazy. I guess it's part of his autism. He's forever getting right in my face when he talks to me. And if he gets going on chocolate cake or his other favorite subjects at TLC meetings, forget it."

"He is different, but to tell you the truth, Cody amazes me. His art is awesome."

"You ought to know," Ashley said, recalling the collage of portraits Cody had painted on the wall of Just As I Am, every one a variation on his favorite theme — Jennifer Hansen. "Cody might make a good missionary," Ashley went on. "I bet he's got most of the Bible memorized. He could probably preach a better sermon than the minister of your church."

"Pastor Andrew would be hard to top."

"I heard him at the country club once. Some group had invited him to be their speaker. He was pretty interesting, I'll admit. But I would still bet Cody knows more Bible verses."

"I haven't found a topic that stumps him. You can mention almost anything, and Cody comes up with Scripture to go along with it."

"See? You should just take him with you. He could be your missionary partner. Your teammate."

As she spoke, Ashley saw a look filter across Jennifer's face that was unmistakable. The young woman's cheeks flushed with pink and she looked away shyly, her blue eyes suddenly sparkling. Though Ashley could hardly believe it, she would know that expression anywhere.

"You *like* Cody," she said in a low voice. "Jen, what's the deal? Are you in love with him?"

Jennifer clenched her hands into fists and shook her head. "No, of course not. That would be ridiculous. I mean, Cody's autistic. At least, we think he is. Besides, he has those irritating habits, and he hasn't been to school a day in his life. He can't do anything with numbers, you know. He reads entire books on Michelangelo or Leonardo da Vinci, but he can't figure out a ruler to save his life. He's horrible at telling time, and he still gets the days of the week mixed up. In many ways, he's like a little kid."

"Yeah, but he's not. He's about your age. And he's handsome. Movie star handsome."

"He is, isn't he?"

"Yep." Ashley picked out a necklace clasp from her supply box and began attaching it to the string of beads. This had to be one of the most unusual conversations she'd ever had. But she liked Jennifer Hansen, and it felt good to talk things over.

"It's okay to like whoever you want, Jen," Ashley said. "You can like Cody if you want. You can even love him."

"I do love him. But not that way. At least, I don't think I love him that way." She gripped the sides of the table. "See? I can't figure out anything these days! It's all a gigantic mess."

"Maybe you should take time off from school and work for a while. What can you do with a major in . . . what was it?"

"Anthropology. Dumb, useless subject. I have no idea what kind of job I could do. I was planning to go to the mission field, so anthropology fit perfectly. Everything used to be logical and comfortable and really right. But now, it's all mixed up."

"Well, try not to get so uptight about what's going on. You don't have to buy your tickets to Timbuktu tomorrow, do you? Be grateful you didn't make a permanent commitment like I did." Ashley paused, reflecting on her Valentine's Day wedding. "You didn't stand up in a church and promise yourself — heart and soul — to someone for the rest of your life."

"Actually, I did. Only my someone was God. He used to be all I thought about, all I cared about."

"God?"

"Yes. I can remember that feeling — that fire I used to have. I knew why I loved the Lord, and I would do anything for Him. Absolutely anything. I was so happy, so sure I was making all the right decisions. It wasn't like I walked into it blindly, either. I went to Africa on a long mission trip. I saw how the rest of the world lives, all the suffering, and it made me more determined. But that was before Mexico."

"It's almost like Brad and me. I just knew marrying him was the best, smartest thing in the world. I truly didn't think my life would be all that different after our wedding. Just like you, I thought I had already tried it out. You'd been to Africa with God, and I'd been to bed with Brad."

"Well, that's really not the same."

"Yeah, but you and I are alike in a lot of ways, Jen. I knew what I was getting into. I saw the future, and I wanted it. But now . . . now that it's a reality, I'm about ready to throw in the towel."

"Are you serious?"

"I think about it all the time. Brad promised to love and protect me, to always be with me, to be faithful to me. But he hangs out at Larry's and comes home drunk and yells at me about money or the laundry or my cooking. He hates my beadwork. His parents are freaks, and he says mine are losers. We have a puppy that piddles all over the floor. Our house is falling down. And I can't count on my husband. I don't trust him anymore." As she was speaking, tears welled in Ashley's eyes again.

"Oh, Ash." Jennifer let out a breath. "I hear what you're saying. We both trusted ourselves to someone we believed in . . . and we both feel let down. I just wish I could get it back."

"That feeling? Me too. I would give anything to see the look of true love in Brad's eyes again."

"Can you win him back?"

Ashley shrugged. "Why should I bother? I used to think he was amazing. Wonderful. The most popular, handsome guy in his class. I couldn't even get him to look at me. He was the quarterback on the football team, Jen."

"I know. Brad and I are the same age."

"Do you know him very well? Maybe you could talk to him for me."

"Me? Talk to Brad?" Jennifer began sorting beads again. "Ashley, I don't think that's a good idea. He's your husband. You should talk to him."

"But I don't know what to say. We always end up in a fight. You're a Christian and all that. Don't you know anything about counseling?"

"I took a class last semester, but it was all about relating to the needs of tribal people."

"Sometimes I think Brad Hanes is a

savage." Ashley focused on attaching the clasp. She didn't like to recall the times that Brad had been drunk and they'd argued. More than once, she had feared he might hit her.

"Maybe he is," Jennifer said. "The football team was his tribe, and he's taking out his feelings on his wife. You should go to a counselor. People say Pastor Andrew is terrific."

"You're the one who should talk to Pastor Andrew. He'll understand all about your missionary stuff. But Brad . . . well, I think he might listen to you, Jen. You were in the same grade, you're the same age, and you're probably as smart as he is — which I'm not."

"Come on, Ash. Why would you say that?"

"Brad graduated with a 4.0, you know."

"Brad Hanes?"

"Believe it or not, but it's true. He says it was just so he could stay on the football team, but the truth is, he liked school. I got by with average grades. I was usually too busy working at the snack shop to get my homework done. I didn't care about anything but the art classes anyway. Brad is way smarter than I am. Look at me and this bead business. You're right — I probably should have asked for the money before I sent out the necklaces. I'm so dumb I never even thought of that."

"You're not dumb. You're just inexperienced."

"Talk to Brad for me, will you? Tell him I'm not such a bad wife. Tell him I'm doing my best, and the way I act is normal for a woman. I'm emotional because I feel things. And tell him to stop going to Larry's. Please, Jen."

Jennifer pushed the newly organized tray across the table toward Ashley. "If I see him, I might try to say something."

"Well, I've got to get going," Ashley said. "I'm supposed to be at work in half an hour."

As Ashley started to pack up her trays, Jennifer caught her arm. "Leave them. I'll sort the rest of the beads for you."

Ashley smiled. "Thanks. Maybe it'll help me not think about Esther so much."

"You know, Ash, you're kind and artistic and sensitive — not to mention gorgeous with all that red hair. If Brad Hanes doesn't realize what he's got, he's a lot dumber than I think he is."

Starting for the sliding door that led out of the basement, Ashley felt better than she had in weeks. She paused and glanced back at the other woman.

"You'll figure out what to do, Jen," she said. "Just be patient."

"You too, Ash. You too."

The two gazed at each other for a moment, and then Ashley pushed open the door and stepped outside.

CHAPTER FOUR

Brad picked up the puppy and set him in a cardboard box. "That's what you get, Yappy. Back where you started. And don't even think about yowling at me, because I'm not letting you out."

"You don't have to let him out," Charlie Moore commented as the puppy leaped up and flung himself over the side of the box. "He's already got that part down pat."

"Well, great." Hooking his thumbs in his pockets, Brad shook his head. The little dog landed on the floor spread-eagled, picked himself up, shook his head, and made a dive for the hem of Brad's jeans. Tiny teeth sank into the denim, and the dog began to back up, growling ferociously as he tried to tug Brad across the room.

"We're not going to get anything done at this rate," he told Charlie. "Do you want to see if he'll play with Boofer?"

"Why not?" The older man stepped to the

door of the new room that he and Brad had built onto the Haneses' house. "Boof's an old cuss like me, but he probably wouldn't mind hanging around with a young whippersnapper every now and then."

With a wink at Brad, he opened the door and let the plump mutt into the room. The moment Boofer entered, Yappy flung himself at the mop of long black hair. Tail end raised high, the pup bowed as if in submission to the larger dog.

"Wow!" Suddenly dancing sideways, Yappy scampered around Boofer with high-pitched yelps of delight. *"Wow, wow, wow!"*

Boofer made an effort at sniffing the little creature bouncing in circles. Tail wagging, the older dog allowed Yappy to take a whiff of him, and then they were off. Both dogs began scurrying around the living room, racing behind the armchair, nearly knocking the television off its stand, skittering across the kitchen floor.

Brad watched in amusement as Yappy ran behind the sofa, Boofer in hot pursuit. The older dog had gained weight in recent years, and he stuck like a cork. But not for long. Backing out, he shook himself and took off after the puppy again.

"I guess you were right," Brad told Charlie. "I had a feeling the box wouldn't hold

Yap for long. Ashley made a nice bed on the floor for him the first night. He howled and carried on so much that we ended up putting him under the covers with us."

"And he's been there ever since." Charlie chuckled. "Same with Boof. I told Esther it was a mistake to let that dog on the bed. Would she listen?"

"Do they ever?" Brad glanced at the empty sink in which he had scrubbed nearly all the pots and pans that he and Ashley owned. The dishwasher was now running, scouring plates and silverware — which he had loaded. The countertops gleamed. Ashley hadn't lifted a finger.

"Women don't listen much," Charlie said, "unless you know how to get their attention. The main thing they want to do is talk — *share feelings* is how Esther used to put it. She cared what I was thinking, of course, but she was a lot more interested in letting me in on her own state of mind. If I wanted to make an important point, I had to get her to focus on me. It was hard sometimes, but I learned a few tricks in my years."

"Have you got a trick that would make a wife clean up the house every now and then? I did all this myself."

"*You?*" Charlie's face feigned amazement. Then he put a hand on Brad's shoulder.

"Listen, son, a man may not like to do the dishes, but he's every bit as capable as a woman. I found that out after Esther's accident. I used to plead ignorance about the dishwasher. I insisted that everything in the laundry room was a mystery to me. I couldn't iron a shirt without burning a hole in it — or so I told Esther. She informed me that if I could run a power saw and a router, I could certainly iron a collar. Turned out she was right. 'Course it took me nearly fifty years to concede that argument. I never would sew on a button. Insisted that was *women's work*. Now look at me."

Charlie indicated the floppy cuff of his plaid flannel shirt. "I reckon I'll have to find Esther's mending box and replace the button one of these days. This ol' dog is going to have to learn a new trick."

"Ashley could sew on a button for you. She's always got a needle and thread in her hand."

"Thanks, but no. I plan to figure this thing out myself just to please Esther. She and my mother are up in heaven right now, probably discussing how my shoes don't match my socks, or my shirt doesn't go with my pants, or I missed a belt loop. Some such thing. Esther was always onto me about my appearance, and I wouldn't listen. I told her it was my business what I wore and not hers. I'm sure you've already learned there are things you and your young bride are going to fuss over from now till one or the other of you goes on to glory."

Brad pondered this comment. At the moment, he could think of about fifty things he and Ashley had been fighting over. His drinking. Her beads. The kitchen. The puppy. The lawn. Money. In-laws. Sex. Friends. Free time. Jobs. Which of them was supposed to make the bed in the morning. Who ought to rake leaves off the driveway. On and on.

"Well, seeing as you've got the kitchen tidied," Charlie continued, "I guess we can get to work prying up these old tiles. Looks like those two fellows wore each other out already."

Brad glanced over his shoulder to find the dogs lying curled together, sound asleep. Yappy was snoring loudly, as usual. Boofer seemed pleased to be snuggled up to the pup.

"I haven't seen Yap that zonked out since I brought him home from Larry's," Brad said as he handed Charlie a shovel. "He'd been shivering inside a cardboard box all day. The minute his stomach was full, he cratered."

"You were a good man to rescue him. Not many people would take in a stray, especially at this time of year. It's so cold, a pup is reluctant to go out and take care of his business." Charlie set the flat edge of his shovel against the seam between two of the old linoleum tiles. With one foot on the blade, he gave a push. The tile snapped in half and popped out of place.

The job didn't look as difficult as Brad had feared it might be. He joined the older man, and within a half hour, they had cleared off a large portion of the old flooring. They chatted a little, as always when they worked. Both men kept up with the NFL standings, and they favored the same teams. As usual, Charlie reminisced about his childhood and his work as a mail carrier. All of his conversation was sprinkled with remarks about Esther. Now each comment carried a tinge of sadness. Once in a while, Charlie choked up and couldn't go on.

Listening to his friend hearken back to events in his long marriage, Brad wondered if he and Ashley would make it through their first year, — let alone almost fifty. He couldn't imagine his wife becoming such a part of his life that he mentioned her every time he talked. These days, Brad didn't much like even to think about the lanky, sensual redhead who had driven him crazy with desire not so long ago. How could a few short months of marriage have turned Ashley from the object of his strongest yearnings into someone he dreaded to wake up to each morning?

"You sure are quiet this evening," Charlie said, leaning on his shovel. "Wishing you'd gone over to Larry's? Probably more fun than scraping up kitchen tile with an old geezer."

A smile twitched the corners of Brad's mouth. "Why don't you come to Larry's with me sometime, Mr. Moore? You could meet the guys from my crew. The music is great — there's a new singer, a smokin' little number who can really belt out the songs. Why not join me and the boys — have a few beers and relax with us? It might take your mind off things."

"Oh, no thanks." Charlie held up a hand. "My drinking days are long behind me. I found out the hard way that never did anybody any good."

"Just a little now and then couldn't hurt."

"Humph. That's what *you* say. You weren't there to see the look on my wife's face the night I got toasted and wound up at a strip joint."

"A strip joint?" Brad couldn't help but laugh out loud. "No way, Mr. Moore."

"Oh yeah. Let me tell you something, kid. A woman may forgive, but she'll never forget."

"How did Mrs. Moore find out?"

"I don't recollect exactly, but they *always* do. Trust me on that." Charlie studied the floor for a moment. "You know, Esther reminded me about that incident not too long before she died."

"How long ago did it happen?"

"Near the start of our marriage. I was young, self-centered, stupid. Esther was idealistic and starry-eyed about me — thought I was her knight in shining armor. Then I staggered home drunk and fell right off my pedestal. You don't think a mistake you make at the beginning of the marriage will affect things down the road, but it will. It sure will."

Charlie went back to shoveling tiles, and Brad joined him. At the sound of their scraping, the dogs woke up and played again, rolling around on the carpet and nipping at each other. Yappy loved to wait until Boofer had settled down again before leaping on the older dog's back and forcing him

93

to his feet.

As Brad tossed a shovelful of tiles into the large garbage can near the dining room table, he thought about Mr. Moore getting drunk and wandering into a strip club. While the image was kind of funny, it made him feel a little sick inside too.

Though Brad had hardly noticed the Moores when he and Ashley moved to Deepwater Cove, the older couple somehow became a part of their lives. In fact, the whole neighborhood seemed involved in what was going on with "the Hanes kids," as they were called. Surrounded by so many siblings as a child, Brad had become something of a loner. He was good at teamwork — on the football field or the construction site — but he didn't like people prying into his affairs.

Only . . . Mr. Moore's presence never felt like an imposition. Brad respected the elderly man. When Mr. Moore called him *son,* the word settled into Brad's chest like a bar of warm, glowing gold. Having grown up with a father too busy and too disinterested to give any of his children much attention, Brad had come to enjoy the evenings and weekends that he and Mr. Moore spent working on the little clapboard house.

In fact, the feeling Brad had developed for

the white-haired gentleman went beyond respect. Brad admired Mr. Moore. He wanted to become like him — able to look back on a long, good life with a loving wife, some kids, and a steady career. A man who could hold his head up and look anyone in the eye.

That vision didn't fit with the story of the episode at the strip joint. It didn't fit with Mr. Moore. How had the one man turned into the other?

"Commitment," Charlie said, wiping his forehead as he leaned on his shovel again. "That's what got Esther and me through the rough spots. I doubt she ever put me on a pedestal again, but that's all right. I didn't belong on one. All the same, she had to work out how she did feel about me after that terrible night. *Committed* is what she finally said. At first, I didn't think that was nearly as good as love, but later on I found out it was better."

"Mrs. Moore forgave you because she was committed to you? Sounds like a word my boss uses about the condominium complex we're building — especially if anyone on the crew shows up late or has a hangover. 'You've got to be committed, men,' he lectures us. We can all imitate the guy's voice and gestures. Bill can be pretty strict, but we do get the job done. Nobody wants to quit, either, because he pays well and the work is steady."

"Well, there you go. Constructing a condo is pretty much like building a marriage. You might not always like the restrictions, but commitment gets the work done anyhow. With strong dedication, neither one is willing to quit. Esther and I were united, you see. We shared a purpose — dreams and goals we wanted to accomplish. And we complemented each other pretty well, too, especially by the . . . by the end."

Charlie set his shovel against a tile and gave it an angry push. The tile popped off, spun into the air, and landed on the floor, breaking into several pieces.

"Wow!" Yappy hurtled over and snatched one of the tiles in his mouth. As the puppy pranced past Charlie, the man scooped him up, buried his face in the soft brown fur, and wept.

Brad leaned his shovel against a counter and brewed a pot of Ashley's favorite tea. He and Charlie sat and drank several cups in comfortable silence. It was a while before they got back to work again.

"It's time for minutes." Cody Goss's deep voice boomed over the chatter of ladies gathered in the tea area of the Just As I Am salon. "Mrs. Moore is in heaven, and she would want us to do minutes."

Patsy Pringle glanced across the table at Pete Roberts. With a smirk on his clean-shaven face, her fiancé was dipping a chocolate chip cookie into his English Afternoon tea — a favorite activity that Patsy had begged him to cease.

Pete had cleaned up a lot in the looks department, but he still had a long way to go with manners. She wondered if Cody might teach him some social skills — an idea that put a wry grin on her own face.

"We need a new president, and I nominate Ashley Hanes." Cody had risen from his chair and clinked the side of his china teacup with a spoon in the same way Esther Moore always had.

"Do I hear any seconds?" Cody asked. He paused a moment. "Meeting seconds are not like seconds at the dinner table, in case you were wondering. Dinner seconds are when you put more food on your plate because you didn't get full the first time around."

At this observation, the entire room fell silent. Cody continued. "According to *Robert's Rules of Order,* meeting minutes are when the president of the organization, who

I think should be Ashley Hanes, reads the old business."

"I don't want to be president," Ashley announced, more or less glowering at the crowd. "I'm too busy, and I'm not in the mood."

The club gatherings had been growing in size, Patsy noted, and the tables seemed extra full today. The one she and Pete had chosen included Cody, Jennifer Hansen, and Ashley. Patsy had observed the two young women engaged in animated discussion as they entered the salon together.

"But Mrs. Moore picked you, Ashley," Cody protested. "When she had her accident, she chose you to be the president *pro tem. Pro tem* is Latin for —"

"I'm not going to take the job," Ashley cut in. "Mrs. Moore was . . . well, nobody could do it the way she did."

When Ashley's voice began to quaver, Cody looked at Jennifer as if she might have the answer to this dilemma. As it turned out, she did.

"Why don't you be president, Cody?" she asked him. "You know parliamentary procedure better than any of us."

"I second that," Pete spoke up.

"But, wait, we didn't open the floor to nominations," Cody objected. "And Jennifer didn't make a motion."

"I move," Jennifer said, "that Cody Goss become president of the Tea Lovers' Club."

"I second the motion," Pete said again. "Any objections? No? Okeydoke, then all in favor say *amen*."

As a chorus of amens echoed around the room, Cody surveyed the gathering in dismay. "Well . . . but that's not exactly right. . . ."

"It's good enough for us," Jennifer told him gently. She touched his arm. "Go on."

"Okay, old business," Cody announced, and without even looking at a written record, he began to describe the Thanksgiving parade, bonfire, and barbecue that had been the club's most recent gathering.

Patsy had to admire the young man's recall of events. Though Cody tended to focus on details others might miss — like the fact that at the Thanksgiving event Miranda Finley's chocolate cake had been cut into triangles instead of squares — he certainly captured the occasion in living color.

When the time arrived for new business, several people mentioned the coming of Christmas and New Year's Day and the fact that the community might want to celebrate those two holidays in some way. But Patsy wasn't too surprised that no one could work up enough enthusiasm to make plans for a special occasion. Without Esther Moore's usual cheerful, chirpy chatter to get the discussion going, the whole thing fell flat.

Realizing that he hadn't been able to get the group to muster up a single bit of new business, Cody ended the meeting and sat down, a deflated expression on his handsome face.

"I really miss Mrs. Moore," he murmured. "She would have suggested another parade, that's for sure. Mrs. Moore liked parades."

"We'll think up some good ideas, Cody," Jennifer assured him. "You did a great job on your first day as president. I suspect no one wanted to talk about Christmas because we're all still sad about Mrs. Moore."

"Christmas is another problem, Jennifer," Cody told her, his blue eyes deep. "I tried to talk to Mrs. Miranda Finley about Christmas the other day when I was walking down to the lake to look for bald eagles. I saw three eagles, but I also had to listen to Mrs. Finley explain about pagan roots."

"Pagan?" Ashley frowned at Cody, then turned to Jennifer. "Christmas is baby Jesus, the manger, the three wise men, and all that, isn't it?"

"Mrs. Finley told me that Christmas is

not really about that," Cody responded. Before continuing, he glanced at Miranda, who sat across the room with another group of women.

"She is a nice lady who made business cards to help me get painting jobs," he explained in a lower voice, "but she says no one knows *when* or *if* Jesus was ever born. Christmas trees and mistletoe and stockings and even Santa Claus all came from ancient pagan earth religions. So, ha ha. Which is when I reminded her that God is bigger and more powerful than anyone can imagine, especially her. So, ha ha back."

Cody took a bite of lemon bar, then added, "Mrs. Miranda Finley and I had a little bit of an argument, if you want to know the truth, but we decided to stay friends anyway."

Patsy focused on Pete, who had been listening with great interest to Cody's latest ramble. Pete surprised his bride-to-be on a regular basis. The man had only a high school education. He wasn't a big talker, had a poor track record where marriage and alcohol were concerned, and only recently had joined the local church. Anyone would suppose such a man might be lacking intellectual depth. As it turned out, Pete *was* a deep thinker, and he enjoyed listening to people's ideas a great deal more than he let on.

"Cody, you're one of the bravest people I've ever met," Pete declared. "I'm not sure I'd want to take on Miranda Finley the way you did."

"Yeah," Ashley added. "You knocked the wind out of her on that Christmas argument. I'll bet you're brave enough to handle just about anything, Cody. You could probably even be a missionary if you wanted to."

At that, Patsy noticed Jennifer elbow Ashley in the side. The redhead suppressed a grin. It appeared the two had been discussing Cody — and not just in a general sense.

"Maybe so," the young man informed Ashley, his blue eyes serious. "But I already know I prefer Deepwater Cove to any other place in the world, because people are nice to me and give me work to do and surprise birthday parties and cut my hair and let me sleep on their porch."

"I think you're happiest here," Jennifer said.

Cody's gaze fastened on her. "I'm happiest to be near you, Jennifer. You're my best friend and also the most beautiful woman I ever met. That's why I love you."

Before Jennifer could come up with a suitable response to another of Cody's regular declarations of love, Ashley spoke again. "But what if Jen moved away? What would you do, Cody? You wouldn't want to leave Deepwater Cove. Maybe you should go with her?"

For a moment, the young man focused on his cup of tea. Then he suddenly grabbed his curls and clenched his hands into fists. "I don't know," he burst out. "I want Jennifer to be happy, but I also want her to stay here. I want to be near her. I love Jennifer so much —"

"Yo, Code." Pete slung an arm around his shoulders. "Jennifer is sitting beside you, and nobody's going anywhere right now. You don't have to make a single decision except whether you're going to eat the rest of that lemon bar. Same with Jennifer. I'm a lot older than both of you kids, and I'll tell you this — the slower you make a decision and the more clearheaded you are when you step up to the plate, the better off you'll be. I've done a lot of dumb things because I was in a hurry, and I sure learned my lesson on that."

"You got engaged to Patsy awfully soon," Ashley reminded him. "You haven't even known her a whole year yet. Brad and I went out for nearly two years before he proposed."

"Hmm." Pete appeared to ponder her words. "So, do you think things are working out better for you and Brad because you waited?"

Ashley's pale cheeks flushed a bright pink, and Patsy gave Pete a little kick under the table. Everyone in Deepwater Cove knew the young couple had lived together a short time before marriage and now were going through a rocky spell.

Though Patsy always did her best to dispel rumors in the salon, she had heard talk of trouble between the young Haneses for several months now. Some of her male clients had told her they thought Brad paid too much attention to the new singer at Larry's. Others had overheard Brad and Ashley arguing at Bitty Sondheim's restaurant next door, the Pop-In. Everyone knew that Brad's pride and joy — the big white truck he had purchased in the spring — had been repossessed. In fact, folks were surprised that Ashley's large diamond engagement ring was still perched on the third finger of her left hand. Word had it the two were deeply in debt, and Ashley's family had been known to frequent the local pawnshop when times got tough.

Furthermore, if Charlie Moore hadn't stepped in to help Brad finish off the

Haneses' room addition and shore up the rest of the termite-eaten walls, people suspected that the entire house would have fallen down around their ears. None of this made for pleasant conversation, and Patsy wished the subject hadn't come up now.

"Brad and I are fine," Ashley fired back at Pete. "You've been married before, haven't you? Was your first marriage one of the *dumb things* you said you'd done?"

Jennifer again elbowed Ashley, but Patsy could see that the young redhead was in no mood to be silenced. She had come into the meeting riled up about something, and Cody's insistence that she become president had only made it worse. Now she was fairly bristling for a fight with Pete.

"Marriage is a risky business," Pete told her. "I had *two* wives in my past life, and I sure don't deserve another. I got married when I was too young and ignorant to know how to treat a fine lady like you or Jennifer or Miss Patsy Pringle. And I was certainly in too big of a hurry to manage things. You're right to call me out on this, Ashley. I probably should have waited longer to ask for Patsy's hand. There's only one thing that makes this time different from the other two, and I'm counting on it to carry us through the rough spots."

" 'Except the Lord build the house,' " Cody piped up, " 'they labour in vain that build it.' Psalm 127:1. The house is a metaphor for marriage. Pete and Patsy are going to start their new marriage with God in the middle and underneath and all around. That's why it's going to work out happily ever after. Isn't that right, Pete?"

"Happily ever after sounds good to me." Pete glanced at Patsy, gave her a wink, and then reached toward Cody's plate. "You weren't planning to eat the rest of that lemon bar, were you?"

"Yes, I was!" Cody cried, snatching it away just in time.

Jennifer laughed and punched Pete in the shoulder as Cody gobbled down his dessert. Patsy's smile faded when she noticed that Ashley's lower lip was quivering as she lifted her teacup to her mouth.

CHAPTER FIVE

"You crazy mutt. I ought to take you over to Mr. Moore's house so he and Boofer can teach you how to do this thing right."

Brad blotted up the latest of Yappy's messes and tossed out the paper towel. As he lifted the plastic liner out of the trash can, he recalled the night Charlie Moore had helped him chip tile off the kitchen floor. A lot of the time, the old man seemed too hopelessly out of date to understand what life was like these days. But once in a while he said something that made good sense.

Charlie had told Brad about the importance of commitment. Both people had to be so resolute in working on the marriage that their commitment to it became more important even than their love for each other. Charlie had said of his wife, *"If I wanted to make an important point, I had to get her to focus on me."*

Though he was exhausted from mudding drywall seams all day, Brad had made up his mind to force his wife to focus on him. He was determined to get what he wanted out of her. For a change, it wasn't a romp in bed. No, Brad was determined to make Ashley notice him. Not only notice him, but say something nice. Admire him the way she used to. Talk about how lucky she was to have him. Tell him how wonderful and smart he was. List all the things she loved about him.

"Is that so hard?" he asked the puppy, who was prancing beside him toward the front door. "I mean, really, Yap. You think I'm pretty great, don't you? Why doesn't she?"

Tossing the trash bag into a larger bin outside the house, Brad reminded himself that he had set a goal for this night. Driven by his purpose, he avoided Larry's bar, made himself a sandwich at home, and began doing what he knew would catch Ashley's attention.

For the second time this month, he was cleaning their entire house from ceiling to floor.

While washing load after load of laundry, he had vacuumed all the floors and scrubbed the toilet bowl. Then he had started on Ashley's side of the bed, stacking her bead magazines, putting her shoes in the closet, and gathering up all the doodads she put in her hair. He cleared his side of shoes, magazines, socks, dog toys, and empty water bottles.

"When did she quit thinking I hung the moon?" Brad asked as he held the door open for Yappy. "I'm the king of the bedroom, if I do say so myself. That ought to keep her happy enough. So why doesn't she ever have a nice word for me?"

Yappy shook his head until his ears flapped loudly. *"Wow!"* he barked. Then the rest of his little body shivered right down to his fluffy tail.

"Yeah, it's cold out there," Brad grunted. His thoughts turned to Larry's for a moment. No doubt Yvonne would be into her second set by now. That long dark hair would be swishing around her shoulders as she swayed back and forth in her tight jeans. Brad could be warm, slightly buzzed, and listening to some good music. Instead he was cleaning house for an icy redhead who rarely gave him the time of day.

Was it really the drinking that had driven Ashley away? Or had she gotten so busy she forgot she was married? Or — worst of all — had she stopped loving him?

Frowning at the thought, Brad switched

off the overhead light, stretched out on the
sofa, and flipped on the television, giving
the room a warm glow. He would *not* fall
asleep, he told himself as Yappy leaped up
and curled into the crook of his arm. He
absolutely would not doze off. Though his
neck ached from staring at the ceiling all
day, he would keep his eyes open until that
woman walked through the door. . . .

"Brad?"

The voice snapped him up from the couch
as though he had touched a live wire. With
a sharp yap, the puppy tumbled onto the
carpet.

"Are you drunk again?" At the tone of
Ashley's voice, Brad cringed. She set her
hands on her hips. "Because I am *not* haul-
ing you into bed tonight. You can just sleep
on the couch with your dog."

"I haven't been drinking," he told her.

"Yeah, right." Ashley tugged off the scarf
around her neck and hung it over a hook on
the rack by the door. "And how were the
ladies at Larry's? Did *Why*-vonne sing all
your favorites?"

She shrugged out of her coat and stamped
her feet on the floor. "It's snowing, for your
information. One of us is going to have to
shovel the driveway tomorrow morning, and
it won't be me. Two dish guys didn't bother

110

to come to work tonight, so the rest of us had to pitch in and wash everything."

Brad rubbed a hand over his eyes and then rumpled his hair to try to wake himself up. "I'll take Yappy out," he mumbled. The puppy's failure to become house-trained had become yet another tension between the couple. He turned on the living room light as he opened the door. Maybe Ashley would notice what he'd done, but at this point, he was beyond caring. Who wanted to be married to the Whine Queen anyway?

Standing outside, Brad watched the white flakes drift downward only to melt as they hit the ground. Yappy ran in circles for a moment, confused and excited by the snow; then he remembered he had more important business to take care of. As the little dog lifted his leg, Brad realized he had actually been praying that Yappy would recall what to do in the yard.

Praying. Praying that a dog wouldn't mess in the house. How nutty was that?

Though the Hanes family had trooped to church most Sundays when Brad was a kid, he hadn't given God much thought since turning sixteen and buying his own car. He told his parents he no longer wanted the weekend routine, and they didn't argue. For them, church was little more than a habit passed down from their own families. Beyond trying to figure out which church to get married in, Ashley never even mentioned religion. Her parents had always used Sundays to rest from the snack shop, and she told Brad she didn't give the subject much thought.

"Yap, what do you know about God?" Brad asked the puppy.

As usual, the moment the dog heard his name, he paused, looked at Brad, and cocked his head. The response was so immediate, so intelligent, and so downright funny that Brad couldn't help laughing. The puppy wagged his tail.

"Did you hear me, Yap?" Brad asked. "Have you ever met God?"

"Wow!" The dog twirled in the falling snow, bouncing on his small feet.

"Is that right? Well, what did you think of Him?"

"Wow wow!"

"I reckon so," Brad said, reaching down to fluff the fur behind the pup's ears. Any sense of the divine had left Brad's life long ago, he admitted. Not even falling snow, glittery and soft and bathed in moonlight, could move him much. He had hardened himself. Turned off the tender, gentle side that might cause him pain. Even his love for

Ashley had been rough and driven, as though he were a diamond miner boring through rock to get to a precious gem. But, as it had turned out, his diamond was flawed. Not even worth the work it had taken to make her his.

"Bradley Hanes!" Ashley's voice in the doorway was filled with joy. "You cleaned up the whole house! Oh, my gosh, I don't believe it!"

Before he could turn, she had thrown her arms around his waist and was kissing his cheek. "It's wonderful! It looks perfect. Beautiful! It's just the way I had always hoped. And the new kitchen floor . . . and the ceiling you patched . . . Oh, Brad, thank you so much!"

Unexpected warmth welling up inside him, Brad lifted his focus to the blue-tinged, misted moon. *Wow,* he thought. *Wow wow.*

"Come inside before you freeze," Ashley was saying. "You too, Yappy. Come on, sweet baby. Did you do your business? I bet you helped Daddy clean the house, didn't you? Was it your idea?"

"Yap is in charge of *messing* the house, remember?"

Ashley laughed, a clear ringing sound that Brad had always loved. "Oh, he'll learn. It takes a while, but they always get it eventually."

The puppy scampered ahead as the young couple stepped back inside the warmth of their living room. "You want some hot chocolate?" she asked.

"Love some." Brad sank onto the couch again. It had been worth it. Ashley had noticed his efforts to straighten and scrub down the house, and her words of praise rang in his ears.

She would mention the laundry and dishes any minute now. He wouldn't mind hearing a little more about how much she liked the floor tiles that he and Charlie had installed in the kitchen, either. That had been quite a job — not only getting out the old tile but putting in the new vinyl. He had gotten her attention with the clean house, and now that she was focused on her husband, things were off to a good start.

Now Ashley would probably ask him about the condominium project, Brad predicted, hope taking hold in his chest. When he told her how hard he had worked on those fourteen-foot foyer ceilings all day, she'd probably be amazed. Mudding was never easy, but a ceiling posed an even more difficult challenge than a wall.

It would be nice to tell his wife that Bill

Walters had referred to him as the best mudder he'd employed in years. Ashley might like to know that. Even boast to her friends about it a little. She had always been so proud of Brad and his accomplishments on the football field that she fawned all over him.

Not only had she made him feel like her hero, but she talked about her boyfriend's accomplishments to everyone she knew. Same thing with her engagement ring, their new house, his permanent job with Walters Construction. Brag, brag, brag. Everywhere they went, Ashley had sung Brad's praises. It was about time for a little more of that admiration and love to start coming back his way.

"You would not believe how hard it is for a restaurant at this lake to keep a good dish guy," Ashley was saying as she walked across the living room floor, a mug of hot cocoa in each hand. "They earn minimum wage, of course, and the job is unbelievably nasty. That garbage disposal at the country club is always getting jammed."

"Oh yeah? You ought to see what happens when someone fails to wash out one of our cement mixers at the end of the day. Talk about a jam."

He took the mug and gazed at his wife.

115

Ashley blew a tendril of red hair from her forehead as she settled into a chair near the sofa.

"That's exactly what I'm saying," she told him. "It's so hard to find responsible employees. Thank goodness I don't have to go near our garbage disposal. They call it Porky. The moment Porky freezes up, this sickening, greasy water explodes out of it and goes all over everyone. An apron does no good whatsoever. And people leave so much food on their plates. Oh, man, I bet the country club could feed half of China with what we throw away. Good stuff, too, like whole shrimp and pieces of steak the size of my hand. I'm glad I don't have to look at those leftovers going down the drain. It's totally disgusting. Just putting the dishes into the washer was bad enough. Tonight was awful."

Brad took a sip of hot cocoa and studied his wife as she talked. Ashley was beautiful, as always. Even after a long, difficult work shift, she came home looking good enough to eat. She had wound up her long hair and poked a couple of chopsticks through the knot to hold it on her head. Tonight, despite her white work shirt and black slacks, she appeared downright exotic. The beads she had chosen added to the effect — blue and white, with intricate designs she had worked into the clay. He ought to admire them, but he really didn't want to bring up the topic of beads. That would get her rambling forever. Better to get back to the subject of his job — the cranky cement mixers, mudding the ceilings, all the things Ashley used to question him about in wonderment.

"Are you listening?" she asked.

"Sure." Brad shook himself inwardly. What had she been saying? "You told me a couple of the dish guys didn't show up for work."

"Yeah, and that meant the rest of us had to take turns going down there and running the washer. Oh, ick. I'll tell you what, if I have to do that again, I'm going on strike. Jay said he's planning to talk to the owners about raising the base pay for dish guys. Because, I mean, what kind of people can you expect to get for that money? It's ridiculous. We get these lowlifes who come in and work a few days, and then they bail out on us."

"Wait a minute . . . Jay?" Brad struggled to draw his attention away from Ashley's long neck. "Who's Jay?"

"I told you the other day. He's the head of customer relations. He checks on the kitchen all the time. It's one of the main service areas. If people aren't happy about their food, they won't come back."

"Do you talk to this guy? this Jay person?"

"Of course I do." She drew a chopstick from her hair. "He is so funny. He can show up and change my whole mood. *You* sure changed my mood tonight. What possessed you to clean the house? It looks wonderful. I'm just blown away. You're amazing!"

Brad felt a shot of adrenaline flow into his chest and make his heart begin to thud heavily. Ashley had taken out the second chopstick, and her hair tumbled down like red-hot lava. Charlie Moore was right, he realized with some surprise. This was working out even better than Brad had hoped. His wife had not only noticed his house-cleaning efforts of the evening, but she was beginning to sing his praises — *and* slowly undressing in front of him.

"It wasn't too bad," he said. "The bathroom was no fun, but the rest was a piece of cake. I know how to handle a broom. At work, there's a lot of sweeping to do after you sand a good mud job. I spent the whole day mudding ceilings. A lot of them were high — cathedral ceilings. It was pretty crazy working way up there. You can't handle that kind of a job unless you really know what you're doing."

Ashley kicked off her shoes and curled her

legs up under her. "I hate to sweep. Thank goodness we have people for that at the country club. If I had to run a vacuum under those tables, I would just about barf. Sweeping was my least favorite thing at the snack shop, and I always had to do it, of course. I felt like such a zero when rich people stopped by for ice cream."

She took a sip of her cocoa, but before Brad could open his mouth to remind her about his mud work, she was off and running again. "Oh, speaking of rich people, guess who showed up at the club tonight. Our next-door neighbor — Miranda Finley. She says she's finally moving into the house. Poor Mr. Moore. I think she has just about run him into the ground doing jobs for her. She invited some friends down from St. Louis for dinner tonight, because she won't be there for Christmas this year. They've always had a girls' night out before the most stressful part of the holidays starts up. I guess their tradition dates back to when they had kids at home — Christmas parties, decorating, wrapping presents, all that fun stuff. I have to say, though, it's hard to imagine having a mom who looks like Miranda Finley, isn't it?"

Aware Ashley had asked a question, Brad focused on his wife again. He'd been admiring her shapely legs and wondering why she had failed to ask more about his work on the condo project. She didn't even give him a chance to report Bill Walters's compliment.

"Sometimes I think about what it would be like to have a child," Ashley continued without waiting for him to answer. "I understand how you feel about it, Brad . . . about waiting. I get that. I really do. But don't you ever wonder about becoming a dad? I think being a mom would be so incredible. I love kids. I wanted to be a kindergarten teacher, remember?"

Brad nodded. "Yeah. I guess I remember that."

"You *guess?* I used to talk about it a lot when we were dating. In fact, for a while I was trying to save up money to go to college so I could get a teaching degree."

Brad swallowed, hoping she wouldn't bring up the fact that her money had gone into the truck he had wrecked just before his second DWI. The truck that was eventually repossessed. He was trying to come up with a way to deflect that topic when Ashley spoke again.

"The other day, I was telling Jennifer Hansen about my dream of teaching little kids. I think my bead designs come from that love I have for children. I don't know, Brad . . . to me, the beads seem so . . . preschool. Jennifer doesn't agree, but I can't figure out why everyone is all gaga about them. Sometimes I feel as though a child could make the same exact patterns. The beads don't *feel* like art. But Miranda tells me that her friends love them because they're so unique. She's always going on and on about my beads, you know?"

If there was one thing Brad knew about, it was his wife's beads. And he definitely did not want to talk about them tonight. Besides, what could he say? They did look sort of kindergartenish to him. He had been interested in math and science in school, and he didn't really understand the appeal of art. Especially these beads that had taken over his life.

"Why aren't you saying anything?" Ashley asked, her voice holding a note of trepidation. "Do you think my beads are stupid? I bet you do. You do, don't you? You don't like them. You think they're ugly."

"I never said that," Brad protested. "I'll just be glad when Christmas is over and things can get back to normal around here."

Ashley's face went pale and her eyes filled with tears.

"Wait, I don't mean it that way." He

121

popped his knuckles, trying to figure out how to fix his error. "Your beads are great, Ash. They're . . . well, the women sure do love them. It's just that I kind of miss the way we were. That's all."

"The way we are now has nothing to do with my beads." Her expression went from disappointed to angry in a flash. "There's not a thing wrong with a woman following her dreams. Jennifer and I have been discussing that."

"Okay," he managed.

"Jen isn't sure she wants to be a missionary now, and I told her it's fine for her to do whatever she chooses. She can't figure out what to do with Cody, either. He's really cute, sure, but he's so different. There's a part of her that loves him. There's another part that wants a regular kind of guy. I said, hey, you can't count on any man turning out the way you thought. I mean, look at us, Brad. I thought we'd go right from dating into marriage without a hitch. But everything is so different now. Jennifer says we should talk about our relationship. So . . . do you want to do that?"

Raking his fingers through his hair, Brad tried to think of an appropriate response to this sudden firebomb. *No,* of course he didn't want to talk about their relationship!

122

That was the last thing in the world he wanted to do. He'd rather scrub toilets and clean out bathroom drains for the rest of his life than talk about their relationship.

"You don't want to talk about it, do you?" she was asking, her brown eyes pleading.

"Well, I mean . . . sure. I guess."

"It's just that I expected we'd keep doing the same things as when we dated. Discussing everything in our lives — all our feelings and dreams and thoughts. Taking walks by the lake. Going to movies. Cuddling. Didn't you like that?"

"Yeah, of course."

Brad felt like he needed to scratch his back — as though he were a bear chased up a tree by a hound dog and unable to get down again. It wasn't that he was afraid. He was just restless. Itchy. He wanted to move. Stand up. Walk around. Anything to get out of this predicament.

"I used to love it when you drove me around and we listened to music for hours." Ashley stretched out, setting her stocking feet on the coffee table and slouching back into the chair. "Remember that? And you would play with my hair. It felt so good when you messed around with my clips and my comb. I think we should try to do that kind of stuff more often."

Brad did remember. He definitely recalled those quiet times when he and Ashley had been alone together, focused on each other and enjoying the intimacy they both felt. In fact, he wouldn't mind running his fingers through his wife's hair right now. He started to move; then he saw that Ashley had once again veered the subject down an unexpected sidetrack.

"There's so much in our way these days," she was lamenting. "Like your mom is always calling to give me recipes. Even though I know she's trying to be nice, that bugs me. It's as if she thinks I'm not good enough for you. I'm doing the best I can in the kitchen. If she's so worried about it, why doesn't she teach *you* how to cook? All our chefs at the country club are men, and yet at home, women are supposed to make the meals. How stupid. Jay agrees with me on that, by the way, Brad. I'm trying to be nice to your parents even though your mom interferes all the time, but I don't understand why you refuse to go to my family's snack shop anymore. You used to hang out there all the time. We'd be together even though I was working. I think the reason you won't go is because you don't like my dad."

Wow. Brad let out a breath as he pushed

himself up from the couch. This was not going as planned at all. Ashley was supposed to be admiring his cleanup job around the house and asking about his work at the condo project. Not this whole relationship discussion. That wasn't the way he had mapped out the evening.

"Do you like my dad?" Ashley was asking.

"Sure." Brad headed into the kitchen, Yappy following at his heels. "He's all right."

He grabbed a beer and popped the top. If he was going to get through the next few minutes of Ashley's discourse on the state of their marriage, he would need some fortification. A buzz would dull some of the discomfort of having to sit and listen to her expound on her family, her friends, her dreams, her beads. . . .

"What are you doing?" Ashley was leaning forward in her chair as he strolled back to the couch.

"I've had a long day, and I'm tired. In case you forgot, I was mudding ceilings."

"Well, I was washing dishes and you don't see me drinking beer, do you? Why do you have to drink?"

"It's one beer, Ash. Chill out. I don't see what the big deal is."

"The big deal is your DWIs."

"Do I look like I'm driving?"

"No, but you do drive when you're drunk."

"I just like to have a cold one now and then — especially when it's getting hot in the house."

"What's that supposed to mean?"

"You're always stirring the pot, Ashley. Heating up trouble between us. Just a minute ago, you were running my mom into the ground, as usual. If I have to listen to that, I might as well pass the time doing *one* thing I enjoy."

"But we were talking, Brad. We were discussing our marriage."

"*You* were talking. And talking and talking. I've been sitting here with Yappy, who's probably ready to go outside again by now."

As he stood, Ashley leaped out of the chair and toppled him back onto the couch. "Don't you dare walk out on me like this, Bradley Hanes! For the first time in our whole marriage, we were having a decent conversation. I was telling you my feelings about my job and our relationship and my friends."

"Your job — the one where you talk to Jay all day? Your friends — like Jennifer who thinks we need to talk ourselves to death? Our relationship — which is in the tank?"

"It is not! Don't say that, Brad." Bursting

into tears, she sank to her knees and covered her face with her hands. "I thought you cleaned up the house as a present for me. I thought you wanted to spend time with me — the way we used to. I thought everything was going to be okay again. Oh, this is terrible!"

"It's not terrible, Ash. I'm having one beer, and you're freaking out."

"But you drink all the time, and you wrecked your truck —"

"I told you I don't want to talk about that truck anymore!" When he got to his feet, the puppy bounced off the sofa and ran to the door. "See, Yappy needs to go out. He's learning. Things are going to be all right, Ashley. You don't have to make such a huge deal over stuff. With you, it's like a constant catastrophe around here. What's going on — is it your time of the month or something?"

"Oh!" She sprang up and squared her shoulders as she shouted at him. "How dare you make that part of our problems? I've been having a period since I was eleven, and it never caused me as much trouble as you do. *You're* what's wrong around here. You can't even talk to me for ten minutes without running to the refrigerator for a beer."

"I cleaned up the house for you, woman! I've listened to you jabber for at least an hour. You never quit. The jaw doesn't stop moving. On and on and on. Gimme a break, would you? For your information, I've worked hard all day mudding ceilings, not to mention the fact that Mr. Moore and I nearly killed ourselves on that kitchen floor. I do all these things for you, and you never utter a word of appreciation. If you're not griping about my family or my drinking, you're blabbing nonstop about your beads. Well, here's a message for you: I've admired your stupid beads and I've complimented every hunk of charred meat you've ever pulled out of our oven. I used to tell you I loved you all the time, and I meant it. But you don't even have time to hear that anymore, do you? You're so busy listing your *feelings* — most of which are put-downs of me — that you don't have time to say one nice thing about me. See if I ever lift a finger around here again. And as for my beer, I'll drink as much as I want, whenever I want, so don't even think about trying to stop me. Come on, Yap. Let's get out of here."

Brad grabbed the doorknob and looked down to find the puppy seated beside several large brown beads. Only they weren't beads. With a snarl of frustration, he scooped up the dog, threw open the door, and stalked out into the yard. He'd rather sleep in his car on a freezing night than stay in the house with that woman.

CHAPTER SIX

Carrying the puppy in one hand and a breakfast burrito in the other, Brad pushed open the door of Rods-N-Ends at six the following morning. He had spent the night shivering in his car with a squirmy, whiny dog curled up against him. Inside the bait and tackle shop, Brad stamped the snow off his work boots. Pete Roberts greeted him from behind the counter, but Brad sure didn't feel like making small talk.

Not until he spotted Yvonne Ratcliff searching a row of shelves along one wall near the cash register.

"Don't you carry smokes, Pete?" she asked in her familiar husky voice as she turned to face the burly storekeeper. "I'm out of Marlboros, and my nerves get so jangly when . . ." Her eye fell on Brad. "Well, hey there, good-lookin'. I figured you'd dropped off the face of the earth. Where've you been hiding?"

Brad shrugged. He felt like he'd been stomped on, rolled through grime, and then spattered with grit. Yvonne didn't look a whole lot better than he felt, to tell the truth. Her hair was silky and her body shapely, but she had dark circles under her eyes. Her mouth might have sported shimmery lipstick earlier, but now her lips appeared smudged and puffy. Her cheeks were a blotchy pink. That short black leather skirt and pair of matching boots would have been sexy if not for the large hole near the knee of her stockings.

"Uh, Brad," Pete spoke up. "You can't bring your dog in here, buddy. I'm sorry, but I serve food, and animals are against the law unless you're disabled."

"He looks pretty disabled to me, Pete," Yvonne drawled, sauntering toward Brad. "You must've had a rough night, honey. What happened — wife kick you and the dog out in the snow?"

One eyebrow arched as she gave Brad a slow smile. She lifted a hand and reached for the dog, but a low growl emanated from deep in Yappy's throat.

Snatching her fingers away, Yvonne gave a derisive laugh.

"What is it, some kind of guard dog?" She flipped a hank of dark brown hair over her

131

shoulder. "Well, I'd better get going. Gotta make it home before my kid wakes up. I've had a long night. Worked on my new set after Larry's closed down. You ought to come by, Brad. I've got a different guy on the guitar now. Name's Josh. He plays pretty decent, and I'm glad he's around to keep me company. 'Course, he's nothing compared to you."

At that blatant flattery, Brad finally mustered a grin. Well, at least *someone* found him attractive. "I'll probably see you tonight. If it keeps snowing, the boss man will let us off early."

"You know where to find me." She passed by, brushing against him in a way that sent ripples down his spine. "See ya, honey."

"Take care, Yvonne," Brad muttered, wishing he'd at least been able to brush his teeth that morning.

"You ought to carry cigarettes and liquor, Pete," she called over her shoulder as she pushed through the door into the icy blast. "Otherwise, you're liable to go out of business this winter. People can't live without their vices, you know."

With a laugh, she let the door swing shut behind her and stepped out into the snow-covered parking lot.

Brad faced Pete. "I can't leave Yappy in

132

the car, man. It's too cold. We both need to warm up, and Bitty doesn't have room for us to sit down inside the Pop-In. Listen, let me eat my wrap in here, and then we'll get out of your way. Have you got any coffee?"

Pete studied him long enough that Brad began to feel uncomfortable — as though somehow the older man was able to see right through to his innermost thoughts. Like Yvonne, Pete surely must have surmised that Brad and Ashley had been fighting. He probably knew Brad had ended up sleeping in the car. With Yvonne's flirting, Pete would suspect something was going on between the two of them. Maybe he even guessed that Brad hadn't been able to pull together enough cash to buy a cup of Bitty Sondheim's gourmet coffee.

"Bring your dog and come on back," Pete offered as he led the way past displays of fishing tackle, thermos bottles, life jackets, and sweatshirts with Lake of the Ozarks logos screened on them. "But keep it down. I've got some guys meeting here, and I don't want anyone spreading the news that I let a dog into my place. Yvonne Ratcliff is a little flaky, but she does know a thing or two about the lake. Without my summer vacationers buying gas and bait, I'm barely making the rent these days. I sure can't have the

133

health department breathing down my neck."

Brad took a bite of his breakfast wrap. Who would be meeting in the back of Pete's shop at this hour of the morning? Usually the only people up and moving were construction workers preparing to start the day and bartenders or lounge singers — like Yvonne — preparing to end it.

"Are you really going to do that?" Charlie Moore was asking Derek Finley. "I'll be honest, my friend. I don't think it's wise."

To Brad's surprise, he recognized most of the men seated on the folding chairs arranged in a circle near the coffeemaker. Several of them owned homes in Deepwater Cove. Steve Hansen, the local real estate broker, spotted him and smiled.

"Well, if it isn't Brad Hanes," Steve said. "Pour yourself a cup of java and join us."

"Brad?" Charlie looked up as if in disbelief. "Are you here for the Bible study?"

"Bible study?" Brad took a step backward. "I just came in for some coffee."

"Sit down for a minute anyhow, young fellow." Charlie patted an empty chair beside him. "Is that Yappy?"

Pete spoke up. "I know it's against the rules, Derek. Don't turn me in, okay?"

"My jurisdiction is the lake," the patrolman returned.

"Hey there, pup," Charlie said, his warm eyes focused on the ball of fur in Brad's arm. "What're you shivering for? It's just me. I bet you smell Boofer, don't you?"

Brad didn't have the heart to admit he'd kept the dog in the chilly car all night. Charlie held out his arms, and Yappy slid happily into the warmth of the older man's flannel-shirted embrace. Pete handed Brad a large mug of hot black coffee, and before he knew it, he was sitting with the other men.

"Welcome to the men's Bible study group," Derek Finley said, handing Brad a booklet. "Steve has been leading us through the Gospel of John. We meet on Wednesday mornings, but I'm afraid you're a little late today, Brad. We've just finished up this week's lesson. At the end of the meeting, we share our prayer requests. This is a closed group — meaning we've all given our word not to talk to others about anything that is said in here."

"Okay," Brad said, reveling in the hot coffee sliding down his throat and settling into his stomach. "I don't plan to stay anyhow."

"All the same —" Derek eyed him — "this is private. We'll have to ask you to abide by our rules."

"Sure. Whatever." Brad cupped his hands

around the warm mug and studied Yappy. The pup had fallen asleep in Charlie's lap and was snoring loudly enough for the whole group to hear.

Derek grinned at the dog as he spoke again. "We've taken part of the format for our group from the Gamblers Anonymous meetings I attend, Brad. That promise of confidentiality makes it easier for a man to speak his heart."

Gamblers Anonymous? Brad couldn't help but gape at the Water Patrol officer. He had no idea that this straight-shouldered, upright citizen of Deepwater Cove had ever known trouble of any kind in his seemingly perfect life. Derek Finley — a gambling addict?

"I was telling the other men that I've offered to try to teach Cody Goss how to drive," Derek explained. "Steve thinks that with his wife and daughter coaching him day and night, Cody's about ready to take the written test. If he gets his learner's permit, someone needs to step up and help him learn how to handle a car on the road. I'm willing to take on the job."

"I'm opposed to the whole kit 'n' caboodle," Charlie spoke up. "The wife and I had enough car troubles to make me extra wary. I realize you mean well, Derek, but you've got one set of twins at home and another set on the way. Cody is a good-natured young fella who wouldn't hurt a fly, but I'd eat my hat before I'd trust him behind a steering wheel."

"He already dented Jennifer's car," Steve reminded the young officer. "Why that daughter of mine let Cody take her nearly new hybrid out for a spin I'll never know. The kid didn't even manage to get out of the parking lot before hitting a lamppost."

The intensity in Derek's eyes showed he wasn't going to back down. "Cody doesn't have the know-how yet, but he will. He's an artist, and that takes fine hand-eye coordination."

"But what about common sense?" Charlie asked.

"I believe he'll catch on if he's given plenty of time to practice. It may take him longer than the average Joe, but look at who's out on our highways and waterways as it is. Personally, I suspect Cody will eventually be able to handle a vehicle better than most."

"You may be right on that," Charlie finally conceded. "All right, we'll pray for you, Derek. Cody, too. And now, I'd like to add a request for the Lord's protection on my trip to California."

"California?" Brad blurted out around a last bite of scrambled egg burrito.

"I thought I told you. I'm going to visit my son, Charles Jr., and his family for Christmas. Esther and I had planned . . . we had planned to . . ."

All at once, Charlie couldn't speak. His eyes reddened as he tried to choke out words, and Brad recognized the pain on his friend's face. Wanting to reach out to him yet afraid to let down his guard in front of the other men, Brad took another sip of coffee. He was surprised to see Derek reach over and squeeze Charlie's hunched shoulder.

"You and Esther had planned to go see the grandkids for Christmas," Derek finished. "We'll be keeping you in our prayers, Charlie."

"We sure will," Pete Roberts echoed.

Brad had noticed that Pete came and went as customers needed service in the front of his store. Though he had missed out on some of the discussion about Cody's driving lessons, he was aware of Charlie's coming journey.

"You'd better pray hard," Charlie said, forcing a smile to his lips. "I believe this is what they call a road trip. In many ways, I'm looking forward to the company. It'll keep my thoughts from dwelling on . . . on things too much. But, men, I've got to tell you that I'm not real sure about accompanying Bitty Sondheim home to see her relatives. She makes a mean fajita wrap, but the woman is a little unusual to say the least."

"Not to mention the lovebirds that you and Bitty will have to keep separated." Steve Hansen shook his head. "If you hadn't offered to supervise Jessica and her fiancé, I'd have had to put my daughter on an airplane to go visit her future in-laws."

"They'll be all right," Charlie said. "If Jessica is even half as sweet and wholesome as her big sister, she won't cause me a bit of trouble. I'm planning to put her with Bitty in the backseat while the boy and I take turns at the wheel."

Finding it difficult to picture this foursome on a Christmas road trip, Brad studied Charlie. The older man was patting Yappy's head while the puppy snoozed. Brad didn't like the idea that his friend would be gone over the holidays. Although he was nothing like the guys Brad considered his buddies, Charlie Moore had become someone to rely on for companionship and good advice about all kinds of things.

When Ashley and he had gotten so angry with each other the night before, Brad's

139

thoughts automatically turned to Charlie. What would he have done if Esther had acted so nutty? Would Charlie have slept in his car on a frigid December night? How would the Moores have repaired their long marriage after such a blowup? In fact, Brad had almost driven to the house down the street and knocked on the door.

"All right," Derek said, ticking things off on his fingers. "We'll be praying for Cody and me as I try to teach him how to drive. And we'll pray for safety for the road trip crew."

"Not only safety," Charlie cut in. "I need God to help me understand Bitty. She's a Californian by birth, and she's headed back to the place where all her troubles happened. I know she's wanting to make peace with her past, but she's got a lot on her plate. I'm not sure where she stands with the Lord. I'm no preacher, but I'd like to be able to talk to her about God in a way that she can understand."

"We'll add that to our prayers," Derek said.

Brad wanted to shake his head in disbelief. Did these grown men really think that God was going to listen to every little thing they had to say? Brad knew some people believed such stuff, but he never imagined intelligent, educated, successful people like the ones around him actually had faith that God cared about them.

"Unless anyone else has a prayer request," Steve Hansen spoke up, "I'd like to ask that you men lift me up before the Lord as a husband and father. I've already told you about this past spring when Brenda and I ran into some problems. We're finding it hard to catch our balance again."

"Is there anything we can do to help you?" another of the men asked. Brad thought he recognized him from the loan department at the bank in Tranquility.

"Mainly just pray." Steve let out a breath. "For a while there, Brenda felt abandoned and alone. Now it's my turn. She's got so much going on that we're finding it hard to spend time together. The new shop is taking a lot out of her. She's working hard to get it set up in time for the Christmas rush."

At this, Brad's attention perked up. He hadn't expected such a candid account from Steve Hansen, but it was comforting to know that another man was having troubles with a too-busy wife. It didn't seem possible that Brenda would yell at her husband for drinking, but maybe they argued about other things.

"If the store was all Brenda had going on,

I think we'd be fine," Steve said. "Trouble is, she's also been working with me to renovate and decorate several properties we purchased. I've got people interested in looking, but the houses aren't presentable yet."

"I reckon that wedding is keeping Brenda busy too." Charlie's face twisted into a wry grin. "Whoo, I thought Esther was going to have kittens after Charles Jr. proposed to Natalie. Even though she was mother of the groom, Esther got caught up in the planning. Then she and Natalie's mother started to clash. What a hullabaloo that was. It was all I could do to keep from hightailing it for the hills."

"Try being the father of the bride," Steve said. "Seems like every time I walk in the door, there's some kind of ruckus going on. Cakes, invitations, flowers, bridesmaid dresses, tuxedos, you name it — some kind of tragedy has occurred. If it can go wrong, it has. And now the happy couple is heading off to California and leaving the whole mess in Brenda's lap. Not to mention the fact that our son — who barely passed his sophomore classes at Missouri State — decided not to come home for Christmas this year. He and some buddies are going to Key West. Brenda's not taking that well."

"How is Jennifer getting along these days?" Pete asked. "Last time she was in here to fill up her tank, I mentioned that trip to Mexico. She still didn't want to talk about it."

"She's feeling a little more chipper these days." Steve glanced at Brad. "She's been helping Brad's wife with the necklace project. Evidently that's going pretty well. Jennifer tells me they're down to the wire on having everything done in time for Christmas. I always hear her and Ashley down in the basement, talking and laughing like a couple of teenagers."

Ashley — talking and laughing? That didn't sound like the shouting, angry young woman Brad had fled the night before. Why was it that women seemed to get along so well with each other but not with their husbands and boyfriends? Men were the same way. Brad and his buddies never argued over things like drinking or housework.

Marriage was for the birds.

Might as well enjoy a good time with a woman — someone carefree and fun like Yvonne — and then move on. Brad couldn't imagine what had possessed Pete Roberts to propose to Patsy Pringle. The man had already been married twice. You'd think he would have learned something. Patsy was nice enough in the beauty salon, but no doubt she'd turn into a crab once they got married.

"Anything else?" Derek asked.

When none of the other men spoke up, Steve Hansen launched into a prayer that Brad felt sure could have set a world record. He began speaking as if God were right there in the room with the men and listening to every word. First, Steve ladled out a bunch of thank-yous — for the lake, the snow, families, friends, on and on until Brad was about ready to try to slip Yappy out of Charlie Moore's arms and sneak out of the tackle shop.

Just when Brad figured Steve was winding down, the man launched into a big apology to God. Sorry for this, sorry for that. Steve — who had earned the right to be one of the proudest guys at the lake — sounded as though he was the low man on the totem pole. And he took everyone in the group down with him. He told God they were sorry for ignoring Him, sorry they hadn't spent enough time reading their Bibles, sorry for harsh words they might have spoken, sorry for looking at women and having inappropriate thoughts —

Now that one caught Brad by surprise.

He had managed to keep his head bowed, but at Steve's confession Brad glanced up to find Yappy gazing at him with big brown eyes. The pup had heard the arguments and shouting the night before. Though silent, that little dog knew his master had been in hot water. And now . . . to Brad's dismay, it appeared that Yappy somehow knew all about Yvonne Ratcliff, too.

Was that possible? Or was Brad's own guilt nagging at him?

As Steve moved on to ask God for help with each specific problem the men had shared, Yappy decided to clamber out of Charlie's lap. The older man tried to hold on, but the wriggling pup did a belly flop onto the floor and then trotted over to Brad.

Lifting the dog into his own arms, Brad caught Charlie gazing at him with almost the same baleful expression Yappy had displayed moments before. Though Steve was now praying about protection for Derek and Cody Goss on the road, Charlie seemed to be speaking in silence. It was as if he were conferring, reading Brad's mind, and transmitting messages of his own.

While working together, the two men had talked often enough that Brad could almost sense what the older man was thinking. In fact, he was sure of it.

Though Charlie Moore's eyes were open and his mouth was unmoving, he was *praying* for Brad and Ashley.

The realization startled Brad to the point that he swallowed to hold back the sudden lump that welled up in his throat. The fact was, Brad loved Ashley — and Charlie knew it. Brad knew it too.

Did Ashley?

Charlie had nearly shipwrecked his own marriage. He'd gotten drunk and staggered into a strip joint. But he loved Esther so much that even now he could barely speak her name without crying.

Brad sensed that Charlie was praying for that same kind of love in the Hanes marriage. Uncomfortable at the intimacy of the moment, Brad bent his head and scratched Yappy behind the ears.

Spending an early morning hour in Bible study and prayer seemed pretty crazy, but the other men must have liked it enough to keep coming. Brad hadn't minded too much, despite the group leader's epic-length prayer. The coffee went down smoothly, and the back area of the tackle shop was toasty warm. If Yappy hadn't been nosing around in Brad's coat pocket in hopes of finding a dog biscuit, the room might have been warm and comfortable enough to put a person to sleep. Especially with Steve now in the midst of praying for the mayor, the governor, the president, and even some of America's enemies.

Just as Brad sensed his eyelids beginning to droop, he heard a chorus of hearty amens. And then they were up, pouring more coffee, patting Yappy, wishing each other a good week, and heading out the back door. Brad figured he shouldn't take the puppy through the store again, so he moved to follow the others.

Charlie caught him at the door. "Good to have you here, Brad," he said. "You're welcome to join us anytime, you know."

"Thanks, Mr. Moore. I'd stay and talk, but I'm about to be late for work. It won't matter too much today because of the snow. The boss won't expect us to be on time. But any other day, my boss would blow a fuse if I got to the site after the other guys had started."

That wasn't exactly true. With the Bible study starting at six and Brad not due at work until seven, he could get there on time. Bill Walters kept the crew busy on the west side of the lake — rarely more than a five- or ten-minute drive from Deepwater Cove. Though Bill wouldn't like him arriving late, the man would probably make an exception for a gathering like this. Walters was so holy he wouldn't even allow the men to cuss when he was within earshot.

"Well then," Charlie said with a nod, "I guess I won't see you until after the new year starts up. Take care of your pup. Boofer's going to miss playing with him. Boof will go to the kennel while I'm away, but he never seems to mind too much."

"Maybe Yap and I could drop by and visit him."

"Now that would be nice." Charlie studied something in the upper corner of the room for a moment. "Your first Christmas with your bride, isn't it? Mmm. I do remember that one well. Make sure you pick out a gift Ashley really likes. Something that says you appreciate her. And spend a little money on it, if you can. I made a pretty big mistake or two in my time. Choosing the right present takes a fair amount of thought."

Brad set his coffee mug on a nearby table. "I reckon I'll get her a bead necklace."

Charlie saw through that comment right away and chuckled over it. But to Brad the anticipation of Christmas with Ashley wasn't exactly humorous. He didn't feel sure they would even be together, let alone opening packages under a tree.

"You have a good trip, Mr. Moore," Brad

said. "Just get Bitty talking about food. That'll occupy her."

"Excellent idea. But, don't forget, Bitty will be in the backseat with Jessica Hansen. It's the fiancé I'm going to have to entertain."

At that Brad tapped his friend on the shoulder. "Come on, Mr. Moore. You don't really think Jessica and her boyfriend are going to ride all the way to California in separate seats, do you? No way. You and Bitty will be taking turns at the steering wheel. And if I were you, I wouldn't aim the rearview mirror toward the occupants in the back. No telling what you might see."

Visibly blanching, Charlie swallowed. "Well, now. Maybe that's exactly where I *will* aim the mirror. We can't have any hanky-panky going on. I'm responsible for those two kids. Steve Hansen will have my hide if I don't keep a close watch on his daughter."

"Man, Mr. Moore, you are so out of it. Nobody's following those old rules these days. If Mr. Hansen thinks his daughter isn't fooling around with her fiancé, he's a lot dumber than he seems. I don't know a single woman who doesn't give it up now and then for the right guy. That's just how it is."

"Maybe that's the trouble." Charlie pointed a finger at Brad. "You may say I'm just an old codger, but I know there are at least a few young people today who value purity. It makes a difference. And it's never too late to ask God to forgive the past and start you out all over again. Don't forget that, you hear?"

"I hear you, Mr. Moore."

Brad shook his head as he and the older man headed out into the predawn morning. An inch of new snow crusted the parking lot, and icicles were forming on the eaves of the shops along the strip of highway in Tranquility. Brad waved good-bye as the older man slipped behind the wheel of his car.

"Young people today value purity," Brad thought, suppressing a snicker as he tucked Yappy close against his denim jacket and made his way toward his own vehicle. When he was a teen, he hadn't given purity a second thought. In fact, he and his friends had actively plotted to end that dreaded state.

Brad had enjoyed the pleasures of more than one girl before he discovered Ashley in the snack shop near the high school. Leaving behind his old wandering ways was one of the things that had worried him most about getting married. Now it seemed he should have listened more carefully to his intuition.

Life was too short to stick to one woman — wife or not. The more Brad thought about it, the idea actually seemed ridiculous. He couldn't imagine that Steve, Derek, or any of the younger men in that pious prayer group had waited until marriage. People just didn't anymore. Girls were the same way. Virginity was for kids.

"Hi, Brad." Jennifer Hansen stepped around the back of her car just as he was opening his door. Her pretty face framed in a brown wool cap and matching coat, the golden-haired young woman beamed shyly at him. "I didn't expect to see you here this morning. Aren't you supposed to be at work?"

"It's no big deal. With the snow and all." Brad's eyes glazed over slightly as Jennifer stepped closer, enveloping him in a sweet, flowery scent. She reached for the puppy and ruffled his ears.

"Ashley called me this morning. She was upset." Jennifer let out a breath that smelled of cinnamon sugar. "Would you mind if we talked for a few minutes? In private?"

"In private?" Brad said, aware that a

length of long blonde hair had blown across
his arm. "Sure. That would be great."

CHAPTER SEVEN

As it turned out, Jennifer was on her way to open her mother's new home-decorating shop, Bless Your Hearth. Brad accompanied her across the parking lot and then followed her into the large, dusky room filled with furniture, lamps, pillows, candles, rugs, and all kinds of other doodads — most of them crafted near the lake, she told him. Before flipping on the lights, she struck a match and began moving from candle to candle. The wicks caught flame, sending a mingled aroma of pine, cloves, pumpkin, and peppermint into the air.

"How long have you and I known each other? Since kindergarten?" Jennifer asked Brad.

"Yeah."

"Mrs. Kirkpatrick's class. You were a troublemaker back then."

"Still am."

She shed her coat, hung it on a hook

behind the counter, and then tugged off her cap. Static electricity made her long hair fan out around her shoulders like sunlight streaming from behind a cloud. With a sigh, she stood for a moment, gazing at the floor.

For some reason he couldn't explain, Brad wanted to take Jennifer Hansen in his arms, stretch her out across one of the soft couches in the store, and kiss her. He could feel the longing well up inside him in mind-numbing waves. Ashley, the Bible study group, Bill Walters, the construction crew, Charlie Moore, Yappy, all scattered from his thoughts like dry leaves in a gust of wind.

The only thing that mattered was this moment. This woman. Heart thudding, he focused on her as though looking at a beautiful deer through the sight of a rifle. His target. In an instant, his greatest desire.

"You and I didn't really know each other in school," Jennifer murmured, switching on a low-watt lamp on a nearby table. "I was kind of shy, I guess. You might not even remember me."

"I remember you. You were in the homecoming court our last year."

"That was my sister. Jessica went on to be elected queen when she was a senior. She's the social butterfly, not me."

Brad took a step closer. Yappy chose that

moment to lift his head and start sniffing the air. The movement of the dog brought Brad back down to earth. This was Brenda Hansen's store. Jennifer was Ashley's friend. He was supposed to be at work.

"My sister and I were friends with Ashley when we were in elementary school," Jennifer said, now wandering through the store, switching on an array of little lamps. "I guess Ashley told you that I've been helping her finish up the bead orders in time for Christmas. We didn't become close friends again until after I got back from the trip I took to Mexico. My group had some trouble there. You may have heard about it."

Trying to sort sense from desire, Brad stood rooted to a braided pink rug. He didn't care about Mexico. He sure didn't want to talk about Ashley's beads. Why had Jennifer led him into the store? Surely she knew how good she looked. She smelled like some kind of dream, and her hair kept slipping back and forth over her shoulders. Who could concentrate with a female like that only five paces away?

"Yeah," he managed. Yappy had decided it was time to explore, so Brad set him on the rug. "Listen, Jennifer. You said you wanted to talk?"

"Oh, sure. I just need to turn on the rest

155

of these lamps. Why don't you go into my mom's office? It's right through that door. I'll be there in a second."

Brad stepped into the small room, its utilitarian desk and chairs a contrast to all the fluff in the store. Could Jennifer really be thinking the same thing he was? Was it possible that she'd been eyeing him since high school, hoping for some kind of connection between them? Maybe Ashley had told her about their problems, and Jennifer had seen her chance to make a move. The idea of someone who looked so angelic having the heart of a vixen made it all the more exciting.

Wow. This was exactly what he'd been considering for the past couple of months. No point in letting an unhappy marriage trap him and bring him down. Just have fun. Make life good. Enjoy the moment.

"Well, anyway," Jennifer said, entering the room with Yappy at her heels, "I've been thinking about everything . . . all the stuff that's been going on."

"Oh yeah? Like what?" She hadn't turned on the light in this room, and he took the opportunity to move toward her. "What's on your mind, girl?"

Just as he reached out to lay a hand on her hair, Jennifer sank down into the office chair and bent over, holding her stomach as if she might be sick. Her voice quavered as she looked up at him. "Things are really hard these days, Brad. Ashley asked me to talk to you. I know we don't know each other very well, but Ashley is my friend, and . . . well, I told her I'd try."

"Ashley asked you to talk to me?" Reality crashing in on him, Brad withdrew his hand. "Why can't she just talk to me herself?"

Jennifer looked at the floor. "She said she's tried, but you won't listen. That you don't ask about her feelings."

"Her *feelings?*" Brad snapped up straight, as if a rubber band had shot him from behind. "Ashley spends every minute we're together pouring out her feelings. I couldn't miss them if I tried. Listen, Jennifer, I've sat through enough mourning over Mrs. Moore to equal fifty funerals. Ashley never stops. I mean, how long does it take for her to accept that the old lady had a stroke and she's dead?"

"It takes a long time!" Jennifer stood up, facing him, her perfume still distracting him. "You can't expect Ashley to just shut off her emotions and move on."

"What do you know about our problems?

157

This really isn't any of your business, you know."

"Yes, I know!" Jennifer sucked in a breath and her beautiful face crumpled. Before the tears spilled onto her cheeks, she covered her eyes with her hands. "But I promised Ashley I would talk to you. She thinks it would be better if she hadn't married you, because you've changed so much since the days when you were dating. She told me she feels alone all the time, but then she pictures her whole life stretching out ahead with no one. No one at all to love her."

The office door suddenly swung open. "Hey, Brenda, did you see that the snow is melting already?"

Cody Goss stopped in his tracks and stood stock-still. His eyes darted from one person to the other. "Oh, it's you, Jennifer. And Brad Hanes. Where's Brenda? What's going on?"

"Nothing," Jennifer blurted. "Why are you here at the store, Cody?" She grabbed a tissue from the box on her mother's desk and blotted her cheeks. "You're supposed to be painting a house for my dad."

"I forgot my sea sponge. You can't do a good faux finish without your sea sponge."

Frustration, attraction, and bewilderment still coursing through him, Brad rubbed the back of his neck. "I'm out of here. Later, you two."

"But what were you and Jennifer doing?" Cody asked, stepping in front of the door. "Were you hiding in Brenda's office? Were you standing in the dark? Why is Jennifer crying?"

"None of your beeswax, kid. Move out of my way. I'm late for work."

"No." Cody squared his shoulders, blocking the only exit. "Did you hurt Jennifer?"

"Of course not, Cody." Jennifer stepped over and touched his shoulder. "Calm down. Everything's fine."

"But you're crying."

"Yes, and Brad is right that this is not your business."

"I will protect Jennifer," Cody growled, piercing what was left of Brad's composure with the steeliness of his bright blue eyes. "I'll take care of her forever. She knows I will. I would never let anyone hurt her — not in the office of Bless Your Hearth or anywhere else in the whole world. Why did you make Jennifer cry?"

"Brad and I were talking, that's all." Jennifer took Cody's arm and tried to move him from the doorway.

"Talking about you?" Cody glanced at Jennifer. "Oh, I bet you were talking about

159

Ashley, right? About how sad she is because of Brad drinking too much and denting his new truck and not being nice about her beads. I know all about that because I listen to the ladies at Just As I Am. Even though Patsy says *no gossip on these premises,* those women do talk, and what they talk about is you, Brad Hanes."

"Me?" He thrust out his chest. "If those old biddies don't have anything better to do than —"

"Hey, it's Yappy!" Cody burst out. "You brought Yappy with you! I like him. He's the best dog except for Boofer, who I like better but only because I've known him longer. I like Yappy a lot."

Before Cody could make a move, Brad bent and snatched up the pup, who was gnawing on the leg of Brenda Hansen's office chair.

Jennifer gasped in horror.

"Oh no! Look what he did — they're soaked!" She knelt over a stack of yellow-stained floor mats. "Mom just got these in yesterday. They're handwoven. Mom nearly broke the bank paying for them. Now how am I supposed to get them clean? My mom is going to kill me for letting that dog in here. And look what he's done to her chair! That's an *antique,* Brad. Your dog just chewed halfway through the wood on a cabriole leg!"

"Ha! That's funny!" Cody said, his face suddenly transforming from concern to hilarity. Laughing, he bent over and slapped his thigh. "Mrs. Miranda Finley thinks that Yappy is really Mrs. Moore reincarnated into a dog. Wait till I tell her what Mrs. Moore did to the floor mats and the old chair! I would like to hear her explain that, wouldn't you?"

"What are you talking about, bozo-brain?" Brad snapped. "Don't say dumb things. And move it before I have to throw you across the room."

Cody sobered as he pointed a finger at Brad's chest. "I am not dumb, and you better not throw me across the room or make Jennifer cry ever again. You ought to just leave forever, Brad. That's what you should do, because in Deepwater Cove, nobody likes you except Mr. Moore — and that's only because Mrs. Moore loved Ashley and told her husband to help fix up your broken-down house."

"Yeah, and you belong in a nuthouse." Brad tucked the puppy into the crook of his arm as he elbowed past Cody into the main room of the shop.

Nobody in Deepwater Cove liked him?

161

Brad heard Cody's words echoing in his head as he stalked toward the door. Well, so what? He had no use for any of them, either. Bible-thumper men spreading rumors about him behind his back. They probably talked about him as one of their "prayer requests." And the salon ladies bad-mouthing him while they got their hair done? They could rot for all Brad cared.

Same for Jennifer Hansen, he thought as he threw open the front door. What had she meant by luring him into the darkened store? Had he been mistaken in thinking that Jennifer was interested in more than a friendly little chat with him?

No way. Brad hadn't read a girl wrong in years — at least, he hadn't until he got married. Now Ashley had found a new way to torment him. Had she really asked Jennifer to talk to him? What did she think that would accomplish?

Boots crunching on the icy snow as he tramped across the parking lot, Brad felt Yappy wriggling to get out of his grip.

"What?" he snapped at the dog. "What do you want? You planning to turn on me too?"

The puppy flinched and looked up at Brad with big brown eyes. *"Wow."* His velvety mouth opened to form the softly uttered sounds. *"Wow, wow."*

"You're right about that," Brad muttered.

As he climbed into his car, he thought about the night he had spent in the cramped, freezing vehicle. He thought about his wife, her tears, his eager willingness to take another woman in his arms. Then he thought about Cody, the large wet spot on the rugs, and Jennifer Hansen's golden hair sifting across her back.

What did it all mean, anyhow?

Brad turned the key, and the cold engine chugged to life. Now he'd definitely be late for work. Bill Walters would not take kindly to him bringing a dog inside the new condo complex. Brad would work all day mudding seams in wallboard. Then he'd go home to his unhappy wife in a neighborhood where no one could stand him. What a jolly holiday *this* was turning out to be.

"Merry Christmas!" Patsy Pringle threw her arms wide as Jennifer opened the front door of the Hansen home. "Oh, come here, you beautiful sweet thing. Let me give you a big hug."

As the fragile younger woman sank into her embrace, Patsy could feel the hurt and confusion making those slender shoulders sag. She knew Jennifer had been troubled lately, but there had to be more going on than the effects of that regrettable trip to Mexico. This girl was actually trembling.

"Are you shivering with the cold, honey?" Patsy stepped into the foyer and shut the door behind her. Picking up a platter of decorated cookies, she hurried into the living room, set it on the coffee table, and began tugging off her gloves.

"I'd bet a gentle breeze would knock you flat, Jennifer." She ran her eyes up and down the young woman. "Have you lost weight? Look at you, all skinny and pale and quaking like some poor puppy left out in the snow — which brings to mind the little dog Brad and Ashley adopted. Have you seen him lately? I'd swear Yappy has doubled in size since they rescued him. And cute! Oh, that little rascal could just tear your heart out."

Tucking her gloves into the pockets of her coat, Patsy studied Jennifer more closely. "What is eating on you? Have you been crying this morning already? It's barely ten o'clock. I took the day off to come help you and Ashley finish up those bead orders, but I walk in to find a girl who looks like she's about to keel over. You'd better start talking, sugarplum, and I mean now."

Jennifer shrugged. "I don't know where Ashley is. She said she'd be here by nine, but she hasn't shown up. She's not answering her phone either."

"That's not like her. I've never seen anyone as responsible and dedicated as Ashley is to her bead business. She wouldn't suddenly drop out on us without a good reason. Especially right before Christmas. This is her last big day to get everything in the mail."

"I know." Jennifer sank down onto the couch. "I checked her Web site, and a bunch more orders came in last night. We've got our work cut out for us."

"Well, mercy's sake." Patsy couldn't think of a thing to do but eat a Christmas cookie. She peeled back the plastic wrap on the glass platter and handed a stocking-shaped gingersnap to Jennifer. Then she chose a chocolate-drizzled pecan bar for herself.

"I didn't make these, you know. One of my customers brought them in." Patsy shook her head as she bit into the delicacy. "The way people can change never ceases to amaze me. Back when I first met the lady who gave me this platter, I thought she'd half lost her mind. She had just been through a divorce and was running wild. I'm telling you — just plain *wild*. She wanted me to do her hair in tiger stripes. I did it, too. Orange and black. Nothing subtle about that color job."

"Are you serious?"

"As a heart attack. But not long afterward, she settled into a little house, made some new friends, learned how to fish, bought herself a johnboat, and even decided to let her gray grow out. When she came into the salon to bring me these cookies, she told me she'd joined the Lions Club and had met a nice widower at the last pancake flip. Can you believe that? Aren't these absolutely delicious? I wish people would include recipes when they bring me snacks. Not that I would ever have time to bake. Pete loves it, though. I've had a few meals over at his place since we got engaged, and let me tell you, that man can cook."

Patsy finished her pecan bar, looked around for a box of tissues, and when she couldn't find one, opened her purse. Even though doing hair for a living was a hard job, she did her best to always look nice. That meant wearing a pretty shade of lipstick and keeping her half-inch nails in polished perfection. After touching up her lips and wiping the chocolate from her fingers with a tissue from her bag, she looked at Jennifer.

"What have you been up to today? Nobody should be crying before noon. That's just wrong."

Jennifer sat staring at her gingersnap so long that Patsy almost decided she wasn't going to answer. Then she spoke.

"I ran into Brad Hanes this morning," she said in a low voice. "Ashley called me last night. She told me they had a big fight and he walked out on her. She didn't know where he went."

"He was at the men's Bible study this morning, if you can believe that," Patsy explained. "After everyone left, Pete practically ran over to the salon to tell me the news. Isn't that wonderful? See what I mean about people changing? That tiger-striped boogie-mama turned into a sweet little lady, and now Brad is joining the men's Bible group. If we could only find Ashley and tell her, I bet she'd be over here in a flash and happy as a lark. Why don't you try calling her again?"

Jennifer pressed the keys on her cell phone. Then she shook her head. "She's still not answering. But . . . I don't think Brad went to the Bible study on purpose, Patsy."

"Maybe not, but that's where he ended up. God works in mysterious ways."

Jennifer studied her gingersnap a little longer before speaking again. "I saw Brad outside Rods-N-Ends. He was getting into his car to head to work. I had just arrived in Tranquility to open up Mom's new shop for her. She had an early meeting with one of Dad's clients. So . . . I asked Brad if I could speak to him for a minute. See, Ashley knew that Brad and I had been in the same graduating class in high school, and she thought maybe I could help him understand how she's been feeling about their marriage. She begged me to talk to him."

"Oh?" Patsy considered the information and decided right away it had been a mistake. The person to talk to Brad about marriage troubles was Pastor Andrew or Charlie Moore or a bona fide counselor. Not little Jennifer.

"So, anyway, Brad and I went into the store together," the young woman was saying, her tone growing more solemn by the moment. "It was still pretty dark outside, and the lights were off in the showroom."

"Oh . . ." Patsy picked up a candy-cane cookie iced with red and white stripes.

"Mom had asked me to light the candles and turn on the lamps for her. She doesn't like overhead fluorescent fixtures. Candles give a better ambience."

"Yes, but what did Brad say to you?" Patsy bit into the cookie. "Did you talk to him about Ashley?"

"It was . . . awkward. I didn't really know what to say. But since Ashley had asked me, I thought I could at least try."

"Oh?" Shifting uneasily, Patsy wiped her fingers on the tissue and then lifted a star-shaped cookie with yellow sprinkles to her lips. "You met with Brad? Where?"

"In the back room. Mom's office." Jennifer set her gingersnap back on the platter. "Those lights were still off. I hadn't gotten to them yet."

For a moment, Patsy couldn't breathe. She swallowed the last crumb of sugar cookie, thankful she hadn't choked on it. "So you talked to Brad. There in the back room. Right?"

"Well, not really. I think . . . I'm pretty sure . . . I don't know exactly, but it seemed like . . ." Jennifer shook her head. "I think Brad might have made a pass at me. He said something in sort of a *tone,* and then he was reaching for me . . . reaching out to touch my hair. . . ."

Patsy grabbed a sandy topped with a chocolate drop and stuffed the whole thing in her mouth. She chewed frantically. Praying. Thinking. Sweating. Why had she worn the wool sweater instead of the cotton one? And look at all the crumbs on her skirt!

What should she say to Jennifer? What

could she say? Was this gossip? Where on earth was Ashley this morning? Had Brad truly intended something improper with Jennifer? And why was she telling Patsy about all this instead of her mother or someone much wiser and more profound?

"So, he reached for you?" she finally repeated, unable to come up with anything else.

"Yes, but I sat down before he touched me. And then I burst into tears."

"Tears . . ." Patsy eyed the cookie platter as if it might be some sort of door through which she could escape. "Were you crying because Brad made a pass at you?"

"I'm not sure he made a pass at me, Patsy. Maybe he didn't. It seemed like he did, but then how would I know? It's been so long since I went on a date, and that was the very thing I starting crying about. Then Cody came in, and he started trying to protect me from Brad, which was totally awful, but kind of sweet, too. And then the puppy wet on Mom's new rugs. Right after that, Brad left the store even angrier at Ashley than when he came in. Oh, Patsy, I totally blew it. I've probably wrecked their marriage, and if they get divorced, it'll be my fault."

"But you didn't make a play for Brad, did you?"

"No, of course not! How can you even say that? Oh, this is so awful!" Jennifer stood, waving her hands around like she was trying to catch flies. "I would never do anything to try to attract Brad Hanes or any married man. Why would I do that? Ashley's my friend. I really care about her, Patsy; you know I do."

Suddenly she folded back onto the couch. "Okay, I might have flirted with him a little bit," she mumbled through her tears. "I don't know if I did or not. He's really handsome, and he was being so nice and sort of saying things to me in a way that I haven't heard for years. Oh, Patsy, I'm afraid I made him think I wanted him to touch me! And even worse, maybe I did!"

"You didn't."

"I might have. I used to watch him all the time at school. I had a big crush on him when I was a junior. Even when I was away at college, I still thought about him sometimes. I really did, Patsy. I thought about him even after I heard he'd married Ashley. And every time I've seen him since I came back to Deepwater Cove, I've felt this little thing inside. And maybe whatever that was came out this morning. Maybe I flirted with a married man. My friend's husband."

She was on her feet again, pacing back

and forth. "How could I have done that? What if Brad says something to Ashley about it? Or what if Ashley asks me what happened?"

"That's enough drama, Jennifer," Patsy said. She stood and took the younger woman by the shoulders. "I've had about all the theatrics I can handle for one day. Now, sit down."

With only the slightest pressure, she dropped Jennifer back onto the couch. Resisting the urge to grab a Christmas tree cookie studded with red hots, Patsy seated herself nearby and tried to figure out what on earth she could say. For about the millionth time in her life, she wished the Lord would just open up a cloud and step out and talk to her.

Taking a deep breath, she laid a hand on Jennifer's thin arm. "First of all," she said as calmly as she could, "nothing happened between you and Brad Hanes. There are too many *maybe*s in this situation for anyone to get all upset. You were trying to do the right thing, and for all you know, he was too."

Jennifer sniffled. "I hope so."

"Second, you need to realize that being a single woman is not the worst thing in the world. I've done it for plenty of years, and I've been happy more or less the whole time. I have friends enough to run me ragged. I get all the hugs I need by doing much hugging myself. If people don't want to hug back, that's fine. But if they see Patsy Pringle, they might as well accept that they're going to get squeezed."

"Yeah." Jennifer's voice came out as a whimper.

"Now, I know what I'm talking about is not the same thing as having a husband and children. I don't pretend it is. Single is single, and sometimes it's lonely. But from what I've heard in the beauty shop, marriage can be a lonely existence too. Being married will not automatically make you happy. It won't guarantee you protection. It won't even promise warm arms in bed at night. Believe you me, honey, I've listened to plenty of sad tales about a husband and wife sleeping in separate rooms. You know as well as I do what the source of real happiness is. True joy only comes from God."

Nodding, Jennifer blotted the last of her tears. "I know that, Patsy. I do. I've just been so caught up in my own fears and worries. I started questioning everything."

"You don't ever have to question God. You've been hurt pretty badly, and now it's time to start healing." Letting out a breath, Patsy glanced down at the cookie platter. It was disturbingly diminished.

"Well," she said, "you and I can probably read Ashley's necklace orders and start packaging them, can't we? Let's go on down to the basement."

"There's one more thing about this morning."

"All right." Finding herself in prayer once again, Patsy carefully rewrapped the cookie platter. "What else happened?"

"Cody. He saw Brad and me."

"In the office?"

"In the dark."

Breaking into a sweat, Patsy grabbed a magazine off the coffee table and began to fan herself. The wool sweater had definitely been a bad idea. But Jennifer was gazing out the window, her expression calm for the first time in a long while.

"Cody offered to protect me," she told Patsy softly. "He would have too. After Brad left, Cody helped me clean up the mess Yappy had made on the rugs. And then he told me he loved me and wanted to marry me, just like he always does."

"What did you say?"

"Nothing." Jennifer leaned over and rested her head on Patsy's shoulder. "I won't marry Cody, you know. He's not ready. Maybe he never will be. And I'm way too

Come on in, boy!" Brad's voice again
k on that loving tone Ashley rarely heard
ected at herself these days. "What a good
 you are, Yappy. Right in the snow, too.
w that's what I call smart."

*Broof!"*Yappy's toenails clicked happily on
 patch of tiles in front of the door. *"Broof-*
! Yow-row-row! Brow-oooo!"

rad laughed. "Let's get you some break-
. Make me a pot of coffee, too. Man,
t a night we had, huh? Look at that mess
made."

e?

d Brad include the dog in his of-
es . . . or had there been someone else
e house with her husband?

nley recalled slipping into the living
 just before midnight. How she had
d to find Brad in their bed waiting for
It had been such an awful day — wak-
p alone, taking part of her paycheck to
arents and suddenly bursting into tears
 in front of them, frantically trying to
 mailing the last of her bead orders
 Patsy and Jennifer gabbed, working
less hours at the country club restau-
nd finally steering back home through
ow, fearful she would run the car into
tch at any moment.

and Brad hadn't spoken at all that

impatient and emotional. It wouldn't work
out well. But, Patsy, I do love Cody Goss. I
love him with all my heart. I believe he's
the best friend anyone could ever have."

Chapter Eight

She hated him. There were few things Ashley felt certain of in her life, but this was one. She hated her husband.

Unable to sleep, lying in bed as the sunlight crept up the slats of the window blinds one by one, Ashley stared at the white ceiling. Brad and Mr. Moore had repaired it together, replacing a patch of stained wallboard that had been saturated by a leak and then painting the whole thing bright white. She had felt proud of Brad that day. He and Mr. Moore had stood in the bedroom, elbowing each other and talking about secret plans for the community Thanksgiving. Mrs. Moore sent down a plate of leftover lasagna, and Ashley and Brad had eaten it together before she left for work. At least she would have *one* happy memory of her wasted marriage.

"Browf?" The muffled sound came from the living room. *"Brrrr. Wowf, wowf?"*

Yappy was awake. How long w for Brad to rouse himself from h stupor and take the dog outsi stiffened as she heard her husb around on the sofa in the living

"What do you want?" he mu gentle voice. "You need to go o a fine boy. Good dog, Yappy. Tl to tell me."

The front door opened. A st words announced Brad's reali snowstorm had blown in over shut her eyes, as if that col block her ears as well. Brad' was one more thing she hat husband. When Mr. Moore v never talked that way. But in around his own wife, the qualms about saying whateve

Not that she cared anymor

The night before, the ne surprised Ashley. She had drive home from work on road as gusts of white drift from her headlights. She l another snow so soon aft evening's light dusting. E had. The plows hadn't ever her car was one of the firs down the pavement.

day. Usually they called each other once or twice to touch base. At the start of their romance, she remembered, their messages had been furtive whispers of love and desire. She had saved every voice mail and text message from him. Those days were certainly over. Even so, when Ashley opened the door that night, she had held every hope that her husband might have returned home, climbed into their bed, and gone to sleep on his pillow beside hers.

But no. There he lay on the sofa, beer cans scattered across the floor around him, the television still blaring. And worst of all — in fact, the killing blow — had been the magazine lying open on Brad's chest.

Porn!

As she recalled the photograph on the cover, Ashley had to grit her teeth to keep from crying. That — or racing into the kitchen and stabbing the creep to death with a butcher knife.

How dare he? How *dare* he!

Oh, she hated him. She despised him. She couldn't wait until he was out of the house so she could throw his clothes into a bag, chuck it out in the snow, and lock the door. *Get out of my life!* she would shout if he even came near her today. *Never touch me again! I hate you. I hate you!*

Whistling the *Andy Griffith Show* theme song, Brad strolled into the bedroom. Her eyes just above the blanket, Ashley watched him strip off his jeans, underwear, and T-shirt, then sniff under his armpits and make a face.

Then he looked at the bed.

Stark naked, he gave a start. "I didn't know you were here."

"Did you think I ran away too?"

For a moment, he didn't speak. Yappy leaped onto the bed and began to lick Ashley's cheek. "Stop," she muttered, pushing the dog away. "Make him stop. I'm trying to sleep."

"Come here, Yappy," Brad said. When the pup didn't obey, he reached over and lifted the ball of brown fluff into his arms. "He's just trying to say hello."

"Shut up, Brad," she snarled.

"What?"

"Get out of my sight."

"What's your problem, Ash? I came home, didn't I? You ought to be glad about that."

"Glad? Are you kidding?" She rose in the bed and hurled the disgusting magazine she had taken from him while he slept. "I'm supposed to be grateful because a man who reads this kind of filth is my husband?"

Brad dodged the magazine, but he wasn't

ready when his wife launched herself across the floor at him. "Get out of this house, you drunk! You sleazeball! You creep! You make me sick."

Grabbing his arms, she pushed him hard. Brad was easily twice as strong as Ashley, but she knew she had the advantage. His hangover would have blurred his vision and given him a headache. With all her energy, she shoved him out of the bedroom toward the front door.

"What are you doing? Are you nuts?" He tried to hold firm against her. When he swayed to one side, she grabbed the doorknob.

"I hope I never see you again!" Ramming her shoulder into her husband's solar plexus, she knocked him backward onto the snow-covered stoop. As he tried to get to his feet, she slammed the door. Where was the key? Wait, the dead bolt. Why couldn't she find it?

There!

Breathing hard, she leaned back against the door. *Gone.* Out of her sight. Out of her life. Thank goodness!

"Ashley!" With a thud that rattled the windows, he kicked the door. The frame cracked and buckled. "Ashley, open this door right now!"

She leaped aside just as he landed another blow and the entire door crashed into the room. Totally bare and pale from the cold air, Brad lunged after her. "You threw me out in the snow!" he shouted.

"I hate you!" She ran back into the bedroom — suddenly afraid of him yet furious at the same time. "Get away from me. Go find one of your bar hussies! You can stay with her!"

Panting, Brad snatched up his jeans and stepped into them. "I'm married to you!" he hollered, pointing a finger as he stalked toward his wife. "The worst mistake of my life."

"I'm no mistake! I'm responsible and loving and caring. You're the drunken loser in this marriage! I don't even know why I liked you to begin with."

At that, he stiffened. "You don't? Have you forgotten who I am? I can have any girl I want."

"What's stopping you?" she cried, grabbing the magazine from the floor. "How about *her?*" She ripped out a page, wadded it into a ball, and flung it at him. "Or this one? She's awfully cute, isn't she? Or maybe you like Miss December better?"

He didn't move as the crumpled paper wads hit him in the chest. Ashley threw the magazine to the floor and stomped on it. "I'm not good enough for you, am I? That's what you're trying to tell me, so why don't you just say it out loud? You hate me as much as I hate you. You want some sexy bar hopper in your bed! Or some nude model! You don't want a wife who loves you and works hard and does everything she can to make you happy. You'd rather get drunk and lust after imaginary women in magazines. You'd rather look at them than hold your own wife!"

"How can I hold you, Ashley?" he asked. "You're never here."

"Neither are you. You're always at Larry's."

"You're always at work."

"I have to work, because you drove your brand-new truck into a ditch and now we have to make payments on it. I'm carrying trays of food half my weight for a vehicle that is gone — wrecked by a drunk."

"Don't talk about that truck."

"Why, because it reminds you what a loser you turned into after your brilliant high school career? That was the peak of your life, Brad. You'll never be anything better than you were back then."

"Stop," he barked. "Don't say that. That's not fair."

"What have you done lately that amounts to anything? Hang drywall in a condo? Slap mud on a few lengths of tape? Wow. I'm so impressed."

He sat down on the edge of the bed and stared at the wrinkled magazine on the floor. For a moment, Ashley thought she had truly wounded her husband, and a tinge of regret crept into her heart.

But then he lifted his head and said with a sneer, "Why shouldn't I read whatever I want? You're always too busy with your *beads* to spend time with your husband. If someone had told me three years ago that my whole life would come unglued because of beads, I'd have laughed in their face."

"My business hasn't caused our problems, Brad. It's you. You pulled away from me right after we married. You started going to Larry's, and then we were hardly in bed together at the same time. But why would you need to hold me? You have your magazine. What good is a real live wife with red hair and skinny legs compared to one of those gorgeous women?"

"It's not like that, Ashley. I know they're not real. You don't understand."

"I don't need to understand your trash. All I need is to finally accept the truth that my husband stopped touching me a long time ago. You know who you hold and stroke and pet these days? A dog. I'm lower than that puppy on your priority list."

Brad suddenly sat up straight. "Wait a minute — where's Yappy?"

"How should I know?" Ashley's anger began to ebb in the realization that the broken front door lay on their living room floor. Snow was blowing into a house they could barely afford to heat. And now the puppy had run off.

"Yappy?" Brad stood and walked past her. "Yap, where are you, boy?"

Ashley pulled her robe off the chair where she'd thrown it the night before. "Yappy!" she called. "Come here, Yappy! Time for breakfast."

"He's not here. The house is empty."

"Help me get the door back in place. You probably scared him to death when you bashed it in. Maybe he's hiding."

Together, they hoisted the door and its splintered frame back into the opening where it had been. Ashley sat down on the sofa amid the discarded cans and tugged on her snow boots. This was awful. What a terrible thing. She and Brad had been fighting so loudly, yelling at each other, tearing down their own house, and now their puppy was missing! What if that dog had been their own child? How had it ever come to this?

Brad stepped into his work boots, pulled his coat over his bare chest, and zipped it up. With some effort, he managed to work the door open enough to slip outside. Ashley followed, unable to shut it tight behind her. Trudging through the drifts of snow, they whistled and called for the puppy.

"He's so small!" Ashley called to Brad as she stopped to catch her breath. "He'll freeze to death."

"He's wily. He'll be okay. Yappy! Come here, fella. Come see Daddy!"

Daddy?

The word ricocheted through Ashley. Brad had always protested the idea of their having a baby. The room she had hoped would become a nursery now sat empty, unfurnished, cold. She had eventually given up hope of children anytime soon, and as it turned out, that was probably wise. Look at the two of them. What a wreck they'd made of their marriage.

But did Brad actually have fatherly feelings tucked away inside him somewhere? He was always so sweet and gentle with the dog, she thought as she worked her way through the trees behind the house. He had been that way toward Ashley once. Why had he turned away from her? Why didn't he

186

even want to cuddle with her anymore? What had she done that was so awful?

If Brad could love a dog as much as he did Yappy, why couldn't he love his own wife?

"Is this who you're looking for?" Miranda Finley's voice echoed between the neighboring houses. Wearing a black fur coat, she held up the little dog. "I noticed him on my deck a minute ago."

"Yappy!" Ashley took off through the prickly brush. As she ran out into the open, she saw Brad just ahead of her. He leaped onto Miranda's deck and wrapped the little dog in his arms.

"Thank you, Mrs. Finley," Ashley said, joining him. "Brad was getting ready for work, and I guess the puppy got out."

"Probably through the front door your husband kicked open with his bare foot." Miranda smiled, her hooded eyes trailing across from Ashley to Brad. "What an interesting sequence of events I witnessed over my morning coffee. Now I truly do know the meaning of a farmer's tan."

Without speaking, Brad turned and stepped off Miranda's deck. As he carried the puppy back toward their house, Ashley studied the older woman.

"I wish you hadn't seen that," she told

Miranda.

"Oh, it wasn't unpleasant. You're a lucky young lady."

Ashley gritted her teeth. Then Miranda reached out and squeezed her shoulder. "Don't worry, dear. Every married woman has her burdens to bear. From a distance, yours didn't look so bad."

"That's not funny, Mrs. Finley."

"I'm teasing. Ashley, you should know better than anyone that I mean well for you. I helped you start your bead business, didn't I? I've tried to be a good friend to you."

"You have, and I'm grateful. But my marriage is private."

"*Nothing* was private this morning." Miranda chuckled and then shook her head. "Oh, don't look so upset. What I saw this morning was a nice surprise for a woman my age. I've heard whispers in the neighborhood about you and Brad having a few spats, but I never pay attention to that sort of thing. My husband and I had our troubles too, when he was alive."

"You did?" Ashley had never heard Miranda speak of her late husband. What sort of man would marry a spiky-haired woman who did nothing but lie in the sun all day or go to tanning salons and bake herself into leather? Derek Finley was nothing like his mother. The gentle Water Patrol officer must have taken after his father.

"What you need, Ashley," Miranda was saying now, "is spiritual grounding. You're floating along through life with no one to guide you, nothing to put your faith in except yourself. Relying on yourself — on your own inner deity — is exactly right, but only if you feel good about who you are. I'll tell you what. For Christmas, I'll give you some of my books. You can come over and we'll do yoga together, too, if you want. That will calm you down and focus you in the right direction — within."

"I don't know about that, Mrs. Finley. You'd better not give me any of your stuff." Ashley didn't want to confess how broken her marriage truly was — and the fact that she might not be able to locate Miranda's books in the midst of a hasty, heated divorce. "I'm so busy. I'm not sure when I could return them."

"Gifts don't have to be returned. This is my way of helping you and Brad. Ashley, you've been running from one thing to the next for such a long time that you haven't had time to focus on what really matters."

"I know. Brad."

"Not your husband. *You.*" She touched the top button of Ashley's coat with her fingertip. "A healthy, whole you. You need to realize that everything in this world is — in its essence — a part of god. You, Ashley Hanes, are one with divinity. Ignorance of this truth is really your only flaw. You don't understand your own nature and how it fits into the wholeness of the universe. These books I'm going to give you will be enlightening. As you begin a personal transformation, things will start to make sense."

"I'm not sure."

"Well, I am. The problem is outside yourself — the ignorance, illusion, and misunderstanding in this world."

Ashley shifted her weight from one foot to the other as Miranda talked. The truth was, she didn't feel the least bit divine.

She was trying to think of a good way out of the conversation when she saw Brad, fully dressed, heading to his car. He carried Yappy in his arms.

"You're right, Mrs. Finley. The problem *is* outside — because outside, it's still snowing, and my front door is broken, and my husband is leaving for work without even saying good-bye to me. So excuse me while I get out of this cold and see if Mr. Moore will come over and help me fix the door."

"Oh, you won't find Charlie Moore at home today," Miranda called after her as

Ashley hurried down the steps of the deck. "He's gone off to California with Bitty Sondheim and Jessica Hansen and her fiancé. You're on your own now, Ashley."

Brad sat by the space heater in the large condo foyer he was helping to build. The other guys on the crew were eating their lunches, but he didn't feel hungry. Yappy, on the other hand, was scampering from one man to the next, taking the bits of sandwich meat, bread, chips, even peanuts they handed him. Brad vaguely wondered what kind of mess he'd have to clean up later.

"You must have been celebrating hard last night, dude." Mack wandered over and hunkered down beside Brad. "I didn't see you at Larry's. Don't tell me you've found another place to hang out. Yvonne was asking about you."

"Buzz off, Mack." Brad pulled his phone from his pocket. "I'm not in the mood for it."

"I'm just saying . . ." Mack shrugged and downed the last bite of a burrito. "The woman likes you. If I had a hot one like Yvonne on my tail —"

Brad cut him off with a glare, and Mack ambled out the door for his after-lunch smoke. Toying with his phone, Brad thought about Ashley.

He didn't like to admit it even to himself, but he had always hoped his wife would be pure and sweet, one of those virginal girls like Jennifer Hansen. Ashley had been almost that way. Not exactly, but near enough that he'd been able to envision a lifetime with her.

How had she turned into this redheaded hornet who hated the very sight of him?

Was he really that bad?

Brad let out a breath. Probably.

He couldn't recall his encounter with Jennifer Hansen without growing uncomfortable. What had he been thinking? He had just walked out of a Bible study, and the next thing he knew, he was making a play for his wife's friend inside her mother's store. Was he insane?

Maybe he was losing some brain cells. Ashley said he drank too much. Could that be it?

He looked around at the other men on the construction crew. They were buddies — guys like him who enjoyed tossing back a few brews now and then. He couldn't say he truly admired any of them. Except his boss, maybe. But Bill Walters held a college degree and ran his company like a drill sergeant. The only tenderness Brad had seen in the man was when Yappy came along to work after the night they had spent in the car. The puppy was shivering and hungry. Bill had taken Yappy into his trailer, fed him, and let him sleep there for the day. In fact, the two had become so attached that Brad felt he'd probably better not show up *without* the puppy the following day.

What about Ashley's accusations of Brad's spending problems? Now there she was dead wrong. He had bought and wrecked the truck, true. But a man could be forgiven for a financial mistake or two, couldn't he? It wasn't like he ordered bead-making supplies day and night.

"Why don't you come to Larry's with us tonight?" Mack was asking as he downed a packaged vanilla cream snack cake in a single bite. "Tomorrow's Christmas Eve, so there won't be much fun going on then. I suspect Larry might even shut down early. Yvonne's been doing a really hot version of 'Jingle Bell Rock,' and I bet you'd —"

"Wait. Did you say Christmas Eve is tomorrow?" Brad sat up. "Are you sure?"

"Man, where have you been?"

Glancing down at his phone, Brad wondered for the umpteenth time if he should call Ashley. There really were a few things he should apologize for. Not everything, of course. But some of it. Like the empty cans around the couch. And breaking down their front door.

On the other hand, he wouldn't have done that if she hadn't locked him out. The look on Miranda Finley's face made him feel sick. What did an old woman like her mean by flirting with Brad right in front of his wife? Had she really seen him buck naked?

"I probably ought to call Ashley." Brad gave Yappy's ears a rub as the dog trotted by. The number was right there, so easy to press. But did he want to hear her harsh accusations all over again?

"Yeah, put that apron on," Mack said. "Run back to the wife with your tail between your legs and see if she'll forgive you. You are so whipped."

Mack wadded up his cake wrapper. With a loud grunt, the heavier man heaved his jeans up on his waist and trudged outside to smoke one last cigarette. Any time now, Bill Walters would step into the foyer and call the crew back to work.

Looking down at his phone again, Brad ran through his stored names and numbers. Charlie Moore's cell number lit up for a moment. What would he say to all of this? He'd probably have a good laugh about

Brad running around naked in the snow. But Mr. Moore wouldn't find the rest of it amusing at all.

Brad hesitated over the number for a moment. With a tap of his finger, he probably could have Mr. Moore on the line. Weird, but it would be nice to hear the old guy's voice. Get an update on the trip to California. No doubt Mr. Moore would want to know how things were going with Ashley. What could Brad say?

"Back to work," Bill called. The other men trooped into the foyer, Brad following right behind. With a yelp of recognition, Yappy raced past his owner and leaped into the man's arms.

"I'll take your pup to the trailer," Bill said.

Though Brad knew it was against regulations to have an animal on the site, he could tell his employer was getting pretty attached to the dog. And vice versa. That bothered him.

"Sure," he said. "Thanks."

"No problem. He's probably ready for a nap anyhow. It's warmer in there." Bill lifted his head. "Listen up, everyone. You guys get that wallboard hung, taped, and mudded in the master bedroom and bath, and I'll let you go early. Tomorrow we quit at noon. If anyone's looking for a Christmas Eve

195

candlelight service, LAMB Chapel has a good one every year. You're all welcome to drop in. Seven sharp."

As he left the site, Mack elbowed Brad. "As if I'd go to a Christmas Eve service. I'll tell you where I *won't* be parking my backside tomorrow night — on a church pew. Nope, I'll be warming up one of Larry's bar stools. You can count on that."

"Aren't you going to have your kids with you this year?"

"Nah. They'll be with their mothers. Good thing, too. I hate Christmas. Me and Scrooge McDuck — birds of a feather."

Laughing, he started up the stairs toward the bedroom the others were finishing. Brad slipped his phone back into his pocket and followed.

CHAPTER NINE

"Where is your Christmas tree, Ashley?" Cody yelled over the loud banging as he hammered the Haneses' doorframe back into place. The overnight snowfall already was melting, though the air outside blew the crisp scent of pine into the small house. "Did you forget that tomorrow is Christmas Eve? Christmas trees don't have anything to do with Christmas, but still, you should have one if you want your house to look festive."

Ashley said nothing. She could hardly hear Cody over the racket, and she had no idea how to respond to his question. With Brad and her both working, arguing, and generally despising each other, neither had even mentioned the approaching holiday.

Instead, the days had passed, and she had done nothing to prepare for Christmas in her own home. Brad never even mentioned the word, as if speaking about such a special holiday would draw attention to the absence of anything joyful or bright in their lives. Would their marriage survive until Christmas? For too long now, it had felt doubtful.

Ashley planned to go home to her parents. Until she'd moved in with Brad, she had always woken in her own bed and run down the stairs to see the presents under the tree. Usually there weren't many, but she loved the excitement of the morning and the noontime gathering of relatives.

Several days ago, Ashley's mother had called. Ashley promised that she and Brad would be at their house in time for lunch on Christmas Day. But with the mess their relationship had become, she hadn't even found time to tell him. Now she planned to go alone. He could spend the day with his own family — and that didn't include Ashley. She felt almost as if they were divorced already.

"Brenda says Christmas trees should have a theme." Cody stopped hammering and climbed down the ladder. "This year her theme is purple and gold. Steve and Brenda bought a tree in the hardware store parking lot. It's chopped off from its roots, so even though Brenda calls it a live tree, it's dead. I mentioned that to her, and she said not to talk about it again. We all decorated the tree before Jessica left with her fiancé to meet her new in-laws in California. Jennifer helped hang ornaments too. She's not so sad anymore since she started working with you on those bead necklaces. I think doing that job made her feel better."

"I'm glad." Ashley pushed on the door and was relieved to see it swing shut. The latch clicked into place. "Thanks, Cody. I couldn't have done this without you. I'll go turn up the heat now."

Though she hoped he would take the hint and leave, Ashley had learned long ago that Cody didn't usually catch understated suggestions. For him, conversation had to be concrete. Tangible. There weren't many subtleties. He did like metaphors, but that was about as close as he came to understanding anything that wasn't spelled out in neon letters.

"Aren't you going to have a tree with a theme?" he asked, trailing behind her. "Or you could not have a theme. Kim and Derek Finley bought a plastic tree because Kim is allergic to live Christmas trees even though they're really dead. The Finleys hung ornaments made by their twins. Kim is having twins again next year, so that will mean lots more ornaments. The Finleys won't ever need to have a theme."

"We're not putting up a tree this year, Cody." Ashley nudged the thermostat as high as she dared. She and Brad were barely paying their bills as it was. If they didn't have a mild winter, she predicted trouble with the propane company.

"No tree?" Cody stood bewildered. "That's like my daddy and me. But we were poor, and you're not. You're rich. You have a big diamond that Brad gave you."

Ashley glanced down at the engagement ring she had been so proud to show off to her friends. "I don't know, Cody. We're just not doing a tree, that's all."

In planning her wedding to Brad Hanes, Ashley had dreamed about their first Christmas as husband and wife. She would decorate their cozy little home, bake gingerbread cookies, wrap presents chosen especially for him. Though her parents had never taken her to church, the idea of attending a Christmas service struck Ashley as romantic and quaint. Mrs. Moore had said that she and Charlie always went to church together on Sundays, and the Christmas Eve service was one of the highlights of their year. After church, Ashley imagined cuddling up with Brad on their sofa and gazing at the twinkling lights on the tree as they sipped apple cider from matching mugs.

"Mrs. Miranda Finley isn't putting up a tree either, alive, dead, or plastic," Cody informed Ashley, taking a seat and stretching out his long legs. "She says her Christmas decorations are still packed from moving to the lake and then moving next door to you. She doesn't mind, though, because she'll go to Derek and Kim's house to celebrate. She told me she loves being a grandmother — especially the part about buying presents."

"Yeah, I bet." Ashley tried to figure out how to send Cody on his way. This was her first day with no beads to make, no necklaces to string, no envelopes to stuff, nothing. She could actually relax until it was time to drive to her job at the country club.

"I made a really nice present for Jennifer, but you can't tell. It's a secret. I'm not good at keeping secrets, but so far, I didn't tell her. You want to know what I did?"

"Sure." Ashley perched on the arm of the old recliner.

"I painted a picture of her."

Ashley had to restrain herself from laughing. "Cody, you've done scads of pictures of Jennifer. You painted her all over the walls of Just As I Am. Your bedroom at the back of the salon is full of sketches of her. Patsy told me about them."

"That's because I like to draw pictures of Jennifer. Paint her too. She's the most beautiful woman in the world. I hope we get married. So far, she didn't say yes. But I'm not going to get discouraged or give up. I am going to keep on asking until she does say yes."

"Maybe you shouldn't, Cody."

"Why?"

"Because . . . well, because maybe Jennifer doesn't want to marry you."

The young man's handsome face sobered. "She doesn't?"

"I don't know, but you have to wonder. You've asked her dozens of times, and she never says she'll marry you. Why don't you get it?"

"Get what?"

"That she probably doesn't want to marry you. When people want to do something, and they can, they do it. If Jennifer wanted to become your wife, she would."

"Maybe I need to ask her some more."

Ashley let out a sigh and slid from the arm into the seat of the chair. "Cody, is there some kind of food you really hate to eat?"

"You changed the subject. It's not good social skills, but that's okay. Anyone can learn social skills if they practice hard enough."

He ran his fingers through his hair, a mass of light brown curls that almost made Ashley jealous. "I hate chicken livers," he told her. "My daddy used to make me eat them whenever we had any money. That's what he bought, chicken livers, and he said they were good for you, and he rolled them in bread crumbs and fried them in bacon grease. But I didn't like them no matter how he cooked them. Yuck."

"Would you like to eat some right now?"

He glanced at his watch, studying it for a long time. "I'm not very good at telling time yet, but I don't think it's twelve o'clock. I think it's somewhere near ten o'clock. That means we don't need to eat lunch for a while. I might be wrong about the time, but thank you, no, I would prefer not to eat chicken livers."

"What if I asked you fifty times to eat them?"

"Umm . . ." He squirmed a little. "Do I have to?"

"No. But I'm just asking if you want to have some right now."

"Thank you, but no thanks. Thanks anyway."

"See, this is what I'm trying to tell you, Cody. You keep asking Jennifer to marry you, and she keeps saying no thanks. If you keep asking and asking, she's still going to say no. She doesn't want to marry you, just like you don't want to eat chicken livers."

Cody stared at Ashley in silence. "You made chicken livers into a metaphor," he said finally in a low voice. "They are a metaphor for me."

"Sort of. I said that so that maybe you could finally get the point. Just be Jennifer's friend. You don't have to marry her."

His blue eyes suddenly filled with tears. "I am chicken livers."

"No, Cody. No, you're not. You're *you*. You're a really great guy. It's just that I don't think Jennifer wants to marry you. She may not want to marry anyone. Maybe she's not the marrying type."

Swallowing hard, he wiped at his cheek. "I understand that metaphor, Ashley. But I never knew Jennifer thought of me as chicken livers. That is a terrible thing, because chicken livers are disgusting and they make you want to vomit. In fact, I have vomited lots of times when I had to eat them. I told my daddy, no more chicken livers. Please, Daddy, please. No more. But he always made me eat them, and that is what I'm doing when I keep asking Jennifer to marry me. I am making her eat chicken livers."

"Oh, great." Ashley leaned forward and propped her elbows on her knees. "Cody, look at me and stop crying. Let's don't talk about chicken livers anymore. Jennifer loves you. She really does. She thinks of you like a good friend or a special brother."

Tears still trickling down his cheeks, Cody looked forlornly out the window. "The snow is melting faster now," he whispered. "I should go over to Jennifer's house and tell her I'm sorry. I won't ask her to marry me anymore. I don't want to be chicken livers. I would rather be chocolate cake cut into squares."

"Wait, don't go over there yet. Just stay here until you calm down."

Cody Goss hanging around the house was the last thing Ashley wanted, but what else could she say? She had tried to explain the situation to him, and as usual lately, she had made a mess of everything.

They sat silently in the living room, both watching melted snow drip off the eaves where the gutter had torn loose from the roof. Ashley thought about giving Brad a call. She definitely had a few reasons to apologize for what had happened between them that morning.

Trying to imagine his voice, she feared he would sound impatient about being inter-

205

rupted at work. And what if they got mad at each other over the phone? He might not come home that night. Or ever again.

Did she want him to? Did she even care?

What had they done? How had they wrecked things so completely?

"Jennifer might marry somebody else," Cody said, his voice flat. "Maybe she will find another person to be her husband."

"Who knows?" Ashley murmured, recalling the conversation she'd had with Jennifer. The truth was, her friend would be overjoyed to find a man she could truly love.

"Jennifer can't marry *Brad,* though," Cody said, "because you already married him. She might want to love him and get married to him, but she can't."

Ashley's skin prickled to life. "What are you saying, Cody? Why would Jennifer want to marry Brad?"

"Because they were talking together in the dark room at Bless Your Hearth one day last week."

"What?"

"At first I thought they were doing kisses and things like that. But Jennifer said no, they weren't, and Brad didn't say anything, because he left with Yappy as fast as he could after I stood up to him and told him to go away."

206

"Brad was with Jennifer? Inside Mrs. Hansen's new store? Are you sure?"

"Yes, and I said, 'Jennifer, I think you were doing kisses with Brad who is Ashley's husband.' She said, 'No, we were talking.' Then we decided to put vinegar on the rugs to get the stains out, and after that, I found my sea sponge and I left too."

By now, Ashley was sitting straight up in the chair. "What were they doing there? Is something going on between them?"

"Not kissing. Jennifer said so, and I believe her. She never tells me lies." He hesitated for a moment. "But she also doesn't tell me the truth. If she did, she would have said, *Cody, I don't want to marry you. I want to be your friend but not your wife.*"

The knot that had been heavy in Ashley's stomach all morning began to twist, making her feel suddenly hot and sick. "What did you see them doing?"

"It was dark, remember? I didn't see anything at first. I heard them talking, and then my eyes got used to the darkness, and it was Brad and Jennifer. She was crying."

"Crying — why?"

"It might have been because of the mess Yappy made on the rugs. We got them clean, so don't worry."

"Don't worry? You've just told me you

walked into a dark room and found my husband and my friend together! Cody, stop talking about rugs and tell me exactly what happened."

"You don't have to get upset, Ashley. I fixed your door, and Brad went to work with Yappy, and Jennifer stopped crying, and the rugs are clean. Everything is all right."

"No, it's not. Why were Brad and Jennifer together? What would they possibly have to talk about except . . . except . . ."

Ashley caught her breath, recalling the day she had begged Jennifer to speak to Brad about the Haneses' marital problems. Jennifer had reluctantly agreed to talk to him. Was this the way she had chosen to carry out Ashley's request — an early morning conversation in a darkened room? That made no sense.

But what if Jennifer and Brad had already talked several times? What if their discussions had turned from his problems with his wife into an attraction between the two of them?

"I have to see Jennifer." Ashley stood suddenly, trying to hold back tears. "I have to talk to her right now. Right this *minute!*"

"But she's not sad anymore. She's happy because the stains are gone."

"Oh no!" Ashley raced to the coat rack

and grabbed her scarf, coat, and gloves. "This is terrible. Why didn't I suspect? I should have known. I'm so stupid. I'm the dumbest person in the world!"

"Ashley, wait." Cody leaped to his feet. "You need to do what I did when you told me about chicken livers. You need to sit down and get calm."

He took her by the shoulders. "Sit on the couch here, because you are too upset to talk to anybody but me. I think I did a bad social skill or something like that. What did I do wrong?"

Ashley slumped on the sofa and shook her head. "Nothing. You didn't do anything wrong, Cody. It's all just a big wreck. I've messed up everything you could possibly mess up in a marriage. I have nothing to show for my life. I hate myself."

Cody sat down next to Ashley and patted her on the back. He was so close she could smell the odor of paint thinner on his hands. "Do you really hate yourself, Ashley?"

"I'm a stupid, ugly girl with skinny legs and long red hair, and I barely graduated, and the one thing I thought I was doing right, I did completely wrong. I was so sure that Brad and I were perfect together. I just knew we would be happy forever and always love each other and have a whole bunch of chi-hi-hildren. . . .”

Sobbing, she covered her face with her hands and bent over, afraid she was going to be ill. Her marriage crumbling was the worst thing in the world. How could it have happened? Had Jennifer fallen in love with Brad? Had Ashley's husband betrayed her?

"I don't think you're stupid and ugly," Cody said, continuing to pat, his hand making a heavy drumbeat on her back. "I think you're like the wife that King Lemuel's mother told him about, that's who. But the trouble is that Brad is not like King Lemuel. The king's mother told her son not to drink alcohol, because he would forget the law and pervert the judgment of the afflicted. And that is exactly what Brad did when he drank alcohol and forgot the law and ran his new truck into the ditch."

"I'm not supposed to talk about the accident or the DWIs, Cody," Ashley moaned. "I'm never to remind Brad what he did. He hates it when *anyone* mentions that stupid truck."

"I know it's not good to gossip, because Patsy says *never spread rumors.* But since you're so upset, I will tell you something that might make you feel better."

Cody stopped patting Ashley's back. "Jennifer said she thinks Brad is a very smart person, even though he acts dumb. That's what she told me."

Ashley sucked down the lump in her throat. "Wait — Jennifer said that? After she and Brad were in the dark room together?" With a deep sniffle, she sat up. "Did Jen really say Brad was smart? Did she say he should be a good husband to me?"

"Yes. But she thinks he acts dumb."

"Oh, I don't believe it," Ashley blurted out as relief swept through her. "Are you telling me that Jennifer is *not* attracted to my husband? You're absolutely positive there's nothing between them?"

"Nothing except talking. Jennifer said she was crying because she wants women to have good husbands, even her. I told her that I would be a very good husband, and I would like to marry her. But she didn't say anything except we need more vinegar or we are never going to get these stains out."

"Oh, thank goodness!"

"I don't feel very thankful at all. I have just found out that I'm chicken livers to Jennifer, and I made you cry, and Brad probably hates me because I told him to leave Bless Your Hearth."

"No, you're sweet, Cody." She rubbed her sleeve across her cheeks. "You try hard to do your best. I'm the loser here."

Ashley felt unexpectedly awkward — sitting on her sofa with Cody Goss pressed up beside her as though the room were crowded with people. Though something inside Ashley rose to defend herself against the charge that she was a loser, her heart overcame it. She knew the truth.

You didn't shove your naked husband out into the snow if you were perfect. You didn't shout at him and call him names. You didn't hate him. She had done all these things . . . and more.

Ashley let out her breath. "I guess you'd probably better go now, Cody. I feel better knowing Brad isn't . . . because what I thought was happening isn't happening after all. At least I don't think it is."

Cody rose from the sofa. "I'm happy that I fixed your door. Sorry if I did bad social skills."

"Everything's okay. I need to call Brad. I think if we talk . . . if we try harder . . . if we can somehow work on our problems, this is going to turn out all right. I haven't been the best wife."

"Jennifer thinks you're a very good wife."

"Jennifer doesn't know me very well. I'm a barely good enough wife."

"Okay." Cody took his coat from the rack and slipped it on. "Well, call me again if you and Brad break something else. I'm a good fixer-upper."

Without another word, Cody turned and strolled to the front door. Ashley felt the tension slide out of her as he stepped outside and shut it behind him. Though she had calmed down a lot, she knew her hands were still trembling.

Brad and Jennifer in the dark? Brad and Jennifer alone together? Why?

What if Jennifer had lied to Cody?

What if Brad was unfaithful?

What would Ashley do? How could a woman ever go on? It was Ashley's greatest fear. Her worst nightmare.

What kind of a husband made his wife feel that way, constantly filled with dread? What sort of man hung out at a bar all hours of the night? And read a pornographic magazine? And failed to pay bills, wrecked his truck, bad-mouthed her parents?

Brad was a *terrible* husband. Ashley didn't know why she put up with him. Had she ever really loved him . . . or had it just been some crazy mix of admiration, awe, wonder, and lust?

What was love really?

Ashley thought of Esther Moore. Mrs. Moore would have known the answer to that question. She could have explained it all.

But now . . . now Mrs. Moore was dead. Just like that. Gone.

"Mail!" Cody sang out the word as he flung the door open and burst back into the living room. "You have lots of letters, Ashley. I saw the mailman putting them into your box, and I thought they must be Christmas cards. Brenda is always happy to get Christmas cards. She puts them in a basket on the table and shows them to Steve and Jennifer and me. Here you go! Merry Christmas!"

He held out a large stack of business-size white envelopes. Ashley recognized her own handwriting on most of them. "What are these? They're not Christmas cards."

She took them and set them on her lap. As realization slowly dawned, she tore one open. "These are my self-addressed stamped envelopes. I sent these out with my bead orders. Oh, Cody! This is a check. It's money. It's a lot of money. They're paying me. My customers are really, truly paying me!"

"Wait till you hear this," Cody said with a laugh. "I played a joke on you, Ashley. Here's more! Lots more. I hid these envelopes in my pocket because I wanted to make a trick! How about that? Did I trick you? Are you surprised?"

As the envelopes fluttered around her like snowflakes, Ashley gasped. "This is wonderful!"

"Ha-ha!" Cody slapped his thighs. "I knew it! I made a great trick. Merry Christmas, Ashley Hanes. Merry Christmas to you!"

CHAPTER TEN

Brad sat up on the edge of the bed and switched off the alarm clock. How long had it been buzzing, he wondered as he rubbed his eyes. The morning of Christmas Eve — and he was going to be late to work.

The snow had all melted before he got home the night before, so he would have no excuse today. He'd have to shower quickly and then grab a breakfast wrap from the Pop-In on his way to the construction site. Bitty Sondheim was in California visiting her family, but she had asked her cook to keep the little restaurant open for its faithful customers. That included Brad, and he was already looking forward to his usual scrambled egg, bacon, and cheese in a biscuit-dough wrap.

As he stood, Brad glanced down at the woman sprawled across the rumpled sheets. Ashley had never shared a bed with a sibling, so she usually yanked off most of the covers and flopped around all night like a dying fish. This morning, in the half-light of dawn, he could see that she was wearing her favorite ugly old flannel gown and the pair of warm gray socks her grandmother had knitted. She hadn't bothered to unbraid her hair. It looked like a frayed auburn rope lying across the pillow. He didn't remember hearing her come home.

In the shower, he reviewed the previous day. It had begun with him being shoved out into the snow by his wife. Next, he had bashed in their front door with his foot. Miranda Finley, their psycho neighbor, had watched the whole episode through her dining room window and obviously thought it was pretty funny. He failed to see the humor.

Toweling off, Brad recalled the many times during the day that he had taken out his phone and considered calling Ashley to apologize. He wasn't a bad man — the sort of guy who beat his wife or tore the house apart in a drunken rage. How had it even happened that he had become so angry with her? What had Ashley said? What had he done? Something was always simmering between them, collecting beneath the surface and waiting to erupt. Ashley had mentioned his drinking, he remembered.

And she had found his magazine. Yappy had gotten mixed up in it too, vanishing into the snow and scaring them half to death. It had been a bad day.

He let out a deep breath and stepped back into the bedroom. Trying to be as quiet as he could, he pulled on his shorts and a pair of jeans. As he was slipping into his T-shirt, he felt a tug on his pant leg.

"Rrrrf! Rrf-rrf!"

"Hush!" he whispered, scooping up the puppy. "Be quiet. I'll take you out in a second."

"I'll do it." Ashley rolled into a sitting position. Cross-legged, she stared at him. Wisps of hair fanned out around her head. "I can take Yappy outside."

"Thanks." He pulled on a plaid flannel shirt and began to button it. "I'm late."

"Are you working a full day?" Her voice was softer than usual. "It's Christmas Eve, you know."

He wanted to repair the damage between them, but he was in a hurry. He didn't even know how to begin. How could he make things better with his wife? How could he show her that he still cared? Did he?

"We don't have much work left to do on this unit," he told her, wondering if they might have time to go out to dinner that

218

night. Even a meal at home together would be good. "We'll get off early. How about you?"

"A churchful of Christmas carolers booked the whole restaurant. They're coming to the club to eat before they go out and sing. I'll probably be late."

Brad nodded. That figured. With his job, a holiday usually meant time off. With Ashley's, it meant extra customers and longer hours. Another point to add to the growing list of reasons why nothing between them was working.

Ashley stepped onto the floor and reached for the puppy. As she gathered Yappy into her arms, Brad felt her warm skin touch his. She looked up at him, her brown eyes deep.

"Brad, I'm sorry," she began. For a moment, she didn't speak. She moistened her lips and swallowed hard. "Sorry I . . . sorry I didn't decorate the house for Christmas. I helped my mom put up their tree a couple of days ago, but I didn't know if we had the money to buy one. I wasn't sure how you felt about . . . about Christmas . . . or anything. I'm sorry."

"Don't worry about it." He turned away, looking for his boots. Why hadn't she apologized for what really mattered? for shoving him out into the snow? That would have been a start.

Frustration welled up in his chest. No doubt Ashley expected him to beg forgiveness for his girlie magazine. Maybe he shouldn't have had it, but there wasn't time to talk through all that now.

"Have you seen my boots?" he asked.

"By the couch."

She had set Yappy down and was pulling on her coat. He grabbed his heavy jacket, still trying to think of some way to ease the resentment between them.

"You working tomorrow?" he asked.

"I'm off. I have seniority." She squared her shoulders. "I got to choose my vacation days before the rest of the staff. Jay let me pick first."

Brad had to refrain from snapping out a smart retort about this *Jay* guy who seemed to have invaded their marriage. If Jay was so wonderful, why didn't Ashley just spend Christmas with him?

No, that was unkind. Brad knew he should keep his mouth shut. If he wanted to say something to Ashley, he needed to make it polite. Something positive.

A thought struck him.

"Mom is expecting us at the house by noon tomorrow," he told her, reaching for

220

the doorknob. "She's got a ham this year. A big one."

Ashley stiffened. "But my mom invited us too."

"*Your* mom?" That possibility hadn't occurred to him. "What did you tell her?"

"I said yes, of course. You never told me your family wanted us to go over there. This is the first I've heard of it."

"You didn't tell me either. And my mom has a ham. That's a huge deal for her. We don't have ham every year."

"Brad, my parents are expecting us."

"Yeah? Well, I'm not eating foot-long chili cheese dogs for Christmas dinner."

"My mother won't make that!"

"That's all she knows how to cook, Ash." He let out a hot breath. "Look, I don't have time to argue. I'm the husband, and I say we're going to *my* parents' house."

"Go ahead. I'll be eating at my house."

"*This* is supposed to be your house!" he bellowed, surprising himself with the sudden rage that flamed inside him. He jabbed an index finger at the floor. "*This* is where you live. This is the place you're supposed to put up Christmas decorations. This is where the presents are supposed to be. Right here — under *our* tree. We're married, in case you forgot."

221

"Married? What's that? Two people who never see each other? who fight all the time? A husband who would rather read a porn magazine than —"

"Stop!" He caught her by the wrist. "Stop talking about the magazine."

"Oh? Is it like all the other things I'm not supposed to talk about? Let's see, so far we've got your truck, your DWIs —"

"Ashley!" He gave her arm a squeeze. "Stop. Stop mocking me. You put me down all the time. You belittle me. I'm sick of it. All I want from you is some respect, okay? I know I'm not perfect. I know I've disappointed you. But you could at least try to find one nice thing to say about me once in a while."

"I might say something nice if I could find the man I married last Valentine's Day. I hardly know *you*. You're either at Larry's or sprawled out on the couch every night when I walk in the door. You never hold me or cuddle with me. Whenever you want me, it's just grab, grab, grab. If you'd like for me to respect you, then be respectable. Be nice to me."

"I work at least forty hours a week at a job I hate so I can bring home a paycheck for you. That's pretty *nice,* if you ask me."

"If you hate your job so much, do something else. Go to college."

"Yeah, right." He yanked open the door. "You could have at least hung stockings, Ash. Any normal wife would have done that much."

As he strode out onto the stoop, he could hear Yappy scrabbling along behind him. Ashley followed, her untied shoes flopping on the wet sidewalk.

"You don't think I'm a normal wife?" she shouted. "Well, you don't know anything about me! You have no idea what I've accomplished! I'm better than normal. I can succeed, Bradley Hanes. I can make a good life for myself, and I don't need you around to do it!"

Brad bent down, picked up Yappy, walked back to his wife, and set the dog in her arms. "Then why don't you and your flannel nightgown get out of my life," he growled, his face an inch from hers, "because I don't need you either."

"I hate you!" she screamed, tears falling as he threw open his car door and got in.

"I hate you too," he muttered. Clenching his jaw, he peeled out of the driveway, screeching the tires on the pavement.

It was hopeless.

Patsy could see that right away. No matter

how many times Derek Finley let Cody maneuver his car around the road that encircled Deepwater Cove, the boy was bound to mess up one way or another.

"Keep trying, honey!" she called out, waving a gloved hand as Cody made another pass by her and Jennifer. With the salon closed for the next few days, the two women had agreed to venture outside and cheer on Cody's latest driving lesson.

"Go, Cody!" Jennifer yelled.

"You can do it!" Patsy pumped her fist as he steered down the hill on the left-hand side of the road.

"He can't do it," she muttered. "He never will, Jennifer, and that's just the plain old truth of the matter. We are going to have to figure out how to tell Cody in the sweetest possible way before he runs Derek's car smack-dab into someone's deck. I don't understand why Derek keeps trying. I'll swear that poor man must have lost a good two years off his life by now."

Jennifer laughed. "We didn't believe Cody could pass the written test, remember? But he did."

"Barely. I think the officer cheated just because Cody's so earnest."

"They can't do that!"

Jennifer was smiling, looking as beautiful

as ever, Patsy saw. She still hadn't sorted out her feelings or made any decisions about her future. But at least the memory of what had happened in Mexico seemed to be fading. Thank the Lord. He could soften terrifying memories, and He could certainly guide a lovely young woman in the right direction. No question about that.

"Do you see them?" Patsy asked, standing on tiptoe to scan the back side of the looping road. "I hope that boy hasn't plowed into a ditch."

"Oh, here they come again." Jennifer clasped her gloved hands together in excitement. "Look, Cody's staying mostly on the right side of the road! He's doing it, Patsy."

The car screeched to a sudden stop right beside the two women. Both Cody and Derek snapped forward, kept from slamming against the windshield only by their seat belts. The driver's window lowered, and Cody stuck his head out, grinning from ear to ear.

"How about that?" His blue eyes fastened on Jennifer. "Did you see me go all the way around without drifting into the middle?"

As Jennifer congratulated him, Patsy studied the man in the passenger seat. Derek had leaned his head back and was breathing as though he'd just completed a half marathon. Despite the chilled air, beads of sweat dotted his hairline.

"You doing okay there, Derek?" she called.

He glanced her way and rolled his eyes. Patsy took the silent message to heart.

Laying her hand on Cody's shoulder, she spoke softly. "You've been working hard on your driving. How about some chocolate cake?"

She could see the struggle. Driving around the circle another time . . . or chocolate cake at Patsy's house. Which would it be?

"I cut the cake into squares," she told him. "Just the way you like it."

"Okay!"

Before she could step back, Cody put the car in gear and started down the road. Patsy and Jennifer gasped in unison. Weaving from side to side, the vehicle was in imminent danger of rolling into someone's yard or dropping into a drainage ditch.

"He's going to crash!" Jennifer cried, clutching at Patsy and squeezing her eyes shut.

"Derek's there, don't forget."

The car veered to the left, missing Opal Jones's mailbox by an inch. Suddenly the horn blared. The car swung right, sending up a spray of gravel from the road shoulder.

"Oh no!" Jennifer grabbed Patsy's hand. "Oh!"

"He's headed for my garage!" Patsy took off running — not an easy feat in her pointy-heeled, knee-high leather boots and pencil skirt.

Jennifer passed her easily, racing down the damp roadway toward the small house Patsy had called home for many years.

"Lord have mercy!" Patsy breathed out as she sprinted along, trying her best to hold things in place. "Lord, make him stop. If You love me at all, Lord, stop that boy's car before he hits my house!"

As Jennifer reached the foot of Patsy's driveway, the car jolted and veered toward the garage as if Cody were aiming to bash right into it. Patsy screamed. The car swerved again. Her heel caught the edge of a crack in the pavement. The fragile dogwood sapling in her front yard disappeared beneath the bumper. Patsy tumbled onto the road, her boot heel snapping off and her ankle twisting beneath her as she landed on her knees.

Looking up, she saw that the car had stopped. The windshield wipers fanned back and forth as Cody hopped out of the driver's seat and began dancing around.

"I goofed up!" he wailed. "I couldn't

remember how to stop! I'm sorry! I nearly hit the garage. I killed Patsy's new tree."

As Jennifer raced toward Cody, Derek rounded the front of his car to assess the damage. And that's when Patsy felt the pain shoot up through her leg like a fire-hot poker. It curled into her hip and then raced back down and around her ankle.

Unable to move, she sat paralyzed, staring at her shredded stockings, scraped knees, torn skirt — and those two legs sticking out oddly from beneath it. Were they hers? Was that what hurt so much? She opened her mouth to wail but nothing came out. Darkness swam across her vision. She was going to be sick.

"Patsy!" Derek Finley's voice rang through the black cloud. "Patsy, can you hear me? You've skinned your knees, and you may have hurt your ankle. I'm going to get this boot off."

She gritted her teeth and grabbed the Water Patrolman's shoulder as he tilted her just a little, unzipped the boot, and worked it carefully off her foot. Tears sprang to her eyes, and there wasn't a thing she could do to stop them.

"It h-h-hurts!" she bawled.

"I know, I know. Let's see if we can

straighten your leg. Does anything feel broken?"

"Everything!" she hollered, all at once unable to hold back the tide of anguish. "I'm bleeding! I'm dying here, Derek! My leg's broken, my foot, my ankle. It's killing me. All of it. Give me morphine! Call an ambulance. I'm fixing to die."

She could hear him chuckle. "Stop laughing at me, Derek Finley. Get me off this road! Now!"

"Calm down, Patsy. If you can yell that loud, you're going to be okay. It's the quiet ones we worry about. I don't carry morphine, and you don't need an ambulance either." He was pressing on her leg, moving things around. "Nothing looks broken. I think you've sprained your ankle."

"Sprained?" The way her foot was throbbing, she felt certain it must be half torn off. She couldn't even look at the thing. Her leg was probably a bloody stump.

"Hey, Patsy." Jennifer knelt beside her on the road. "I've brought Derek's car back around. Do you think you can get in?"

"Get in? Do I look like a woman who can get into a car?"

Derek slid one hand under her arm. "Come on, Patsy. Let's get you inside and warm you up. Then we'll decide if we need to go to the hospital."

Unsuccessfully fighting tears, Patsy allowed Jennifer and Derek to help her off the road and into the backseat of his car. For some reason, her pain and tears opened the floodgates inside her, and everything sad in her life came flowing out all at once. Her father's early death. Her mother's long battle with Alzheimer's. Her endless struggle to keep her salon afloat. Her loneliness.

Wait. That wasn't on the list anymore.

"Where's Pete?" she sniffled. "I need Pete."

Jennifer glanced at her and smiled as she pulled the car into the driveway and they came to a gentle stop. "I'll call him in a minute when you're settled. We have to deal with Cody, too."

Oh, Patsy thought, *Cody.* How long would it take him to recover from this latest calamity? She had witnessed his breakdowns before. When he'd first come to Deepwater Cove, frightening things caused him to emit an animal's scream and bolt away in terror. As he had settled in and become less fearful, his episodes evolved into bouts of crying, wailing, and even yanking at his own hair. Nowadays, he still wept sometimes, but he had learned to make less of a scene. She recalled him dancing in her driveway.

"My dogwood tree," she moaned. "I planted it in the spring."

Derek opened the back door and reached for her. "It took a hit. But it's just a sapling. It may not be a goner. How're you doing?"

"*I'm* the goner. Are you sure you don't have any morphine? Someone needs to knock me out."

Again he laughed. "I'm not on duty, and I only carry first aid supplies when I am. You'll be all right, Patsy. Lean on me."

With Jennifer and Derek supporting her on each side, she hobbled onto the deck and through the front door. They eased her down onto a sofa. As Jennifer placed Patsy's leg on a pillow, Derek returned from the kitchen with a bag of frozen peas.

"Those are the expensive kind, you know." She glanced at him. "I was going to serve them for . . . oh, rats. Tomorrow's Christmas, isn't it? And here I am, nearly dead."

"I'm 99 percent sure this is a sprain, Patsy," Derek told her as he wrapped the peas in a dish towel and packed them around the swelling joint. "Your boots were tight enough that they protected the ankle."

"My boots are what did me in." She sighed and closed her eyes. "Where's Cody?"

"Hiding in the bathroom," Jennifer told

her. She had finished blotting and cleaning Patsy's skinned knees, which somehow didn't even need bandages. With a sigh, Jennifer focused on the powder room's door. "I'm going to serve the cake. That'll bring him out."

"I'm afraid I'll have to excuse myself from the dessert portion of this event," Derek said with a wry smile. "I've had about as much excitement as I can stand for one day."

"Are you going to give up on Cody?" Jennifer's question came out in a whisper. "Do you think he can ever learn to drive?"

Derek studied the ceiling for a moment. "Not sure. He does tend to have a one-track mind. Driving involves doing a lot of different actions all at the same time. If he's working to stay to the right of the roadway, he can't seem to remember to check his rearview mirror or watch for a car that might be pulling out of a driveway. If we're approaching a corner, Cody will put the blinker on but then forget to slow down, look both ways, and turn the steering wheel. He just sort of leans his whole body to one side, as if that will somehow cause the car to follow suit. We've driven over more curbs than I care to think about."

"That's autism," Jennifer murmured. "I've

done a lot of reading on the subject. It can be hard for an autistic person to multitask. Apparently they can master one behavior but then forget about all the accompanying actions. It takes a long time to integrate everything they're learning."

"Well, the words *give up* are not in my vocabulary, and I've got plenty of time to work with Cody," Derek said, giving her a smile. "With another set of twins on the way and Kim starting to slow down, I'm not planning to go anywhere. They're boys — did you hear? Mom wants us to call them Eric and Derek, after my father and me. But no way. Kim and I have decided we want Bible names. Names that have meaning, like . . ."

From her position on the couch, Patsy tried to focus on the genteel sharing of information between Derek and Jennifer. But she found it hard to keep from butting in and ordering one of them to get her something for this pain. And fast!

"That's a great idea," Jennifer was saying. "My parents went with the whole *J* concept — Jennifer, Justin, and Jessica. But it caused a lot of confusion for us. People can't remember who is who, so we —"

"Excuse me," Patsy said finally. "I hate to interrupt, but I could use a slice of that chocolate cake, Jennifer. And could you gather up a nice mix of painkillers for me while you're at it?"

"Oh, Patsy, I'm so sorry."

Within moments, Derek had headed out the door and Jennifer was returning to the living room with the sheet cake Patsy had baked that morning.

"It was for my first Christmas dinner with Pete," she said, mourning the beautiful decorative star she had created out of whole pecans. "That cake and the peas. I guess since I'm already wearing the peas, we might as well go ahead and cut the cake. I want a big piece, too. Comfort food. Who-ever said that was a bad thing?"

As Jennifer dipped a knife into the cake, Patsy saw the bathroom door swing open to reveal Cody's silhouette. Like a duck to water, she thought.

"Come on out, honey," she called. With a sip of water, she downed the two over-the-counter painkillers Jennifer had brought. "Nobody's mad at you. Let's all have cake and talk about something nice."

"Christmas?" Cody said hopefully. He crept out and settled on the edge of a chair near the sofa. With a glance at her knees and swollen ankle, he appeared to tear up again. But Jennifer pressed a plate of cake into his hands, and Cody cheered up immediately.

"Do you have a theme?" he asked Patsy. "At Jennifer's house, the theme is purple and gold."

"On the Christmas tree," Jennifer clarified.

Patsy eyed the scraggly artificial pine she'd had since childhood. "Love," she said. "I guess that's my theme. Those ornaments came down to me from my parents, and theirs, and who knows how far back. Every year, they come out of their boxes, and we hang them on the tree so we can remember all the love in our family. So next Christmas — if Pete and I are married by then — we'll hang those very same ornaments on our own tree."

"You haven't set a wedding date yet, have you?" Jennifer asked. "Patsy, it's been a month since Pete proposed. What are you waiting for?"

"I don't think we're waiting for anything. We just haven't gotten around to talking about it much."

"Because they like to kiss instead of talk," Cody inserted.

"What do you know about Pete and me?" Patsy reached out with her good foot and tapped him on the knee. "You'd better not be peeking in any windows."

"I don't peek in windows. I think kissing is what people do when they're in love." Cody slid a glance at Jennifer. "But if they're not . . . if they think the other person is chicken livers, then they don't want to kiss them, and there's nothing anyone can do about it. Or if you're married already, but you hate each other like Brad and Ashley and push each other out in the snow without any clothes on, which is what Mrs. Miranda Finley told me Ashley did to Brad, then you probably don't want to kiss. But otherwise, I think that's what you do."

Patsy and Jennifer looked at each other. This one was going to take some time.

CHAPTER ELEVEN

Brad scrolled through the names stored on his phone and wondered what Mr. Moore was doing this Christmas Eve. The lights inside Larry's Lake Lounge were turned down low, and it was pitch-dark outside. Yvonne Ratcliff had already sung two sets. One was a collection of her usual country numbers. She could cover the most popular hits very well, in Brad's opinion. The other set had been Christmas songs full of words like *jolly, merry,* and *joyful.* The folks gathered at Larry's didn't appear to have much happiness to spare. Still . . . with a small rotating tree in one corner of the bar and silver garlands taped to the ceiling, it was better than being at home alone.

"Don't call her," Mack said, gesturing at Brad's phone. "She's workin', anyhow. No point in getting yourself all riled up."

"I wasn't thinking about Ashley." Brad knew that was a lie. He had been thinking about her all night. But he didn't correct his untruth as he slipped the phone back into his pocket. "You know the guy who helped me with my remodeling — Charlie Moore?" he asked Mack. "He's in California. Went out there to see his son. I was just wondering what he's up to tonight."

Mack took a swig. Brad eyed his own empty mug. The two of them had downed more than usual, but why not? This was a holiday. Celebrate. Whoopee.

"Probably puttin' together a bike for his son," Mack said and then laughed. "Does anybody do that these days? You know, like in them old movies when the father was down in the basement tryin' to build his daughter a dollhouse and finish assembling his son's bicycle before midnight? The mother would come down in her ruffled white apron and ask him how he was getting along, and he was always havin' trouble. I'll tell you what. My mama didn't wear no apron, and my daddy sure never put a bike together for me. I stole the only one I ever had."

"Mr. Moore's son is an adult," Brad told him. "He doesn't need a bicycle for Christmas. They're probably sitting around the fireplace singing carols."

"In California? Do they have fireplaces there?"

"Maybe not. I'll bet Mr. Moore is missing his wife, though. She died right before Thanksgiving. They were married nearly fifty years."

"Rah, rah, rah." Mack lifted his mug and waved it back and forth as he cheered. "Fifty years of bondage!"

"Shut up, you idiot."

"What's the matter, boys?" Yvonne slid onto the bar stool next to Brad. She had on tight black suede pants and a red sweater that hugged her curves. Red and green earrings in the shape of tree lights dangled around her shoulders. "Don't tell me you're having an argument on Christmas Eve."

"Brad's in mourning," Mack told her. "His marriage died."

"Really?" Yvonne's voice sounded way too perky for this hour of the night.

"Kaput," Mack pronounced.

"Awww." Yvonne leaned against Brad. "Too bad, honey. It happens to the best of us. But on Christmas Eve? Now that's a rotten deal. What happened?"

Brad studied the foam drying on his mug. What *had* happened? He hardly knew. He remembered so well the day he had spotted Ashley making a milk shake at her parents'

239

snack shop. Her back was to him, and he was amazed at that lava flow of flaming hair that ran down her back. Rumples and waves, it fell all the way to her unbelievably perfect little hips. She was tall, slender, and standing at the milk shake machine with the kind of slouch that set up a roar inside his chest.

No way could this creature be as beautiful from the front as she was from the back, he had thought. But then she had turned and looked right at him with those big brown eyes. On seeing him, her cheeks had flushed a pretty pink, and his heart stumbled.

"Hey," she had greeted him. *"Aren't you Brad Hanes? You used to play quarterback for the Lakers. Your team won State."*

All he'd been able to do was stare at her. Where had she been during his high school years? Why hadn't he ever noticed her?

She twined her index finger through a long strand of beads looped around her neck. *"What do you want?"* she had asked him.

"You," he almost blurted out. *"You, you, you, and nobody else. For the rest of my life."*

That's how he had felt on seeing Ashley, and he hadn't stopped feeling that way right through the engagement, the wedding, and the first few months of the marriage. Nothing and nobody could satisfy him like his wife.

He would do anything to please her. Starting right after their first date, he never gave another woman a second look. He had bought Ashley a whopping big diamond ring — spent most of his savings on it. Within a couple months of their meeting, he was looking for a house to put her in after he made her his wife. She was as sweet, pretty, smart, and supportive as he could have dreamed possible.

And there was something extra, too. Ashley was spicy. Her long red hair drove him crazy, and he loved the way she dressed in funky skirts and beaded necklaces. She always surprised him with her creativity and imagination, and he couldn't believe his good luck.

That whole time, she had been focused completely on him. They couldn't see anything but each other. Ashley raved about everything he had done in the past and everything he did after meeting her. She adored all that he was, constantly reminded him of all that he meant in her life. They dreamed and planned their future until it took on a reality of its own. And he wanted nothing more than to hold her in his arms from dusk till dawn.

What had happened?

"Brad don't feel much like talkin'," Mack told Yvonne. "I reckon he needs a refill. Hey, Bub! How about another brewski for ol' Brad here? He's singin' the blues tonight."

Bartender Bubba Jones, grandson of Opal Jones, made a face. "Who's driving him home? You sure ain't fit to be on the road, Mack."

"I'll take care of him," Yvonne said, edging closer. She leaned up and pressed her soft lips to Brad's cheek. "This boy's in good hands tonight."

"Awright!" Mack chuckled. "I wish I could say the same."

"You don't try hard enough, Mack. Look at all the women in this place. It's Christmas Eve, honey. Everyone's lonely and wanting some comfort. Get over there and play a game of pool with Dixie and Brandy and them gals. You don't have nothin' to lose."

Mack took another swig. "Naw, I ain't fallin' for that, Yvonne. Dixie and them are like sisters to me — I see 'em here every night."

"You're just a big chicken, Mack." She ran her fingertips through Brad's hair. "You don't see *me* as a sister, do you, sweetie?"

Brad swallowed. Red flags waved inside

242

him. *Don't do this. Don't let her come on to you that way. Go home, fool. You can patch things up with Ashley.*

But he couldn't. He knew that. He didn't have a clue how to fix the mess they'd made. Ashley had flat out told him she hated him. She didn't need him anymore.

What hope could you have when your wife said something like that? What reason could he possibly have for denying his own need? He was lonely. Hurt. Angry. Frustrated. And yeah, Mack had spoken the truth. Brad was in mourning. The marriage he had dreamed about was dead, and he might as well accept it.

Swallowing down the pain, he leaned over. "I never felt this way about any of my sisters," he murmured in Yvonne's ear.

With a giggle, she nuzzled up and slipped her arm around his neck. "My kid's with his daddy tonight. You got any reason to go home?"

Brad knew what Yvonne wanted. No doubt about that.

He thought about the bed he and Ashley had purchased on credit just before they moved into their new house. That and everything else they owned would probably be repossessed or pawned.

"Yappy," he told her, gazing at her lips

through the fog in his head. "The puppy's at home."

"You'd turn down my Christmas present for a dog?"

Recalling the night he had found Yappy, Brad realized how much had changed. On that evening, he had resisted the allure of the bar and the long-haired, sexy singer. Though he and Ashley had been having a fair amount of trouble even then, on that cold winter evening, saving the dog had allowed him to resist the siren call of temptation.

But tonight, Yappy was warm and well fed. Ashley would be home in time to let him out. Or clean up the mess. Brad had nothing to hold him back.

"Nah," he whispered, slipping his arm around her waist. "I got nothing. Nothing but you, honey."

Ashley bit her lower lip as she steered her car toward Deepwater Cove. To everyone's surprise, the church Christmas carolers had eaten quickly and left the restaurant much earlier than expected. It hadn't taken long to bus the tables, set them up again, and clock out. Even the dishwashers had it easy. Jay from customer service dropped by to wish everyone a merry Christmas and hand out bonus checks, and then the dining room and kitchen staff were free to go home.

Home.

The word sent a lump into Ashley's throat. Would Brad be there? Would he have seen what she'd done in his absence that day — her valiant effort to salvage their marriage? Would he understand what her gesture had meant?

Surely he would. He must.

Dear God, please let Brad see that I don't hate him! she pleaded in silence.

Though she hadn't been brought up in church, Ashley had decided long ago that there must be a God worth praying to. Did maples just happen to turn brilliant red every autumn? Blue herons stood like soldiers on the docks at dusk. Had they decided to grow long legs, beaks, and curved necks — perfect for plucking fish from the lake?

Someone must have designed it all. Such miracles didn't just happen. If God had made all these things, surely He cared at least a little bit about Ashley and Brad. Surely He could do something to heal a broken marriage.

Trying to concentrate on the narrow road, Ashley continued in silent prayer to the Creator. He knitted torn skin and broken bones. He sealed the bark on a tree that had been struck by lightning. He brought flowers out of thorny rosebushes. Surely He could do something to fix this terrible mess.

Please! Please help us!

Approaching Tranquility, Ashley couldn't help but glance at the site of her greatest rival for Brad's time and attention. Larry's Lake Lounge sat in darkness except for the icicle lights that hung glittering from the roofline. The parking lot was empty.

Empty except for one car.

Her breath catching, Ashley suddenly swerved into the driveway pockmarked with potholes. Yes, that was Brad's car.

What was it doing there by itself? Was he still in the bar? Had everyone gone home and shut the place down with one lone drunk passed out inside?

Ashley pulled her car to a stop beside Brad's and stepped out into the chilly breeze. Peering through the window, she saw that his old car was empty. She tried the door. Locked.

Dread and confusion gathering in her chest, she stepped to the front door of the bar. It, too, was locked. And then the icicle lights went out overhead.

Someone was still here.

"Brad?" she called.

Ashley jogged around to the back of the building. In the moonlight, she could make out the figure of a man emptying trash into the large metal Dumpster. She thought she recognized him.

"Bubba Jones?" She stepped nearer.

"That's me. What do you need?"

"Bubba, it's Ashley Hanes. I live near your grandma in Deepwater Cove. Have you seen Brad? Brad Hanes?"

Setting the trash can on the ground, he shook his head. "What are you doing out at this time of night on Christmas Eve, kid?"

"I'm looking for my husband."

As she reached him, she could see the weary expression on his face, the resignation in his eyes. "Brad's gone. I've locked up for the night."

"But his car is still here." She shoved her hands into the pockets of her coat. "I was on my way home from work, and I saw it sitting in your parking lot. He must be inside."

Bubba heaved a sigh. "Nope. I checked her out like I do every night. The place is empty."

"Did you see Brad leave? Did Mack drive him home?"

"Mack left with Dixie Barnes." Bubba picked up the can again. "Why don't you go

247

on home? He'll probably show up after a while."

"Bubba, where is my husband?"

The man lifted his cap and studied the streetlight in the distance. "I'm just the bartender, you know. I don't even own the place. And I've gotta get home."

As he turned toward the tavern's back door, Ashley caught his arm. "Bubba, tell me where Brad went. Please. I have to know."

"There's a lot of things I hate about my job. Rowdy drunks. Bad singing. Cussing. This is one of them."

Ashley went cold and stiff. "Is he with that singer? That Yvonne woman? Where does she live?"

She could read the answer in his eyes as he pointed a finger over her shoulder. "Yvonne Ratcliff. She lives right down the road behind the bar. There's a fourplex. First door on the left. Black door."

Unable to accept what she was hearing, Ashley clung to the man's arm. "Are you sure?"

"I didn't tell you nothin'. You never even saw me tonight. That's how it goes."

Brusquely drawing away from her, he carried the trash can back inside and shut the door behind him.

Ashley sucked down a sob.

No.

It couldn't be true. Brad wouldn't do that. He was her husband. He had made a vow in church. He had loved her, and he promised to stay with her throughout his whole life.

Aching, she returned to her car and sat in silence for a moment. They had spoken such harsh words over the past months. Words filled with venom and malice. They had spat their hatred, anger, disgust at each other that morning. She had truly felt all those things she said to him — every one.

But did that mean the end? Had Brad left her? Had he gone with the bar singer? Could it be possible that their marriage really was over?

Ashley turned the key in the ignition. In a daze, she drove behind the bar, found the narrow road, pulled up in front of the run-down fourplex.

Again, she sat. Unable to move. The lights in the apartment on the lower floor were off. Four cars lined the parking area. The one nearest the door was a battered Honda with too many bumper stickers.

Mechanically, Ashley pushed open her car door and stepped out. So this was what you did when marriages died. This was how you knew. This was it, in the worst possible way.

She knocked on the black door. Muffled voices sounded inside, and the dead bolt slid open. The door opened a crack, and a woman with tousled brown hair peered out.

"I'm Ashley Hanes." She spoke quietly. "Is Brad in there?"

The woman wiped her mouth with the back of her hand. She unchained the door, swung it open, and flicked on the overhead light. "I'm not sure, honey. He told me he was Santa Claus."

Brad sat up on the couch — a lumpy sofa bed with grayed sheets. Clothing lay scattered across the floor. A red sweater. His jeans.

"Ashley?" he muttered, confusion narrowing his brow. His blue eyes clouded. Then he yanked a sheet up over his bare chest. "Shut the door, Yvonne!"

To the sound of his cursing, the woman flicked a length of brown hair over her shoulder. "Night-night, sweetie," she said. One dark eyebrow lifted and a smile flitted across her lips. "Maybe you can find yourself an elf."

Ashley turned away and heard the door click shut. She swallowed. So. This was adultery, that mysterious word she had never quite understood.

This was it.

The end.

Robotic, she returned to her car. Opened the door. Sat down. Closed the door. Turned the key. Put the car in reverse. Backed out of the parking lot.

The yellow lines on the road slid by. Somehow she arrived in front of the little house in Deepwater Cove. The house with the newly built room — a nursery for a baby, she had dreamed once. The house where so much was supposed to have happened but now never would.

Ashley left the car, entered the house, stood staring. Yappy burst out past her, racing for his favorite spot in the yard. Leaving the front door standing wide, she walked into the bedroom she had shared with her husband for ten months. Not even a year. Not even one year.

She opened the closet and dragged out a stack of empty plastic laundry baskets. Pink, the color of romance, she had thought when she bought them. Now these would hold everything she owned. Setting them out on the bed, she began to pull dresses off hangers.

As she folded the first one and put it in a basket, Yappy raced into the room and leaped onto the bed. Muddy paws marking a pattern of excitement, he sniffed all over. Then he jumped into the basket and let out a high-pitched yip. His tail wagged as he sat down and looked at her with a quizzical tilt of the head.

"I see you, Yappy," Ashley said. "You're a good boy for waiting so long to go out. And now it's time for us to pack. That's what people do at the end. They pack their things and leave. So, we'll do that together. We'll put my clothes, my necklaces, my beads, and maybe some silverware and a pan or two into these baskets. We'll put your food and bowl in the car. And then we'll go."

"Wow!" The puppy stood up in the basket and turned in a circle. *"Wow-wow!"*

Ashley rubbed his long ears as her tears began to fall.

CHAPTER TWELVE

"How about another piece of chocolate cake, sugar? Would that help?"

"No, I'm stuffed to the gills. Oh, I feel awful." Fighting the pain in her ankle as well as the disappointment in her heart, Patsy ran her gaze over the large man seated at the end of her sofa.

Pete was trying his best to be of comfort. On learning about her tumble the day before, he had baked a ham, whipped up some mashed potatoes and gravy, put together a green bean casserole, and tossed a beautiful salad for their Christmas lunch. After the meal — which he brought to Patsy on a tray — he covered her with an afghan and propped her sock-clad feet on his leg. Then he began to massage the uninjured ankle.

"I'll call Kim Finley," he suggested. "She works for Dr. Groene. I bet she's got some dandy painkillers over at her house."

"Dr. Groene is a dentist, Pete."

"That's my point. Who dishes out more pain than a dentist? Dr. Groene probably prescribes narcotics left and right. Or maybe Kim could call and get him to order something for you."

"Oh, hush, you silly goober. I'm fine. I know it's just a sprain and I'm being a big baby. But honestly, this has put such a damper on my Christmas."

"You didn't like the sweater I got you?"

"I love *you*, Pete honey. And the sweater is so bright and cheerful . . . isn't it, Ashley?"

Patsy looked across the room at the young woman who had appeared on her doorstep in the middle of the night. Truth to tell, the sweater Pete had selected and wrapped in bright gold paper hardly had a redeeming feature. Not to mention that it was a couple of sizes too small. Patsy would have to take it back to the outlet mall, and the chances of finding the same sweater in her size were next to zero. Fortunately.

"I like the neckline."

Ashley finally produced something positive. She was seated across from the sofa, her eyes hollow. Her little dog dozed on her lap. Patsy knew the poor girl hadn't slept a wink. Between the pain in her ankle and her worry about Ashley, Patsy hadn't slept much either.

"Yes, it does have a pretty neckline," Patsy agreed. "I'm griping because I hate being stuck on this couch. I feel so bad that you had to cook all the food, Pete. Yesterday we ruined the frozen peas. And we dug into the Christmas star pecan-chocolate cake. I didn't get your present wrapped, either. And poor Ashley . . . well, it hasn't been the best of times."

"Do you want me to leave, Patsy?" At the sound of Ashley's plaintive voice, the puppy lifted his head. He fixed his dark eyes on the young woman as she continued. "I could move in with my parents. They wouldn't mind."

"No, I think you did the right thing to come to my house. We'll let Brad spend a little time wondering where you are. That will give him the opportunity to think things over."

"I'd like to give Brad a punch in the nose," Pete muttered.

"Listen to you, Mr. Perfect." Patsy reached for her fiancé's hand. "You remember what Jesus told the men who wanted to kill that woman they'd caught breaking the law? Let the person who is without sin cast the first stone."

"I know I'm not perfect," Pete acknowledged. "But there's no excuse for what Brad did."

"Of course not." Patsy squeezed his hand. "I can't think of anything worse. It was terribly wrong, and I'm sure Brad knows that."

Pete shrugged. "You're right, Patsy. But still . . . I think a black eye would suit him right about now."

"Or Yvonne Ratcliff," Ashley spoke up. "I'm not sure which of them I hate more."

Patsy tried to think of the right response. How did one discuss such an incident? The very idea of finding one's husband in bed with another woman was enough to make her shudder. If Pete ever did anything like that . . . well, Patsy couldn't imagine how she would react.

"I don't even know what to tell you, Ashley," she admitted finally. "I can't think of anything that will fix this situation. All I can do is make sure you know I love you, and I'm here for you. You can stay with me as long as you like."

The barest hint of a smile crossed Ashley's face. "Thank you for not trying to make it better by saying dumb things, Patsy. Like when Mrs. Moore died and people said, 'Well, she lived a long, happy life.' Or, 'Well, it must have been her time to go.' That stuff doesn't help at all. Nothing can change how

I feel. Right now I just want to disappear."

"You've done that for sure," Pete told her. "With your car parked in Patsy's garage, no one will have any idea you're here. But don't you think you ought to call your folks? They'll be worried."

"I don't want to talk to them. All those questions. I'm not up to answering anything. I need to hide for a while. Maybe forever."

"People are going to find out eventually." Pete focused on Patsy. "There's no way you can keep a secret in Deepwater Cove."

Patsy thought for a moment. It was true that Ashley would have to face reality again soon enough. But maybe there was a way to let the young woman rest in silence for a little while longer.

"I have an idea," she said. "It's worth a try."

She picked up the phone and dialed. When Brenda Hansen's voice came on, Patsy greeted her friend and then asked to speak to Cody. "Merry Christmas, punkin! Did you open your present from me yet?"

"Hey, Patsy! You gave me five boxes of chocolate cake mix and five cans of chocolate icing and one sheet cake pan and also a knife. But, Patsy, you forgot that I don't know how to bake."

"You'll learn. That's the whole point of

my present. I bet Brenda or Jennifer will help you turn one of those mixes into a cake. After you learn how, you can make your own any time."

"Thank you, Patsy. And guess what. Jennifer gave me a set of watercolors. I'm painting a picture of her right now. The paper is getting very soggy."

Knowing Cody could talk about his own interests for hours, Patsy changed the subject. "Pete came over to my house. I couldn't stand up to cook, so he made our lunch. We're having a great time this afternoon. We opened presents and sang carols and ate some more of that cake with the pecan star on top. Ashley Hanes is doing pretty well, and we all feel so stuffed we hardly know what to do with ourselves. Did you have a nice meal?"

"I ate a whole turkey leg."

"All by yourself?"

"Yep. But nobody made cake over here."

"Well, ask Jennifer to help you use one of your new mixes. Maybe even this afternoon. How about that?"

"Okay."

"Merry Christmas, then. I sure love you, Cody."

"I love you too."

As she hung up, Patsy grinned. "Just you

wait. Our curly-haired neighborhood tele-gram service will soon spread that news around — including the little tidbit I put in about Ashley."

"Patsy, you're nuts if you think Cody can keep a secret," Pete said. "People are going to figure out she's staying here with you."

"You know how Cody mixes up details — and I didn't really say Ashley was here. We'll let him do his thing and see how it turns out. It's all going to be fine."

Having made such an optimistic state-ment, Patsy couldn't help but glance at Ash-ley. The pretty young redhead was staring out the window. She looked as though her world had come to an end. And it had.

"I miss Mrs. Moore," she murmured. "I wonder what she would have told me to do."

"We could call Charlie and ask him," Patsy offered. "He's in California, but I've got his number."

"I don't want to bother him. The last thing he'll want to do on Christmas Day is think about his wife being gone. Being dead." A sniffle betrayed Ashley's heart. "Who wants to talk about a totally wrecked marriage anyway?"

Pete shifted on the sofa. "I don't know what Esther Moore would have said, but I can pretty much tell you what Charlie would say."

Both women turned to him.

"He'd say Brad is a fool for hurting his wife that way and for thinking he could do it without her finding out. Charlie would say Brad deserves every bit of misery he gets. Then he'd tell you to go find your husband, talk to him, and see if you can work things out. He and Esther seemed like they had a perfect marriage, but Charlie said enough things at our men's Bible study for me to know it wasn't always rosy in the Moore household. The main thing was that they *tried.* They always kept trying. Working on their problems. Seeing if they could figure out a way to be happy together."

"And forgive," Ashley said softly. "Mrs. Moore told me forgiveness was important. But I don't think she ever had to forgive anything as bad as this."

Patsy felt Pete's hand tighten on her own. Ashley was right, of course. This was it . . . the very worst. Patsy wasn't sure she herself could pardon such a thing. Was such mercy even possible?

"I don't know what the Moores would say," Patsy told her. "But I think Cody might remind us of a verse in the Bible. There's one that says the things that seem impossible to man are possible with God."

Ashley's eyes narrowed. "If God loved me, He never would have let something like this happen. I used to believe in God, Patsy. But not anymore. Now I know I never will."

Brad opened his eyes. A stab of pain angled down through one side of his skull and into his brain. He couldn't move his head. Where was he?

He looked up and tried to focus. The familiar ceiling over the sofa stared back at him. He was home.

"Ashley?" He managed to call out the word, even though the sound of his own voice intensified the throbbing in his head.

"Hey, Ash?"

When she didn't answer, he tried to recall the events of the night before. It hadn't been a good day — he did remember that. He and Ashley had fought in the morning. Then he'd gone to work. Finished early. Stopped at Larry's.

Oh no.

With a groan, Brad watched the vague images of the previous night flash through his mind. Larry's. Mack. Bubba. Yvonne.

Cringing, he rubbed his hand over his face. Yes, he had left Larry's with Yvonne. He remembered now. And later, he had seen Ashley standing in the doorway of Yvonne's apartment. His wife's brown eyes had focused on him. Then she turned away.

Yvonne had laughed. Lit a cigarette. Tried to touch him. He shook her off. Fought her off. Shouted at her. She had pleaded, threatened, whined.

The night air had hit him like a blast from an open freezer as he staggered outside. Yvonne pulled on him. He looked for his car. She began screaming, throwing things at him. From another apartment, a man had hollered at them to shut up.

Somehow he had found his way back to Larry's and his car. He had no memory of the trip home. He might have driven into a ditch. Or hit another vehicle head-on. But he hadn't. Here he was. On the sofa.

"Ashley?" he called again. "Ashley, what time is it? Where are you?"

The house felt empty, and Brad knew why. She was gone. The puppy, too. She had taken Yappy. Afraid to leave the dog alone, she must have packed him up with her other stuff and left the house.

Fighting revulsion at himself, Brad pushed up into a sitting position. His ears rang, and his head felt like it might explode. What had he done?

What had he done?

The phone in his jeans' pocket warbled.

262

He fished it out and looked at the name. His mother. The digital clock on the side table read 2:00 p.m.

Letting out a breath, he hurled the phone across the room. This was *Christmas Day.* He was supposed to have eaten lunch with his parents. He and Ashley had argued about where to spend the noon hour, just as they'd argued about everything lately.

Where was she? He needed to talk to her. She would be at her folks' place.

Rising, he realized he had no shirt on. He must have left it at Yvonne's house. Yvonne Ratcliff. What had he said to her last night? Why had he gone to her apartment? How could he have been so stupid?

Beer. That was the culprit. He'd been drunk. Ashley would believe that. But could it make any difference? No. He had done this thing, this terrible thing, and his wife knew. Because of it, she had left him forever.

He picked up the phone and pressed the number for her parents' house. Ashley's mother answered.

"Where are you two?" she demanded at the sound of Brad's voice. Peeved, she sounded like a gong inside his head. "I held the lunch in the oven until one, but then we gave up and ate. Let me talk to my daughter. I've been calling that girl's cell number for

263

hours. Ashley promised you would be here."

Brad focused on the phone as he shut it off without responding. Ashley wasn't at home? Where could she have gone? What if something had happened to her? Or what if she had . . . no. She wouldn't have killed herself. Not over this. Would she?

Fear steered a course through his chest, reigniting the pain in his head. What if Ashley was dead? It would be his fault.

No, she must be at the Hansens' house with Jennifer and her family. Ashley liked Jennifer, and she would have sought shelter with someone who cared about her. At the memory of his inappropriate thoughts and behavior toward Ashley's friend, Brad winced. How could he call over there? By now, they would all know about his night with Yvonne. They would despise him.

Yet he had to find his wife. The phone book lay on the counter. He flipped it open and finally located Steve and Brenda's number.

"Hey, this is Cody!" The answering voice was so loud that Brad flinched as sparks of pain shot through his brain. "I'm over at the Hansens' house because it's Christmas, and we opened presents and guess what! I got a big set of professional watercolor paints from Jennifer and cake mixes from

Patsy, and lots of other stuff."

"Is Ashley over there?"

"No, and I hope it won't be bad social skills if I say good-bye. We're getting ready to eat pecan pie. It's not as good as choco-late cake, but —"

Unable to bear Cody's chatter any longer, Brad again cut the connection. Ashley wasn't at her mother's house. She wasn't with the Hansens. Where could she have gone? What might she have done?

Seeing your husband like that . . . in another woman's bed . . . what would that do? Again he pictured Ashley's luminous brown eyes staring at him through Yvonne's doorway.

Nausea rising, he pressed another button on the phone. It rang just once.

"Hello, this is Charlie." The voice sounded so familiar. So jovial. So sane.

"Hey, Mr. Moore."

"Brad? Is that you?"

He sagged down onto the floor, his knees bent and his head hanging low. "Yeah. It's me."

"Well, this is a nice surprise! I'd wish you a merry Christmas, but you don't sound so good. Are you sick?"

"Uh . . . sort of." Looking up, Brad sud-denly noticed the one unfamiliar thing in the room. A Christmas tree.

Branches fanning out to fill the place where the recliner had sat, the fragrant pine rose to the ceiling. From top to bottom, it dripped with beads. Ashley's beads. Beads of every color and design imaginable. Beads strung together on wire and fashioned into stars. Beads crafted into the shape of snowflakes. Beads dangling from every twig, glistening in the slanting rays of sunlight.

Brad's eyes brimmed, blurring the tree as he realized what Ashley had done. After shouting at him, telling him she hated him, insisting she didn't need him, she had gone out and bought a Christmas tree. Then she had spent her whole day decorating it. For him. For them.

"Do you have a bad cold?"

"Huh?" Brad looked down at the phone.

"What's eating on you, kid?" Charlie asked. "Did you pick up some kind of bug? I hope Ashley's not sick too. Somebody needs to be there ladling chicken soup down your throat."

Brad brushed at the damp spot under his eye. "No, I'm not sick. Not like that."

"You sound like you're at the bottom of a barrel. What's going on, Brad?"

"Nothing, Mr. Moore. I'd better go."

"Now, hold your horses there. You called

me for a reason, and I'd like to know what it is. If you won't tell me, put Ashley on."

After a second's pause, Charlie spoke again. "How long has she been gone, Brad?"

"She wasn't here this morning. I think she left last night."

"You *think?* Where were you? Not at that bar, I hope. Not on Christmas Eve."

Brad couldn't respond.

"I see. Well." Charlie cleared his throat. "All right, boy. What happened? Give it to me straight."

"We had an argument."

"And what else? I know you two have been fighting like a pair of wet cats lately. That can't be all there is to this."

Brad shook his head. "No. That's not all."

"Did you do something wrong?"

"Yeah." The word came out in an unexpected falsetto as waves of anguish began to push up through his chest.

"All right," Charlie said, his voice softening. "Did you hit Ashley?"

"Worse."

The silence on the phone was so final that Brad couldn't stifle the sob. He bent over on the floor, curled into a ball of agony. Tears welled, spilled from his eyes, ran down his cheeks, dampened the carpet. He sucked down a choking gasp.

"Brad." Charlie's voice was calm. "I want you to tell me exactly what happened — every bit of it. Spit it up and get it out, because this is the only way to begin fixing it."

"I can't talk, Mr. Moore. I've gotta go. I don't know where Ashley is. I can't find her."

"Start at the beginning. The last argument between the two of you. That's as good a place as any."

"I don't want to talk about it."

"Confession is good for the soul. Besides, you're not going to get past this feeling you have in your gut right now until you talk everything through with your wife. You might as well practice on me."

"Ashley said she hated me. She didn't need me anymore." The anger Brad felt in recalling that moment stopped his tears. "I haven't been the best husband, but I didn't deserve *that*. Man, I've tried, Mr. Moore. The problems between us aren't all my fault."

"Yeah, yeah, yeah. Stop defending yourself and get on with it."

Brad wasn't sure why, but he suddenly poured out everything. Maybe it was because Charlie Moore was far away in California. Or because he was too honorable a man to gossip about what he was told. Whatever the reason, Brad outlined the previous day — all the way from the morning argument until the sight of Ashley's face at the door of Yvonne Ratcliff's apartment.

"So, you're home now, and she's gone," Charlie said. "Any idea where she went?"

Swallowing, Brad rubbed his chin. "Wait — aren't you going to yell at me, Mr. Moore? I mean, you heard what I did. I did that to Ashley. To my wife. Aren't you going to say anything about it?"

"You already know what I think. The job now is to figure out where to go from here. First of all, you've got to find your wife. The two of you need to figure out how to stay married. No matter what, boy, you've got some serious apologizing to do. And I'm talking about groveling. None of this *I tried to be a good husband* nonsense. You committed adultery. You promised to love and cherish Ashley forever, and you cheated on her. In the eyes of God, the two of you had become one, but you tore that union apart. Now, anyone with a lick of sense knows these marriage problems go two ways. You both contributed to the trouble. But the bottom line is that you're the one who violated your vows."

At Charlie's concluding statement, Brad

felt sobs building up inside him again. "She's not gonna take me back, Mr. Moore."

"Do you want to go back? You sure haven't been acting like it."

"I don't know. She's . . . well, she's a pain. Marriage stinks. It's nothing like I thought it would be. Ashley is into her beads and her job and wanting to have a baby and all that. One time I tried to sit down and listen to her, and she never stopped talking for a minute. It was all about her and the ideas she was having and gossip from work and that kind of junk. She didn't say or ask one thing about me."

Charlie gave a laugh of disbelief. "About *you?*"

"What's wrong with that? She used to always brag on me and ask about what I was doing and admire me, you know? Now she just talks about her own stuff. It took me about ten minutes to figure out that if I was going to listen to her ramble, I needed a beer just to sit through it. I went to get one out of the fridge, and she started screaming at me. She hates it when I drink."

"You drink too much, Brad. Everyone knows that. You've got a couple of DWIs on your record. You hang out at that bar. And now you've gone and whooped it up with some woman you hardly know. All because you were drunk."

"But it's not as though I drink hard stuff. I don't even like whisky."

"Look here, boy, if you're going to sit there and defend yourself, I don't have time to listen. I haven't seen my two grandkids in a long time, and we were playing a pretty interesting game when you called. So either stop talking about what a stand-up guy you are, or I'm heading back to the children."

"Yes, sir." Brad rubbed his face. "I'm sorry, Mr. Moore."

"I'll tell you one thing before I let you go. If you quit on this marriage, you won't ever be trading up. Ashley's not that different from any other woman. They love to jabber, they've got moods coming and going till you can't keep up, and they don't want you grabbing at them unless you've spent some time being nice first. You're not going to find a wife *better* than Ashley. You might find one who's a little *different,* but not much."

"I understand, sir."

"Then make up your mind, act like a man, and quit being so doggone foolish. Go over to the church and visit with Pastor Andrew. He's a smart fellow. Start attending the men's Bible study at Rods-N-Ends. Talk to

Steve Hansen and Derek Finley. They've been married longer than you, and they'll help you out. Most of all, you've got to do everything possible to win back your wife's heart. You got that?"

"Yes, Mr. Moore."

"Are you sober right now?"

"Yes."

"Well, drowning your sorrows isn't going to make this any better. Stay clearheaded, you hear?"

"All right."

"And, Brad? I love you, and I'll be praying for you."

"Thank you, sir."

As he slipped the phone back into his pocket, Brad gazed at the Christmas tree across the room. There were no presents under it, but that was okay. The tree was enough.

CHAPTER THIRTEEN

Brad paced the floor from the living room into the kitchen and back again. It was the first morning of the new year, and he had a vicious hangover.

The day after Christmas, Brad had called in sick with what he thought was a bad cold. When the fever, chills, headache, and nausea continued day after day, he decided he must have the flu. And he knew he deserved it.

Not until New Year's Eve had he begun to feel halfway human. Mack had shown up that night with a cooler full of beer. Brad declined at first, recalling Charlie Moore's admonitions, then gave in to Mack's urging to drink just one. Many hours, many beers, and many tears over women later, the two men had toasted in the new year.

Now, rummaging through a kitchen cabinet for an aspirin, the ridiculousness of his situation struck Brad. He had been sicker than a dog for days. Then just as he was finally starting to feel better, he had gotten drunk and made himself sick again.

Jerking open the fridge door, he began grabbing cans of beer and throwing them into an empty paper bag. One by one, he filled the bag to the brim. Then he opened the pantry door and took out the imported six-pack he had bought the week before. Hefting both into his arms, he crossed the living room.

As he tugged open the front door, he thought of Yappy. The pup hadn't lived there long, but Brad was accustomed to hearing the skitter of tiny toenails on the tile as he left the house. He missed his dog's voice — and no one could deny that Yappy had a voice. The yowls, yaps, wows, browfs, and other vocalizations charmed everyone who met the little fur ball.

But Ashley had taken Yappy away, and rightly so. Brad didn't deserve either the joy or the responsibility of owning a dog. Berating himself for leaving the puppy alone while he whiled away Christmas Eve at Larry's and then broke his marriage vows in Yvonne's apartment, Brad carried the six-pack and the bag of beer down to the lake.

As he reached the shoreline, he set them on the bank, grabbed a can, and flung it as far out into the water as he could. He knew people would frown on finding it floating in the lake, but he didn't care. He'd been a quarterback, and this was what he did best.

"This is for you, Camdenton Lakers football," Brad growled as he launched another can. "Good-for-nothing sport."

Another sailed across the water. "What am I supposed to do with my quarterback fame now?" he shouted as it made a splash. "What's that total yardage record done for me lately? Can anyone tell me that?"

His anger turned to a lump in his throat as Brad thought of his fleeting popularity and empty pride. What did high school honors matter in real life?

"Nothing!" he snarled as he threw another can beyond the rippling circles left from the previous one. He bent down and tore open the six-pack, flinging bottles now as the tears fell and his voice cried out.

"Take that, 4.0 GPA!" *Splash.*

"And here's one for you, Mack, good buddy!" *Splash.*

"Yvonne!" *Splash.*

"Drywall!" *Splash.*

"Ten bucks an hour! Whoopee!" *Splash.*

"New truck!" *Splash.*

He had emptied the six-pack, so he returned to the paper bag.

"Spare room! Larry's! Bubba!" *Splash,*

splash, splash.

"Hey there."

The voice behind Brad startled him. He swung around to find Cody Goss standing on the bank. In a denim jacket and jeans, the guy looked almost normal. But Brad knew all about the homeless nut-job who had turned up in Deepwater Cove that spring.

"Get away from me, you idiot," he ground out. "Leave me alone."

Cody swallowed. "You know, every year at the spring cleanup, they find refrigerators and foam and glass bottles and all kinds of things by the lake. We're not supposed to throw stuff in the water."

"Shut up, you stupid creep."

"Don't talk to me like that. It's not polite."

"Polite?" Brad stalked toward Cody and gave his shoulder a shove. "Polite is leaving people alone when they ask you to."

"I could hear you yelling all the way over at the Hansens' house, and Brenda said —"

"Can you hear me *now?*" Brad shouted, his face an inch from Cody's. "I said *get.*"

"I thought I should check on you, because —"

"Stop!" Brad threw a shoulder into Cody's chest. Cody flung out his arms as if he could stop himself in midair. Then he hit the ground, sprawling across the stiff brown grass and lying still, his blue eyes wide.

Brad dropped to one knee and grabbed Cody by the collar of his jacket, then jerked him into a sitting position. "I told you to shut up. Just shut up and leave me alone."

"You are not being reasonable," Cody managed to huff out.

"What?" Brad let go and pushed Cody back to the ground.

"Reasonable." Cody blinked at tears that filled his eyes. His voice came out in a whispery croak. "It's not good social skills to litter. Or knock people down."

"What do you know about social skills, weirdo? What do you know about anything?"

"I know that you and I are both crying. I'm crying because I'm a little bit scared of you. I think you're crying about Ashley."

Breathing hard, Brad stared down at the figure splayed out on the ground. Half of him wanted to beat the guy into a pulp. The other half wanted to . . . what?

What on earth could Brad possibly do that would change anything? Unexpected sobs welled up past the lump in his throat. He sank down onto the ground beside Cody, covered his face with his hands, and wept. Rough, hoarse wails heaved up through his chest and emerged from his mouth.

"Brad?" Cody touched him on the arm.

"Buzz off, jerk." Brad swung his arm randomly, barely getting the words out.

"Mr. Moore is coming back home from California in two days," Cody said, his tone subdued. "He'll be glad to know that you threw away your beer."

Charlie Moore's advice on the phone filtered back into Brad's mind. "Mr. Moore doesn't get it. He's too old. I'm a young guy. That's what we do. My friends and I, we drink."

"I'm a young guy, and I don't drink. You know why? Because Steve Hansen said, 'Cody, alcohol can get you into all kinds of trouble.' Derek Finley said, 'Cody, we have had nine people drown in the lake this year, and every one of them was drunk. Do not drink.' And Pete Roberts told me that he used to be an alcoholic and go to alcoholic meetings and then fall off a wagon and go to more meetings and then fall off *another* wagon until he finally decided it is not worth it to even taste the stuff. He said, 'Cody, it is the devil's poison.' "

Brad wiped his face with the back of his hand. "You're the weirdest kid I've ever met, you know that?"

Cody was silent for a moment. "At least I don't break down my own front door and leave my wife and her weird friend — which is *me* — to put it back up again."

"You fixed our door?"

"Yes." Cody elbowed himself up into a sitting position. "And you're welcome, even though you didn't say thank you."

"Well . . . yeah, thanks."

"Okay."

The two sat side by side, looking out over the water. "Ashley's gone," Brad said finally. "She left me."

"But she's all right. She's fine."

Brad turned. "How do you know? Have you seen her? Where is she?"

Cody winced. "I'm not sure. There have been lots of people talking to me, and somebody said Ashley Hanes is doing pretty well. I don't remember who said it. It has been a very talkative time lately."

Rubbing his hands over his eyes, Brad shook his head. "Her mother said she didn't show up at home on Christmas Day."

"Ashley's home is right over there with you."

Together they studied the small house with its newly added room tacked onto the side. Brad felt the lump trying to form in his throat again, so he took a can from the paper bag and rifled it out into the lake.

"Litterbug." Cody looked over, a smirk on

his face.

"Weirdo."

"Litterbug."

Brad couldn't hold back the trace of a smile that sneaked past the hard lump. "You're not so weird, Cody. At least you have a life. I wrecked mine. Now I don't have a clue what to do."

"I think Ashley ran away because you did something bad with another lady. You're that kind of man. I can tell, because when women see me, they say, 'Oh hi, Cody. How are you, sweetie pie?' When they see you, they giggle and turn pink."

"Not Ashley. Not anymore. She took her stuff and our dog, and she left."

"You need to ask forgiveness from God. Then maybe you will have a chance to be forgiven by Ashley."

"I quit religion a long time ago, man. I don't go to church."

"God doesn't live in a church. He lives in people. You can apologize to Him anywhere. Don't you know that?"

Brad checked the paper sack and noted a single remaining can. Fighting the urge to take a drink, he could feel Cody's eyes on him.

"Hey, quit looking at me like I'm some kind of doofus. For your information, I earned a 4.0 in school."

"I don't know what a 4.0 is, but I know what Exodus 20:14 is — 'Thou shalt not commit adultery.' That is what I think you did wrong, Brad. Also drinking too much. And breaking your door."

"Okay, I get the picture." Brad pushed his fingers back through his hair. "Sheesh. What did you do when you were a kid — memorize the whole Bible or something?"

"My daddy taught me lots of it. I didn't go to school. The Bible is my 4.0." Cody stood. "Well, I'll go now. I'm getting cold."

Still seated on the hard ground, Brad looked out across the lake. Flat and glassy, it had gone silver in the waning light. "What made you say that about me — the adultery stuff?" he asked in a low voice. "What do you know?"

"I know you're like me when my daddy put me out on the side of the road and drove away. I was alone and lost before I found the road to Deepwater Cove. I could have been happier a lot sooner if I had known which direction to go. I think you know which direction to go, Brad Hanes."

Reaching down into the paper sack, Cody picked up the last can. Rearing back, he hurled it toward the lake in a glimmering silver arc. Far in the distance, it splashed into the water, leaving a circle of ripples.

"Happy New Year," he said as he turned away.

Brad watched Cody cross the sloped lawn beside the docks and head toward the Hansens' house.

"Pete thinks I've lost my mind spending hard-earned money on paint and curtains." Patsy gingerly stepped into the living room carrying a tray of sliced caramel apples and cups of hot spiced cider for herself and Ashley. "He reminded me it wasn't so long ago I painted the tearoom that beautiful shade of purple."

Ashley had offered to help, but Patsy said she had a special way of making cider and would prepare it herself. Ashley didn't mind waiting. Though she had taken a week off from work, she felt exhausted all the time. Patsy, too, was tired. She had worked late New Year's Eve — hobbling around on her sore ankle while fixing hair and polishing nails for partygoers. This first morning of the new year the two women had risen late and eaten a lazy breakfast.

Now Ashley took a handful of popcorn from the bowl in her lap and tossed a piece to the floor for Yappy. The air in the room smelled of cinnamon, cloves, and pine-scented candles. Reflections from a crackling fire lit the walls and danced on the chair cushions that cradled her.

Dropping onto the nearby sofa, Patsy let out a breath. "Did you know Esther Moore was the one who suggested I paint the tea area purple? Oh, how I miss that woman."

"Me too."

"She'd be thrilled about Brenda's new shop. It sets a different tone — makes the whole strip seem more genteel and high-class."

"Yeah," Ashley murmured. "Tranquility is starting to feel like a quaint little town instead of a pit stop for gas and tackle."

"The other day I got to looking around the salon, and I realized it was just plain-old, been-through-the-washer-too-many-times shabby. It needs a paint job in the worst way."

"What about Cody's mural of all the Jennifers with their different hairstyles? You won't paint over that, will you?"

"Heavens, no. That's a treasure." Patsy took a sip of cider from her china cup. "I want to get this work done before summer starts up and things get too busy. Charlie Moore is going to help Bitty remodel the Pop-In into a bona fide bistro, so I feel like I simply have to make some changes to Just

As I Am."

"After you're done, maybe you can re-name it Better Than I Was."

Patsy laughed. "Actually, the name is very important to me. The words are from an old hymn."

"I was kidding, Patsy. I like the salon's name." Ashley hadn't heard of the hymn, but she had always thought Patsy's beauty shop had a welcoming feel. Both her place of business and her home mirrored the woman herself. Patsy was warm, encouraging, quick to offer a hug or a tissue, always ready with a word of sympathy.

Most people weren't like that. At the snack shop Ashley's parents owned, she had seen more than her share of humanity's nasty side. Same thing at the country club. Rich or poor, young or old, it didn't matter. Customers loved to find fault. Always ready with a complaint, they were rarely grateful or complimentary. Their snide comments sometimes rang in her ears.

"I asked for mustard on this hot dog," one would say.

Another — fury rising like mist off the lake — would march up to the snack shop window. *"Why on earth did you put mustard on my hot dog?"*

In the country club dining room, she often

heard, *"My steak is overcooked. Take it back to the kitchen."*

Or, *"This meat is so rare I can almost hear it moo."*

"What are you thinking about, honey?" Patsy asked. "You look like you're a million miles away."

"People can be so rude." Ashley dipped her fingers into the bowl of popcorn again. "I'm glad you're not like that."

"I have my moments. Don't let anyone tell you different."

"Patsy . . . I really appreciate you taking me in on Christmas Eve."

"Mercy's sake, you were a godsend. With my sprained ankle swollen up like an over-ripe plum, I could hardly get around. A week later, it still gets to hurting if I don't rest it now and then."

"I heard sprains can take a long time to heal." Ashley didn't want to remember who had given her that piece of information — a former football player who'd experienced his share of injuries. Fighting the memory, she dropped a few more kernels of popcorn down to Yappy, who was growing larger and more shaggy by the day. The dog crunched the popcorn, licked his lips, then sat staring up at her, his tail wagging and his brown eyes filled with hope.

For a couple of days, Ashley had been trying to figure out a way to discuss something important with her friend. Now she decided simply to blurt it out.

"Patsy, I've decided to rent an apartment in Osage Beach. I already put down a deposit."

Patsy paused, caramel apple halfway to her mouth. "An apartment?"

"I found one in the paper last week. I haven't seen the place, but I called and got it at a reasonable price. And I can cancel the lease with two weeks' notice, in case I don't like it. When the summer crowd comes in, the owner said he'll raise the rent, and I'll have to find something else. But this gives me four months to look. Also . . . I'm going to quit my job at the country club."

"Quit?" Patsy sat up and put the apple slice back on the tray. Then she looked at it, popped it into her mouth, and began to chew.

Ashley lifted her chin. "I made a lot of money on my beads, Patsy. I mean, a *whole* lot. I can hardly believe it, but it's true. Since the holidays are over, I expected things to slow down, but they haven't. I checked my Web site the other day, and orders are still coming in."

"Well, my goodness."

"And guess what else." She shivered at the news she had kept secret from everyone. "You'll never guess, so I'll tell you. One of my customers, a lady in St. Louis, owns a small chain of gift and furniture boutiques. She has five of them, all in Missouri. Plus, two people are talking to her about buying franchises for out-of-state stores. She called me and said she got so many compliments on the necklace I made that she wants to carry my beads in her stores. I got a huge order, Patsy. She paid me a chunk of money up front. I have enough for several months' rent and food and bead-making supplies, too. I have so much work to do that I'm almost overwhelmed."

"Are you going to keep working in Brenda's basement?"

"No, I'm moving everything to the apartment. I've decided to ask Jennifer to be my partner, and I'll give her a share of the profits. Before Christmas, she told me she's not going to take any missionary classes this semester. I know she and I can string the necklaces and bracelets and headbands and things. Then while I create more beads, she can do the packaging and mailing. I haven't told Miranda Finley yet, but I'm sure she'll keep my Web site running. Patsy, isn't it amazing? I'll have a real company."

"Ah." Patsy was trying to swallow the bite of apple. "A company."

"Yes, and why shouldn't I?" Ashley's eyes narrowed in resentment at the memory that filled her mind. "My former husband used to tell me that I was a dreamer just like my father. He said I was nuts to believe I could do anything besides work at a regular job, but I know I can do this."

"Wait. Did you say your *former* husband? Ashley, have you filed for divorce?"

"Not yet, but I plan to. I need to settle everything. The debts. The house. And Yappy. I'm not giving back my dog. There's no way I'm letting him take Yappy away. He's mine now. I'm the one who takes care of him, and I'm the one who's keeping him."

"You're doing a lot of *him*-ing, Ashley. Is one of those *him*s Brad?"

"Don't even say that name around me, Patsy. You know how I feel."

"Honey, you can't file for divorce yet. It's only been a week. You two haven't even *tried* to fix your problems."

"Our problems started right after we got married. Besides, why would I want to try to fix anything? I don't care if I lay eyes on the man ever again. I saw all I needed to see that night."

The tears that misted her vision mortified

Ashley. She had already done all the crying she intended to do. The husband she had loved and believed in was nothing but a cheat. Who needed that? Not her, that's for sure.

"Honey, please don't give up yet." Patsy's eyes went deep. "I realize it was a shock to find Brad the way you did. I can't imagine . . . though at work I do hear so much about this kind of thing. It happens more often than I would have thought."

Ashley sniffled. "Yeah, I know lots of people. My cousin, for one. She told me her affair was a long, drawn-out thing at her job. She said it started with flirting. Then they fell in love, and finally they just did it."

"I guess her husband found out."

"He saw the calls on the phone bill. They're divorced now. The man she had the affair with stayed married. My cousin was tempted to call and tell his wife, but she didn't. The wife never found out, and now he's seeing another woman. The guy's a scuzzbucket."

Patsy shook her head. "I reckon I've heard every possible thing that could go wrong in a marriage. The real trouble is patching it back together."

"Why would anyone want to? I sure don't."

"Yes, you do, honey. Your brain is angry, but your heart remembers falling in love with Brad Hanes. A heart never forgets."

At that, Ashley grabbed her teacup and drained it, hoping the hot liquid would stop her tears. "It's too late. I don't trust him, Patsy. For all I know, he's just like my cousin . . . or the guy she was with. Maybe he's had more than one affair. Maybe he and that bar singer have been hooking up for months — even before we got married."

"I doubt that."

"What if he's in love with her? She's probably crazy about him. Who wouldn't be? Look at him. He's got the perfect body. He's handsome, and he charms the socks off everyone. The girls in school were nuts about him. If he loves that woman . . . if he tells her the same things he told me . . ." She clenched her fists, battling the agony in her heart. "We'll never get back together. It's impossible."

"Impossible," Patsy repeated.

For a moment, she sat gazing at the candles on the coffee table. When she spoke again, her voice was soft. "Ashley, do you remember those antique teacups Pete knocked off the wall when he first moved into Rods-N-Ends last spring? I was so mad I wanted to bite his head off."

"You tried."

Patsy smiled. "After that, he started buying cups for me — one by one, until he had replaced the whole collection."

"Pete's a good man."

"He's good enough for me. Are you done with your cider?" She glanced over. "Take your empty cup and hold it up to the lamp beside you. Tell me what you see."

To her surprise, Ashley noted a spiderweb of thin lines running across and around the yellow-flowered cup.

"That one's from my original collection," Patsy said. "You just drank hot apple cider out of it."

Ashley turned the cup upside down and studied the almost seamless base with its maker's mark. "No way. Those cups were shattered. You couldn't possibly have glued this back together, Patsy."

"I sure could — and I did. I had all the pieces. Those cups were very precious to me, so I figured it was worth a try. I sorted the chips into piles and began gluing them back together while I watched TV. You know, honey . . . nothing is so broken that it can't be fixed."

Ashley set the cup back on its saucer. "Is this supposed to be like one of Cody's metaphors, Patsy? Get real. Marriage is not

291

a teacup. You can't fix a relationship with glue. It's impossible."

"That word again. But couldn't you at least give it a try?"

"*No.* I couldn't. How would you feel, Patsy? If you opened a door and found Pete in another woman's bed? If you saw his . . . his jeans lying on the . . ." Ashley gritted her teeth. "I am not going to cry anymore! I'm done with that man. It's over. The thought of him ever, ever, ever touching me again makes me sick! Don't you get it? The places he touched her . . . the things she did to him . . . Patsy, he belonged to *me!* He promised himself to *me!*"

The flash of an image tore through Ashley's brain like summer lightning. She was standing at the altar in her glorious white satin gown, a bouquet of red roses in her hands. Brad waited beside her, so tall and handsome in his black tuxedo. They looked at each other as they exchanged vows. His blue eyes were filled with love. That day, she had believed she was the happiest woman in the universe.

"I think I'm going to throw up." Ashley bent over, holding her stomach.

"Oh, dear. Do you need help getting to the bathroom?"

"Ugh . . . no, I'll be okay. It's just that

every time I remember opening that woman's apartment door, I feel sick all over again." Covering her face with one hand, Ashley held her stomach with the other and gave in to her tears. "I hate him, Patsy. I hate him forever. I'll never forgive him. Never!"

As sobs racked her, she sensed Patsy coming to kneel on the floor in front of her. Warm arms encircled Ashley's quaking shoulders. As the women embraced, Yappy began to worm his way between them. He snuffled and wiggled and clawed until he had clambered onto Patsy's knees and was able to put his head on Ashley's lap.

"Brooo," he mouthed softly. His wet nose pressed against Ashley's cheek as his soft pink tongue licked her tears.

"Aw, looky there." Patsy leaned back and stroked the puppy's head. "We've got Yappy all upset. Maybe he heard us talking bad about Brad. Don't tell me your husband was mean to this little guy."

Ashley wiped her cheeks. "He was okay. He taught Yappy to go outside and do his business."

"Did he? Well, at least Brad is good for something. He's a fine potty trainer — let's give him a point for that."

With some effort Patsy edged back onto

the sofa. "Oh, I've got to lose some weight or I won't be worth beans on my wedding day. Who knows when that will be? I can't get Pete to set a date, let alone talk about the honeymoon."

Ashley reflected on the man she had married. "On the way to Branson for our honeymoon, Brad wouldn't let go of me for a second. He drove the whole time with one arm around me, kissing me and holding me. He knew how much I loved being close to him. But back home, it turned out he wasn't as great as I'd thought. He expected me to cook, but then he griped about what I'd made. Neither of us had the energy to pick stuff up and keep the place looking decent. You know, he never once cleaned the shower drain. He said it was all my hair, but it wasn't. What a jerk."

Patsy picked up another slice of caramel apple and chewed on it for a while. "Sounds like you both stopped taking care of things . . . including your marriage."

"That is *not* true. I loved Brad. I never did anything to hurt him."

"I'm afraid I can't agree with that one, petunia. You had a death grip on the late shift at the country club. Exactly what did you expect your husband to do from four in the afternoon until you got home at midnight?"

"But I made twice the money from tips in the evenings. That income was important."

"Uh-huh." Patsy sniffed, clearly unimpressed.

Yappy had crawled onto Ashley's lap. She'd been trying to break him of getting on the furniture. He had chewed a big hole in the corner of one of Patsy's sofa pillows. Several legs on the dining room chairs bore tiny tooth marks too. If the woman hadn't been so kind, she would have kicked the dog and his owner out long before.

"Patsy, you don't really believe I should stay with Brad, do you?" Ashley asked. "You know how cocky and self-centered he is. If he betrayed me once, he'll do it again. Won't he? Be honest."

"People *can* change — especially if they're motivated."

"My husband was never motivated to change — not for me."

"He is now. He's been looking for you the whole time you've been hiding. People have told me he called them trying to find you. Brad is raw and ignorant. Definitely immature. Arrogant, too. I won't deny that about him. But the boy has always been respectful and polite to me. Now he's become downright humble. Who knows what could happen next? He might just turn into the best husband a girl could ever want."

It was hard to imagine. Too hard. Ashley tried to picture herself back inside the little house she had thought would be their happy home. She made an effort to conjure up children and Thanksgiving dinners and Christmas trees and snuggling on the sofa. But all she could see was Yvonne Ratcliff's red sweater lying on the floor next to Brad's blue jeans.

"I can't." She shook her head. "I'm sorry, Patsy, but I just can't do it."

"You *won't*."

"I'm not as good as you. You're all spiritual — reading your Bible every morning and going to church on Sundays."

"I never said I was good. And that's not the point, anyway. But I do know one thing — when I hold on to my anger, the person I hurt the most is *me*. And if you don't find a way to forgive Brad Hanes, the person who will suffer the rest of her life is a pretty little redhead with a broken heart."

Ashley bent over and laid her cheek on the top of Yappy's head. She wanted to believe Patsy. Truly she did. But her own experience had taught her not to trust people . . . not even someone as kind as the friend who had taken her in on a dark, cold night.

And certainly not the man who had betrayed her, broken her heart, turned her life upside down, and given her a memory that would never fade.

CHAPTER FOURTEEN

"Things look a little bedraggled around here — including you." Charlie Moore stepped into the living room and began taking off his jacket. "I'll tell you what, Brad. It was sure a lot warmer in California. We're not even a month into the new year, and the humidity and chill are making every bone in my body ache. Boofer doesn't like it any more than I do. Speaking of dogs — where's Yappy?"

In the kitchen making hot chocolate, Brad found he couldn't respond. Instead he focused on stirring a powdery mix into mugs of water he had heated in the microwave.

"Don't tell me you let your puppy get away too?" Charlie seated himself on the sofa. "I leave town for a couple of weeks, and you go and lose your wife and your dog. Well, if that doesn't beat all."

"I messed up."

"You sure did." Charlie scratched his head as if the explanation for Brad's behavior was hidden in his white hair somewhere. Finally he sighed. "Well, at least you've stopped drinking. Wouldn't it be nice if we could learn from what people tell us? But most of us are too stubborn to listen. We've got to go ahead and make our own mistakes."

When Brad didn't respond, Charlie chuckled woefully. "How's the hot chocolate coming along? This house must be hovering around the freezing point. Have you got your thermostat turned off, boy?"

A package of discount store cookies under one arm, Brad carried two steaming mugs across the floor. "It's as low as I can stand it. Sorry, but I don't have much choice, Mr. Moore. The house payment, the utilities, the credit cards, the bank. I've got people trying to take away more money than I can possibly bring in."

"That's what you call debt, kid. My father used to caution me against owing anybody anything, and I'm glad he did. I never ran up a credit card in my life. Paid every bill before it came due. I tried to teach Charles Jr. that lesson too, but I don't know how well he learned it. You should see the house they live in. Hoo-wee. I know my son is a vice president with his company now, but *onions?* How much can onions really pay?"

"You'd have to ask Bitty Sondheim. She probably buys them by the bushel."

"Bitty and I talked about onions till we were blue in the face. In fact, I think we said everything there is to say on the subject." Charlie took a sip of cocoa and smiled in contentment. "Ahh. Now that's tasty. I guess winter isn't too unbearable if you can have a cup of hot chocolate now and then to pull you through."

Brad took the chair nearest the sofa. Despite Mr. Moore's rebukes, he felt the need to be close to the older man. Ashamed to call his parents and too disgusted with himself and his friends to phone any of them, he had been alone in the evenings with nothing but the TV and the temptation to drink keeping him company.

"So you had a good time in California?" he asked. "How was the trip?"

"Bitty and I talked the whole way there and back. That woman has had quite a life, let me tell you. She's been through some rough spots. I admire her. I sure do. You know, I'd planned for Bitty to sit in the backseat with Jessica Hansen, but that young lady flatly refused to go anywhere unless she was right beside her fiancé. Bitty made a fine traveling companion, though.

We took turns behind the wheel. There was a little too much smooching going on in the back to make me comfortable. Afraid I had to take a peek in the rearview mirror every now and then just to let the kids know I was watching. Bitty did too."

"So you like Bitty, huh?" Brad said, giving Charlie a knowing smirk.

The older man didn't balk. "I do like her. Enjoyed the trip. But I can't deny I'm happy to be home. I missed Deepwater Cove. Even winter began to look good to me. Much as the seasons throw things helter-skelter, I'm fond of them. A man needs a change now and then."

He glanced at Brad. "Maybe you've had more of a change than you bargained for."

"You were right about what you told me on the phone, Mr. Moore. I caused my own problems." Brad studied the Christmas tree near the window, its brown needles lying scattered on the carpet. "Well, not all the problems. Ashley's bead business got in the way of our relationship. The only thing she wanted to do in her spare time was make jewelry. She didn't want to talk about anything else. Beads, beads, beads."

"If a person really enjoys something, that's to be expected. I used to talk about my mail route in the evenings when I got home from work. I'd tell Esther how many packages and letters I had delivered and where. I'd ramble on and on about who I had met that day and what we discussed and the things I had noticed along the way. Probably drove her to distraction, but she never complained. Didn't you ever want to talk to Ashley about your construction job?"

Brad reflected on his desire to tell his wife how well he could tape and mud the seam between two sheets of wallboard. He had taken pride in Bill Walters's compliment, but he was never able to share that with Ashley. Now that he thought about it, she probably wouldn't have been interested anyway.

"My job is boring," he told Charlie. "I'm good at it, but I'm just part of a crew. Nothing I do matters in the big scheme of things. Almost anyone could take my place, and those condos would still get built. In high school, I stood out. What I did mattered — especially on the football field. Now I'm just one of the chain gang."

"What would you rather do?"

"No idea. I used to want to go to college and become a teacher. Believe it or not, I liked school. Around the other guys, I faked it, of course. Told them I thought it was a waste of time and all that. But I did well because I was interested in what I was learning, and I wanted good grades so I could stay on the football team. The counselor called me an all-around outstanding student."

"Outstanding, huh?"

"In the end, though, it turned out to be a waste of time. English class — Shakespeare and Mark Twain and all those writers? Forget it. No point in having read any of their stuff. Geography? Who cares where Venezuela is? Civics? None of the guys I hang with even bothers to vote. I used to love math, but now all I use it for is figuring out where to mark a two-by-four before I saw through it."

"Why didn't you go to college, Brad? You could have become a teacher and coached football, too."

Brad shrugged. "I bombed the ACT. Had a hangover when I took it. I didn't get a football scholarship either — knee injury kept me off the field when recruiters were scouting the team. Coach spoke up for me, but it didn't do any good. Now I'm so deep in debt I'll never work my way out. I couldn't afford college even if I still wanted to go. Ashley and I used to talk about it before we got married. She wanted to teach kindergartners, and I figured I'd be over at the high school."

As he took a sip of cocoa, Brad pictured himself standing in front of a classroom. He would know what the kids were going through. And he would certainly understand the pressures of family, grades, athletics, dating. He knew how it felt to have everything weighing you down until you didn't think you could take another minute.

"Anyhow, I probably wouldn't last a month in college. Didn't even make it through the first year of marriage."

"Do you think Ashley is gone for good?"

"Yeah. I can't even find her. She probably went to visit her cousin in Texas. She hasn't returned any of my calls. Her parents know where she is, but they won't say."

Brad studied the ceiling, willing away his emotion.

"Ashley despises me. Mack said the woman . . . the singer . . . packed up and left town. Went back to Tennessee to give the music business another shot. If you can believe it, I even hurt her."

"Of course I believe it. I don't suspect there are many women who take relationships lightly. She probably thought she had you hog-tied."

"She thought wrong. And we didn't have a relationship. I hardly knew Yvonne Ratcliff. I would never marry a woman like her. She's trash."

"And you're not?" Charlie reached for a cookie. "My dad used to say, takes one to know one. If you act like trash, then you're trash."

"Okay! Man. I feel bad enough. You don't have to rub it in."

"Do you really feel bad enough, Brad? Are you so sorry that you want to start over?"

Brad leaned back in the chair and stretched out his legs. "No one can start over. My dad says you make your own bed and you lie in it."

"That doesn't mean you can never climb out of it."

"Come on, Mr. Moore. Nothing's going to bring back my wife or erase my debts or unwreck that truck I bought."

"That may be true." Charlie closed his eyes, his hands cupped around the warm mug. "On the other hand, there's always Jesus."

Groaning, Brad set his own empty mug on the table near his chair. "You're not go-ing to start in again on that religious stuff, are you? I don't get why people make it such a big deal. If you do good things, you go to heaven. If you're bad, you roast. That's where I'm bound after what I did to my wife. And I deserve it."

Brad was beginning to wish he hadn't agreed to let Charlie come over. At first, he thought it might be nice to have a visitor. When Charlie had called and asked to stop by for a cup of cocoa that evening, Brad had welcomed the idea. Now he realized he'd rather be watching television.

"Despite what you think, Christianity does *not* say good deeds will get you into heaven," Charlie said.

"Whatever. I'm not interested in religion, okay? I'm smart enough to know that no matter what I believe, I can never go back in time and undo the damage."

"Yes, you can. You can ask God's forgiveness. Once you begin to *act* different, you'll find out that you *are* different. And Ashley might give you a second chance too."

"Ashley's not into religion either. That's one thing we had in common."

"And look how well it worked out for you."

Brad let out his breath with a low groan. Charlie's voice faded behind the plan that had begun to form in Brad's brain. He could drive over to Larry's, hang out with his friends, and have a few laughs. He wouldn't have to drink if he didn't want to.

But Charlie was still speaking. "People are

too flawed to come into the presence of God. Good deeds can't erase our faults. In order to really become clean, you have to put your life under the control of Jesus Christ."

"Yeah." Brad nodded, glancing at his lined denim jacket on the coat stand beside the sofa. "Listen, Mr. Moore, I've enjoyed the visit, but I'm beat."

"You don't, then?"

"Don't what?"

"Don't want to be forgiven. Don't want your sins erased."

"I do. I mean, it sounds great. The way you put it, wow. It makes sense."

Charlie stuck out an index finger. "Brad Hanes, you haven't been listening to a word I said. You know how I know? Because I used to be just like you. I was too smart and too busy and too all-around amazing to care about anything other than myself and my own interests. Oh, Esther and I went to church. I believed everything the pastor said. Everything! Sure I did. Just not quite deeply enough to *act* on it. And that's what I told you while you were sitting there thinking about Larry's Lake Lounge and yukking it up with your friends."

Brad stiffened. "What made you say I was thinking about Larry's?"

307

"I told you about the strip joint, didn't I?"

"Yeah." Brad chuckled. "I'm sorry, Mr. Moore, but that is a pretty funny image."

"Maybe to you, but not to Esther. Not to me either, after a while. You know why? Because every time I thought about God or tried to read the Bible or made love to my wife or walked my mail route or just about anything else, you know what came into my mind? Those women in the strip joint. One in particular. Oh yes. She had long blonde hair and that's about all. She sauntered right into my brain and set up housekeeping. Oh, I told Esther I was sorry about what I'd done, and I was. But that did not get rid of Miss Shimmy-hips. Not at all."

"Miss Shimmy-hips!" Brad leaned back and laughed.

"I can see her now, if I try. But I don't try. In fact, I worked long and hard to get her out of my thoughts. You see, real belief takes action. I discovered that if I really wanted to change, I had to do more than sit around on my bohunkus. Because if I didn't get up and *act* like a godly man, Miss Shimmy-hips would come sashaying back into my thoughts. Just the way Larry's Lounge and ice-cold beer and probably Yvonne came sashaying into yours while I was talking. Am I right?"

308

"I guess."

"You bet I am. There's more to faith than belief. The Bible says even the demons believe — and they tremble. No, the important part of coming clean is repentance and change."

"You're starting to sound like Cody."

"I don't mind if I do. He's a smart kid. Smarter than most of us, in some ways. Repent, surrender, admit you're powerless, stop trying to justify yourself. Once you're there, *then* the change begins."

Brad was still thinking about Miss Shimmy-hips. In a way, Yvonne Ratcliff had the same effect on him. He didn't love her. Didn't even care about her much. But he sure had wanted her. He had thought about that woman with her long brown hair, dark eyes, tight jeans, and curvy hips, especially as things got worse with Ashley. His wife began to look irritating and harsh and annoying. Yvonne, on the other hand, appeared warm and welcoming. She was full of admiration for him. Just what he had needed. Or so he thought.

"Do you intend to change, Brad?" Charlie was leaning forward, his elbows on his thighs. "Do you want to make a fresh start of it?"

"Sure." Brad met the older man's gaze.

"It's just . . . hard."

Charlie stood. "All I can tell you is it took faith and repentance to get Miss Shimmy-hips out of my brain and a bunch of other junk out of my life. God healed my marriage and kept on healing it through nearly fifty years of good and bad times. Because of my faith, I know Esther is in heaven. And I know I'm going to be all right here without her. Most important, I have no doubt that I am loved and forgiven. Now if you can figure out a way to do that for yourself, you just let me know, Brad. Because I do believe we could write ourselves a best seller and go on TV talk shows and make a million bucks or two."

Reaching for his coat, Charlie took out his cell phone and checked it. "I guess I'd better head on out. Boofer will be wanting to go for a ride on the golf cart, and it looks like Bitty has left me a couple of messages."

He gave a farewell smile and was out the door before Brad could respond. *Bitty?*

"Have you seen Ashley Hanes?"

"No, have you?"

"I heard she took off work the whole week between Christmas and New Year's Eve."

"I heard she quit."

Patsy glanced at Pete, who was seated

across the table from her at the TLC meeting. Around them, the women were abuzz with gossip about the latest events in their lakeside community.

Pete was talking to Cody. Actually, it was the other way around. These days it was hard to get a word in edgewise with the young man. Patsy recalled the previous spring when Cody had first arrived in Deepwater Cove. No one had been able to get him to say much. He was scared to death, filthy, and barely mumbling anything except how hungry he was.

Now he blabbered about one thing after another. Learning to read — which had shocked everyone at how fast it happened — had opened a whole new world to Cody. When he wasn't working or painting portraits of Jennifer Hansen, he was at the Camden County Library reading books.

Pete had suggested that Cody might now know too much for his own good. The young man never hesitated to tell anyone what he thought — without the slightest hint of guile. Areas that interested him — painting, the Bible, metaphors, and several other topics — had taken possession of his mind. He was particularly knowledgeable about impressionist art, and he seemed determined to educate Patsy, as well. She'd about had it up to here with Renoir . . . or, as Cody called him, *Reenor.*

Of course, Cody still could barely add two and two. Jennifer had used Ashley's beads to try to teach him some basic math, but evidently he had spent more time talking about the merits of square cakes than he had learning to add or subtract.

A voice broke into Patsy's musings.

"I suspect she's around here close by," Miranda Finley observed to her daughter-in-law, Kim. "Ashley has a certain flair, an avantgarde creative side, but she isn't the type to globe-trot. She may move to Jefferson City or Springfield once the divorce is final, but I doubt it."

"Divorce?" Patsy couldn't help but speak out at this. "Where did you get the idea that Ashley and Brad were divorcing? Did he tell you that?"

Miranda self-consciously touched the spikes of bottle-blonde hair on her head. "Well, no. But what else could happen? I saw Brad getting into his car yesterday morning, and he told me he hasn't spoken to his wife since Christmas. Poor kid. He does nothing but go to work and then come home. I doubt he's been to the grocery store since she left. I told him I thought he was wasting away, but he just shook his head and drove off. It's obvious to me, he's terribly depressed about all this."

"I thought Mrs. Moore came back to life as Yappy so she could fix all their problems," Cody said. Laughing, he licked a dollop of chocolate icing off the side of his mouth. "That's funny!"

Unaware that no one else was joining in his mirth, Cody stood and rapped his spoon on the side of his teacup. "Time to start the meeting of the Tea Lovers' Club," he called out. "There's no old business to report. How about new business, because if not, I am planning to get another one of those brownies with frosting on top. That's why I'm skipping most of the parts of *Robert's Rules of Order,* in case you were wondering. Those brownies are good, and there are only two left in the dessert case. I would like one of them to be mine."

"I have some new business," Brenda Hansen announced. "First, I'd like to thank everyone for making the opening of Bless Your Hearth a success. It was touch and go getting ready for the ribbon cutting, but we're off to a strong start and we look forward to playing an important part in our community. In order to help with that —"

"Okay, Brenda, but what about new business?" Cody cut in. Seeing the expression on Brenda's face, he dropped back down in his chair. "Sorry. Bad social skills."

Patsy couldn't hold back a smile. If anyone had been a mother to Cody over the past year, it was Brenda. Of course, the love between them was mutual. Though Cody had his eyes fixed on the glass case holding the last two brownies, he kept his mouth shut while Brenda continued to speak.

"I want you all to know," she said, "Bless Your Hearth is planning a very special celebration."

The announcement was met with a hubbub of excitement among the group. Opal Jones leaned over to hear Kim Finley explain the news. Even Miranda, who had been looking bored, perked up.

Brenda took a breath. "Steve and I are coming up on our twenty-fifth anniversary, and we think spring is a great time to celebrate life and love, new birth and weddings, hope and joy — everything good in this world. So the weekend of the Camdenton Dogwood Festival, we're going to rent a large tent and set it up in the parking lot. Pastor Andrew has agreed to perform marriage vow renewal ceremonies and baby dedications. The feed store will bring in chicks for the kids to watch. The conservation department will be giving out dogwoods and redbud seedlings like they always do. And to top it off, Color of Mercy is going to sing."

Patsy felt the urge to raise a cheer. Her favorite group. She played their music almost nonstop in the salon. Though the women of Color of Mercy lived at the lake, they traveled so much she rarely got to hear them in person. What a treat!

Brenda continued. "After the vow renewals and baby dedications — which we'll do in small groups — families can pose for a picture. Charlie Moore has agreed to photograph everyone, and we'll give the portraits away free. We plan to have an arch with ivy and roses twined through it for the background, and there will be punch and cake, too."

"Chocolate cake?" Cody asked.

Brenda pursed her lips for a moment. "We'll see."

"I think it's a wonderful idea," Miranda spoke up. "I'll head the decorating committee. Kim and I will do it together."

Everyone looked at Kim, whose middle was beginning to pop out in a big way. Patsy could see that those twin boys she was carrying had decided to strut their stuff. Their poor mother seemed to be having a hard time of it.

"I'd be glad to take Kim's place," Jennifer offered. "I think it would be fun."

"Wonderful," Brenda said, smiling at her beautiful daughter. "Does anyone have a question? We'd love to take ideas from —"

A sudden murmuring among the TLC members silenced her. Ashley Hanes had entered the salon.

CHAPTER FIFTEEN

Her face pale and her neck bare of jewelry, Ashley walked steadily toward the group. Patsy hardly knew how to react. For nearly three weeks, the young woman had remained holed up in her spare room, hiding from the world. She had quit her job, and she refused to step outside in case someone saw her. She wouldn't hear of going to church or venturing out to eat with Pete and Patsy. Thus far, she had not even summoned the energy to visit the apartment she'd rented or start working on her big bead order.

Poor Yappy clearly had been confused. But the puppy soon learned to sneak out the back door with Patsy and scurry into the woods to do his business. The rest of the time, he stayed with his grieving owner. Patsy knew Ashley clung to the dog for comfort.

But now here she came, striding straight

into the midst of the TLC just as she always had. Though the women in the group had good intentions, Patsy couldn't deny how often their chitchat turned to gossip and even criticism. As Ashley stepped into the tea area, Patsy flashed on the biblical image of Daniel entering the lion's den. *Oh, Lord, please shut their mouths,* she prayed silently. But then Cody stood.

"Hey, Ashley," he said loudly. "Sit down at our table. Oh yes, everybody — I declare that this meeting of the TLC is hereby over. Amen."

Before anyone could move, he made a beeline to the dessert case. Miranda rose as well, and Patsy scooted her chair over to make room for another at the round table. Ashley slipped into Cody's empty place. Like deep pots of coffee, her brown eyes looked around the silent group.

"Hey," she said in greeting.

"It's good to see you, Ash," Jennifer responded. There was another awkward moment before Jennifer spoke again. "Cody told me the payments for your necklaces have started coming in."

A wan smile crossed Ashley's face. "Yeah. I need to talk to you about that."

Patsy cleared her throat as she tried to think of something to ease the tension at the table. "Charlie Moore said he had a wonderful time in California," she said. "It's good to have him back home, though."

Pete nodded. "Deepwater Cove didn't seem right without Charlie cruising around in his golf cart."

"Not to mention Bitty Sondheim." Patsy reflected on her friend. "I don't think this community could survive without the Pop-In. If I don't eat one of Bitty's turkey, gravy, and biscuit wraps once a week, I get downright cranky."

Falling silent, she looked around the table in hopes that someone else would take up the thread of conversation. If nobody spoke soon, she and Pete might have to carry the ball for the rest of the afternoon. As much as she loved talking to her fiancé, that didn't sound like fun.

"I got it!" Cody exclaimed. He pulled up another chair and sat down, his eyes focused on his treat. As usual, he seemed mostly unaware of those around him, oblivious to the fact that the composition of their group had changed.

"Mrs. Miranda Finley acted like she was going to take both of the brownies, but it was a trick. I don't think tricks like that are funny, and I told her so. She said 'Well, Cody, if you can't take a joke, I don't know what will become of you.' "

With that, he bit into the brownie. Jennifer eyed him, a grin tugging at her lips. "Cody has abandoned his watercolor efforts for the time being," she told the group. "He says the paper gets too wet."

"And besides that, Pierre-Auguste Reenor painted mostly in oil." Cody chewed his brownie as he spoke. "He started out painting on china, but he didn't have to do that long."

"The artist's name is *Ren-wah*," Jennifer corrected him gently. "Not *Reenor*."

"My books said that even when Reenor didn't have enough money to buy paint, he was a happy man." Cody clearly was so enthralled with his topic that he continued to pronounce Renoir's name as he'd first read it in a book in the library. "Reenor got arthritis and had to learn how to paint by strapping a brush to his arm, but he still thought everything he saw was amazing. People made fun of him for painting beautiful things all the time, but Reenor said, *Why shouldn't art be pretty? There are enough unpleasant things in the world.* And that is very true, which is why I always paint pictures of Jennifer. She's the prettiest person I have ever met."

"Okay, Cody." Jennifer rolled her eyes.

"That's enough about Renoir — and me."

Cody stared at her for a moment. Chocolate brownie crumbs had collected in the corners of his mouth, as usual. For once he had nothing to say.

"I'd like to hear Pete and Patsy's wedding plans." Jennifer pointedly avoided Cody's confused stare. "Have you two chosen a date?"

Now it was Patsy's turn to get uncomfortable. Pete had told her he'd had two fancy weddings already, and neither marriage had gone well. He confessed that he was scared to death about having a big ceremony and all the hoopla that went with it. On the other hand, he didn't want to run away to some quickie wedding chapel either. He hoped to have a real ceremony that would signify God's blessing on the couple.

"We're still discussing it," Patsy told Jennifer. "It's hard to find time in our schedule."

"The one thing I don't like about Reenor is that he had a mistress." Cody took another bite of brownie as he spoke. "I looked up *mistress* in the dictionary, and it's when you are married and you have a girlfriend who is not your wife. Reenor had a mistress. That is bad. Brad Hanes and I were discussing that very sin on New Year's Day when he threw all his full beer cans into the lake. Okay, I know it was littering, but I threw one in too. We did it because we felt like it."

"Cody, we were talking about my wedding, not Renoir!" Patsy told him a little more emphatically than she had intended. How on earth could she gloss over his pointed comment about Brad? Flustered, she plunged ahead, focusing on the others at the table. "You see, I want to get married in church and have all our friends there, but Pete isn't so sure. And, Cody, my wedding has nothing to do with Renoir."

"I thought you were finished with that topic," Cody returned. "And I wanted to tell about Reenor."

"I want to know about the beer cans," Ashley said. "Was Brad really throwing his beer into the lake?"

"One can at a time and also crying. When I walked over and started talking, he knocked me down. But it turned out okay."

"Brad cried?" Ashley's pale face suddenly flushed with two pink spots on her cheeks. "What about?"

"About you, because you ran away and hid just like I did after someone was mean to me. He was very sad about losing you."

Patsy swallowed as she watched Ashley carefully. The younger woman's cheeks had gone from pink to red, and now her eyes brimmed with tears.

Suddenly Ashley stood.

"I'm going to get a cup of tea."

"There's fresh Earl Grey," Patsy called after her. Then she turned to Cody. "Listen here, Buster Brown, this is a public place and you'd better watch what you say. Brad and Ashley are having a very hard time. The last thing they need is for you to spill the beans about their problems."

Cody's jaw dropped. "Patsy, you are speaking sternly."

"I think this is okay, Patsy. I really do." Jennifer hooked her arm around Cody's. "Ashley needs to hear that Brad is upset. Do you have any idea where she's been staying?"

Just then, Ashley arrived back at the table with her teacup. "You might as well know my situation," she said softly as she sat down. "I can't pretend it's a big secret. Everyone knows Brad drinks too much. Mrs. Finley saw him kick our door down, as I'm sure you all heard. We're separated now. I'm sure there aren't any secrets. Especially with Cody around."

"Me?" Cody blinked. "Did I do another bad social skill?"

Ashley shrugged. "Everyone has flaws,

Cody. If I didn't know that before, I sure do now."

She lifted her cup and took a sip of tea. Patsy studied each face around the table. Miranda Finley hadn't returned, but everyone else was gazing at Ashley with great sympathy.

Patsy had been worrying about her own future marriage more than usual. The prospect of ever ending up as miserable as Ashley made her question her sanity in agreeing to wed Pete. They got along fairly well — when they weren't arguing. Fussing. Disagreeing on one thing or another.

Pete liked to provoke Patsy. And she had trouble keeping her criticisms about him to herself. How many times had she called him a big hairy bear or a shaggy sheepdog? What if they started to get on each other's nerves too much? What if one day Patsy found herself seated forlornly at the tea table, knowing everyone's eyes were on her, realizing she had made the biggest mistake in her life?

"Speaking of flaws, Ashley," Pete spoke up, "I'll admit I've made more than my share of mistakes. I hope I've learned a thing or two from them, because I want Patsy and me to be able to work through our hard times."

Patsy's mouth opened in surprise. She knew Pete had his opinions, but he'd never been much of a talker. This public confession was a side of him she had rarely seen.

"What have you learned, honey?" she asked.

He slipped his arm around her. "Well, you can't focus on a person's bad side too much. If you do, after a while, that's all you'll see. Ashley, your husband is just a kid. He's messed up one thing after another. But he's got some positive qualities too."

"Like building," Cody remarked. "Brad and Mr. Moore built a nice room together. And Brad is also smart."

"He's a good athlete," Jennifer said. "Isn't he, Ash?"

"See there," Pete said. "I sure hope Patsy doesn't keep a record of my flaws, because if she does, I'll feel lower than a snake in a wagon rut. I did so much wrong that I didn't believe I could ever work my way past it. Still do wrong things, sometimes. But I believe my sweet Patsy will try her best to love me the way God does. Instead of writing down my failures in a logbook, she'll see how hard I'm trying, and she'll forgive me."

By now, it was all Patsy could do to keep from throwing her arms around Pete and kissing him up one side and down the other. "Of course I will, sweetie pie," she managed to say around the lump of love in her throat.

"My, my, what do we have here?" Miranda set her teacup down on the table and took an empty chair. "This sounds a little too sugary for my taste!"

"Nothing can be too sugary," Cody told her firmly. "This conversation is not about chicken livers or snakes in the road. We are talking about marriage and love and being nice to each other."

"Please!" She raised her hands in mock horror. "Everyone knows success in marriage is a matter of good luck — which is exactly why I haven't tried it again. And it certainly helps if your husband is a magazine photographer who's gone more than half the year, like mine was."

As she laughed, Patsy spoke up. "I don't think luck has anything to do with it. Faith strengthens us —"

"Hey!" Cody blurted out. "Look who just came in the front door. It's Brad."

The acrid tang of nail polish and permanent curling solution hit Brad full in the face as he stepped into Just As I Am.

Crossing the salon, he could feel the eyes of the women in their swivel chairs as they watched him. He tried not to look around. It was bad enough to get his hair trimmed in the midst of all that spray and gel and blow-dryers. No man could remain inconspicuous in such a place. Today — in his dusty jeans, flannel shirt, and heavy leather work boots — he knew he stuck out like a flat tire on a boat trailer.

Focusing ahead, Brad searched the tea area for a single shade of red-gold. How well he knew that color. Long ago, he had memorized it, engraving the coppery hue onto his heart.

Not ten minutes ago, Miranda Finley had called him to say that Ashley was at the meeting of the Tea Lovers' Club. Bill Walters — unexpectedly generous after learning of Brad's problems — had agreed to let the young man take an hour off in the middle of the workday. Personal time, Bill had called it.

Driving down the highway from the condo project, Brad knew that nothing in Deepwater Cove was truly private. As he approached the salon filled with people, he had wondered at his sanity. But Mrs. Finley had told him Ashley had emerged from hiding at last. What else could he do but go in search of her?

There.

He spotted Ashley seated at a table. Lips parted, she stared at him. Her large brown eyes were deeply set into dark hollows in her pale face. As realization dawned, she sucked in a deep breath.

"Hey," he addressed the group awkwardly. Ashley flinched at the sound of his voice.

"Sit down, Brad." Cody reached for an empty chair.

"No, thanks."

"Don't you want to be a member of the TLC? You could be our . . . one, two, three . . . our third member who is a man. It would be me, Pete, and you."

Ashley suddenly let out the breath she'd been holding. "Excuse me, everyone. I have to go."

She rose and broke from the group as though fleeing a swarm of bees. Without a glance at Brad, she started through the salon at a fast walk. And in a moment, she was running.

"Did I do another bad social skill?"

Cody's voice echoed remorsefully as Brad swung around and dashed after Ashley. Ahead of him, she pushed open the salon door. It didn't have time to swing shut before he had exited the building too.

"Ashley!" he called as she ran toward her car. "Ashley, wait!"

She was fumbling with her keys when he caught her arm. As she turned, he could see the tears streaming down her cheeks. "Leave me alone," she gasped through her sobs. She jerked her arm away. "Let go of me. Don't touch me ever again."

"We need to talk. Please, can you just give me a minute?"

"I have nothing to say. Nothing."

Ashley's key finally found the lock, and she turned it. As she flung herself into the driver's seat, he stepped between the open door and the car. In order to back out of the parking space, she would have to knock him down. Seeing the tormented expression on her face, he didn't doubt she would.

"Ashley, please listen to me," he pleaded. "I'm sorry. I'm sorry for everything I did to you. I'm sorry I hurt you. Please forgive me."

Brushing a strand of red hair from her cheek, she leaned her forehead against the steering wheel. "I hate you. I told you that before, and I meant it. I mean it even more now."

"You don't hate me. You're mad at me, but you don't hate me. We love each other, remember? We fell in love, and we got married. Please, just give me a chance to explain."

"Explain?" Her eyes flashed as she turned on him. "Explain what? That you spent the first Christmas Eve of our marriage in another woman's bed? That you woke up on our first Christmas morning with Yvonne Ratcliff by your side instead of your own wife? How can you possibly explain that?"

"I was drunk. I was totally drunk —"

"And that's supposed to be an excuse? That's supposed to make me feel better?"

"No, of course not. But if I hadn't been drinking —"

"But you *were* drinking, Bradley Hanes. You were drinking just like you've been drinking every single day of our entire marriage."

"I've stopped. Cold turkey. I swear. I haven't touched a drop since New Year's Eve. I'm clean, Ash. I'm clean."

"You're filthy! You're disgusting and dirty. You're nothing but a big pile of smut!"

He tried not to react to the malice in Ashley's voice. For a moment, he struggled to keep his temper. But he had to accept the truth. He had hungered for his wife's words of admiration once, and now he deserved her contempt.

"I got rid of everything," he confessed. "It's gone. The beer, the magazine. All of it. I'm telling you, I'm clean."

"Clean? How can you even say that? You're the man who . . . who took off Yvonne Ratcliff's red sweater. You're the man whose jeans were . . . were lying crumpled on her floor."

"Ashley," he said, reaching for her hand but missing as she shrugged away from him. At the memory of what she had seen, she began to cry even harder. He bowed his head, feeling shamed.

"Don't ever say that name again, Ash. Please. She left town, and I'm glad. It was all a mistake."

"A mistake is when I fill a saltshaker with sugar at the country club," she choked out. "A mistake is when I drop a tray of plates. Those are mistakes. Having sex with a woman who isn't your wife is a *choice.* You made a decision to do what you did."

"But I was drunk. I —"

"No, Brad! Stop trying to defend yourself. Now get out of the way before I back over you."

As she reached to pull her car door shut, Brad finally was able to take her hand. "Ashley, please listen to me. I'm not trying to excuse what I did. I know it was wrong. And yes, it was a deliberate act. Driving to Larry's was deliberate. Drinking too much was deliberate. What I did was . . . was . . ."

He couldn't hold back his own tears any longer.

"I don't know what happened to us," he said, his voice husky. He knelt on the parking lot and wove his fingers through hers. "I loved you so much, Ash. I still love you. I don't know how things got so bad. I don't understand it, but I'm sure most of it was my fault. I was lonely after work, so I went to Larry's. I drank too much, even at home. I know I did, and I didn't try to stop myself. I bought the truck. I crashed it. And that magazine . . . I didn't know it would upset you so much."

"You probably thought I'd be happy about it."

"Okay, I'm stupid. I've done a lot of stupid things, and I'm telling you I'm sorry."

For a moment, they fell silent. Brad wiped his cheek with the heel of his hand. Ashley was sniffling. He sensed movement around them, people opening the salon door and stepping outside, chatting, whispering, walking by the car, their shoes crunching on the gravel of the parking lot.

Looking at Ashley's hand, he realized how much he loved those long fingers and beautifully manicured nails. She always kept her hands perfect, and they had tantalized him from the start. How could he ever win her back?

"You don't know, do you?" she asked finally.

"Know what?" He lifted his head and looked into her eyes. "Tell me."

She pulled her hand away. "Things have changed so much, Brad. Everything has changed forever — and you haven't even figured that out."

"Don't say that. Listen, we could find a counselor, or talk to the preacher at Mr. Moore's church. I'd be glad to. I know I messed up. I admit it. I love you, Ash, and I think we can make our marriage work if we try."

"Why would I want to try?" She shook her head. "Move out of the way, Brad. I have to go check on Yappy."

As he stood and stepped back from the car, Brad fought tears. "How is he? How's Yappy doing?"

"He's fine. He doesn't miss you. I don't think he remembers you."

She pulled the door shut. Before leaving the parking space, she lowered her window. "You haven't taken down the Christmas tree yet. It's time to do that. Then you'll know how I feel."

"I saw the tree, Ashley. I know you spent

the whole day decorating it, and I thought it was so great. The beads and the snowflakes and all of that. It was beautiful."

"Take it down, Brad. Do it now." She raised the window and turned the ignition.

Bordering on desperation, he watched as she backed out. Without looking at him again, she drove her car across the parking lot toward the highway.

"Last time I saw you, young fella," Charlie Moore said, "you looked like something the cat threw up. What are you up to this evening? I've been thinking about us having another visit."

At the sound of Charlie Moore's voice, the older man's face emerged through the void that had encroached on Brad's vision. White hair. Wrinkled, leathery skin. That voice. Those words. Faith. Belief. Repentance. Miss Shimmy-hips.

"Brad? Are you there, boy?"

"Yes, sir." Carrying a sack of groceries in one arm and holding the phone to his ear with his free hand, Brad stepped into his house and kicked the door shut behind him with his bootheel.

"What? I didn't hear you. Speak up. I'm over seventy years old. You think I can understand a whisper? What's going on there?"

"Nothing, sir."

"Have you been drinking? You sound odd."

"No. I haven't been drinking. I just got home from work."

As he carried the groceries through the living room, Brad recalled his conviction that January was the longest, coldest, and most miserable month on Missouri's calendar. The holidays were over and spring lay far in the future. As a rule, January stunk. This one was no exception.

He had gone thirty days, nine hours, and eighteen minutes of this particular January without a drink. In order to save propane, he had lived that entire time with his thermostat turned to a maximum of forty-two degrees. Just warm enough to keep the water pipes from freezing. Running the vacuum cleaner, washing machine, dryer, or dishwasher would eat up electricity, so he no longer had a stitch of laundered clothing or a single clean plate. He kept forgetting to shave.

"What are you planning to do tonight?" Charlie asked. "Sit around moping? Feeling sorry for yourself as usual?"

Brad couldn't summon up any indignation at the dig. "No, sir. I'll probably watch some TV and then go to bed."

Sleep had become more and more appealing lately. When he could manage to drift off, the hours slipped by and nothing mattered.

Charlie's voice piped up again. "Well, listen here. I've been thinking about pie. Now, Aunt Mamie's Good Food in Camdenton has some of the best pecan pie you ever sank a tooth into. How about we drive over there, get a bite to eat, and then have us a couple of slices of pie?"

Passing the Christmas tree, Brad looked at the needles that littered the floor around what was left of it. He had tracked them back and forth to the kitchen, and now they were embedded in the carpet. Walking barefoot had become a hazard.

He recalled Ashley's order to take down the tree. *Then you'll know how I feel. . . . Then you'll know . . .* How had she known it was still standing? Despite her admonition, Brad hadn't had the energy to take off the beaded decorations and haul the tree outside.

He reflected on the conversation with his wife more than two weeks previously in the parking lot outside the beauty shop. Ashley had told him that everything had changed forever. Did she really mean that? Was it possible that no matter how desperately he apologized, no matter how hard he begged her forgiveness, no matter how much he changed himself, she was determined to end their marriage?

"Brad, did you hear what I just said?" Charlie asked.

"I heard you, Mr. Moore."

"Are you all right? You sound different to me tonight. Your voice is a little hollow."

"I *feel* hollow."

"I can sure understand that. But you're not hollow, boy. You're full up, see? You've got good sense and a fine work ethic. Now listen to me, young man. I enjoy your company very much. Why do you suppose I thought about you when I had my pecan pie craving just now? It's because we're friends, that's why. You are a good friend to me. Do you hear what I'm saying?"

Brad dropped the grocery sack on the kitchen counter. For meals, he had resorted to dry cereal and the occasional can of soup. Sometimes he ate boxed macaroni-and-cheese dinners. At the very worst, it was cold weenies and saltines.

As he shrugged out of his denim jacket, he accepted the blunt truth. He was worthless. Never mind what Charlie Moore said about their friendship. Never mind the sports trophies on the shelf over the television set. Never mind his 4.0 grade point average. Never mind his steady job and regular — though insufficient — paycheck. None of it meant anything.

After setting a loaf of bread and a jar of peanut butter on the counter, he carried the phone into the living room again.

Charlie was still speaking. "You are a good friend to me," he repeated. "Do you understand that?"

Brad tried to answer. "I'm not a good person, Mr. Moore."

"None of us is perfect. Don't you remember me telling you about Miss Shimmy-hips? Just telling you about her the other day put the woman right back into my brain. Esther would have a fit if she knew, and she probably does. Sometimes I feel like an old goat being led by a rope around my neck. Parade a pretty girl in front of me, and I'll follow. Sure, even a geezer like me. And now I've got to get Miss Shimmy-hips out of my mind again. You know what I'm saying? Brad? Brad, are you still there?"

"Yes."

"Well, what about that pecan pie?"

"I'm tired, Mr. Moore. It's been a long day."

Though normally intolerant of any let-

338

down by his crew, Bill Walters seemed to accept the fact that Brad was working on not enough sleep and wearing jeans so dirty they could stand up on their own. So far, no one at the job site acted like they knew anything had gone wrong in Brad's life, even though they did. He was grateful.

Now that he knew where Ashley was staying, Brad studied Patsy Pringle's house each time he drove by. His wife's car remained in the garage, though, and he never caught sight of her long red hair. He even drove past at times when he thought she should be on her way to work, but their cars never met. She didn't answer when he called and left voice mails on her cell phone or sent her text messages. Nor did he spot the puppy he had rescued from a cardboard box on a freezing night in Tranquility.

"All right, then," Charlie said. "I'll let you go. But if you change your mind about that pecan pie, just give me a call."

"I will, Mr. Moore."

A glint of silver beneath the Christmas tree caught Brad's eye as he dropped the phone into his pocket. One of Ashley's beads, he guessed. Curiosity allowing him a brief respite from his misery, Brad pushed his hand through the stiff branches toward the silvery glimmer. His skin, chapped from the cold, caught on the rough pine needles and began to bleed. When his fingertips touched the shining thing, he saw that it wasn't a bead. It was a box. A small square wrapped in silver paper and tied with a silver bow.

A gift.

For the first time in weeks, the rhythm of his heart increased its tempo. Was this a present from Ashley? Had she put it under the tree after she decorated it? Maybe, despite his harsh words of accusation to her that last morning they spent together, she had begun to anticipate a happy Christmas day with him.

But of course . . . after decorating the tree, she had discovered Brad in Yvonne Ratcliff's apartment. Maybe in her haste, Ashley had left the present behind when she took her clothes and the puppy and fled to Patsy Pringle's house. Even so, it was something of his wife. A remnant of what they might have had.

His mouth dry, Brad carried the small box to the sofa. In the silence, he untied the bow and took off the wrapping paper. What could be inside? He almost hated to open the lid. Had Ashley made him something? Or had she spent her bead money on a special gift?

Filled with a mixture of dread and hope, he took off the lid. A sheet of folded paper lay inside. When he lifted it out, he saw that Ashley had placed something beneath the note. Her diamond engagement ring.

The large gem glittered in the dim afternoon light filtering through the blinds behind the sofa. Brad picked up the slender gold circle with its crowning jewel. It barely fit over the tip of his index finger. He would never forget Ashley's response the night he gave it to her. She had burst into tears, thrown her arms around him, and vowed she would love him forever. The ring had become her pride and joy — always on display for friends and family to admire.

Now Brad recalled that he had held Ashley's hand in the parking lot outside Just As I Am, and he hadn't even noticed the ring was missing. With trepidation, he unfolded the note and began to read her familiar loopy handwriting.

Brad,
     This morning after you told me that a *normal* wife would put up a Christmas tree, Yappy and I walked a long way back into the woods and found this little tree growing near some taller ones. I think the trees might be on Pete Roberts's

property, so please don't tell him. I cut the tree down and dragged it home. Then I spent the day making ornaments. I wanted you to be happy when you came home from work.

I have always wanted you to be happy.

I guess I just wasn't enough for you. So here is the ring you gave me. Merry Christmas. Maybe it will make you happy. You can give it to your girlfriend. Or you can hock it to pay off some of the bills.

I'm not sorry I married you. I loved you once, and I thought you loved me, too. Well, I was wrong about you. Anyway, have a good life.

Ashley

Brad gazed down at the signature. This was final. All the way back on Christmas Eve, after she had found him with Yvonne, Ashley had wrapped up her engagement ring and walked out of the marriage forever. Only now did he truly understand that.

He refolded the note, laid the ring back inside the box, and put the note on top of it. Then he set the lid in place.

Slipping off the sofa, Brad knelt. As tears welled, he began to pray.

CHAPTER SIXTEEN

"It smells funny." Jennifer Hansen made a face. "I think the people who rented this apartment before you must have had cats."

Ashley shrugged. "I can't complain. I'm planning to bring Yappy even though I know the place is supposed to be pet-free. I signed the lease agreeing to abide by that rule. I guess we're all liars and cheaters, aren't we?"

When Jennifer didn't respond, Ashley closed the door. The two women stood without speaking inside the empty room. Ashley had rented the place almost a month ago, but she hadn't been able to summon the energy to drive over and take a look at it until now.

Jennifer remained motionless as Ashley stepped to the bare window. The one-level apartment building backed up against a stretch of forest running between the highway and a steep limestone bluff that dropped forty feet straight down into the chilly waters of the lake. A dense thicket of leafless oaks, maples, redbuds, and dogwoods enclosed the occasional scraggly pine. The perfect place to walk Yappy.

The parking area had never been paved, so tracked-in mud had stained the low-pile carpet. The walls wore toddlers' handprints, spots of purple jelly, splatters of spaghetti sauce. A knob-size hole in the drywall revealed that someone had once thrown open the front door. In excitement? Ashley wondered. Or in anger?

"I could bring over some candles from Mom's shop," Jennifer remarked as she moved toward the open kitchen area. Still wearing her knitted gloves, she touched the countertop with a fingertip. "She put the Christmas things on sale at the start of the new year. I love the cinnamon candles. The fragrance is sweet with a hint of cloves and vanilla. It's just strong enough that it doesn't overpower a room. Of course, in this room . . . well, anything would help."

Ashley took off her coat and hung it over a hook someone had screwed into the wall near the door. "It's going to smell better soon. I can scrub the kitchen and rent a carpet steamer. At the snack shop, we used to clean the carpet a couple of times a year.

I never understood why my dad carpeted the bathrooms. But they always looked pretty good after I tackled them."

"Ick."

Maybe Jennifer had never had to clean a bathroom, Ashley thought as she wandered into the single bedroom. "Mom says I can bring my old bed over here. I can even have the sheets."

At the memory of the sunny midwinter afternoon when she and Brad had picked out their new king-size bed, Ashley felt a familiar lump in her throat. While planning their purchase, they had viewed themselves as so very adult. It was a somber event, this premarital acquisition of their first piece of real furniture.

But once inside the store, they'd acted like a couple of children. Brad had chased Ashley from one display to another, tickling her and making her squeal and giggle. They had bounced on every available mattress until the manager nearly asked them to leave. In the end, they chose a beautiful pillow-topped set along with a cherry headboard and metal frame. The store had been happy to let them open a charge account and buy it all on credit.

"Stupid," she muttered.

"What?" Jennifer followed her into the

bedroom. "Did you say something?"

"We were like kids playing house. Wave the magic card and everything appears — a bed, a pickup truck, a refrigerator, a sofa and matching chairs. Presto!"

As Ashley tossed out her left hand in a flourish, Jennifer grabbed it. She peered down at her friend's bare fingers. "Your ring is gone! What did you do with it?"

"I left it at the house. Brad's getting the mail — except for the bead money, which Pete Roberts picks up for me — so he's got to have something to help pay the bills."

"But, Ash, it was your ring! Your beautiful engagement ring with that huge diamond!"

"Yeah." The lump in her throat hardened. "It's the only thing that was ever really mine. I don't even own my car, you know. My parents hold the title. The house and all the furniture Brad and I got for it . . . we were making payments. Big payments. But Brad had bought the ring for me outright. He used his savings."

"Oh, Ashley."

She shrugged. "He thought he wanted to go to college, so he had saved quite a bit of money from his summer jobs. He had a good GPA, but he didn't do so great on the ACT test. His counselor told him to keep taking it until he got a good score. She said he should apply for scholarships, but he didn't. He thought he would get a full ride to play football somewhere. That didn't pan out, and then he found the construction job and met me."

"And fell in love with you and spent every last hard-earned dime on a diamond ring for you." Jennifer took Ashley's shoulders. "Brad loved you, Ash, and he still does. I know you don't believe it because of what he did. But he stopped drinking. Cody swears they threw every can and bottle into the lake. And my dad told me that Brad has been coming to the men's Bible study at Rods-N-Ends on Wednesday mornings."

"Bible study." Ashley had heard these rumors, but she didn't trust them. She didn't trust *him.*

"Brad's faith will make a difference in him." Jennifer's face was earnest. "God can change people's lives."

"You know, Jen . . . sometimes I think you're trying so hard to be holy that you're not even real. We're total opposites. You don't want to face the truth about people, but it's all I can see. What was your big plan anyhow? To be so isolated that your children wouldn't ever need to meet kids whose moms had meth labs in the kitchen or whose uncles messed with them when nobody was looking?"

"No."

"Yes!" Angry for some reason she didn't understand, Ashley pushed her friend's hands from her shoulders. "This is what's real, Jen. *Me.* Look at me! The world is full of people like me. Stupid girls who sleep with their selfish boyfriends and then get married and find out that their husband drinks too much and has sex with a barfly on Christmas Eve. I'm real. You're not."

"I am too."

"Oh yeah? You got so buried in your Bible and your missionary dream that when the real world intruded, it knocked you flat. Well, I'm not going down with this punch!"

Without waiting for a response, Ashley squared her shoulders. "I'm a strong person. I'm tough enough to make it without a man. I don't need your friendship either. And I don't need your help with my bead business. I don't need anything. I may be ignorant, but at least I'm not weak."

Her fury at its peak, Ashley stormed into the bathroom. She didn't know what she would find behind the door, but she didn't care. She could scrub the toilet and clean the tub and do whatever it took to make it on her own.

But what she saw behind the door was

herself. The image in the mirror tipped her heart off rhythm for a moment. Who was that?

Ashley leaned across the sink and peered at her own reflection. Rumpled red hair caught up in a band of loose elastic. Eyes, once large and brown, now swollen, filled with pain and distrust. Lips tight with anger. Hollows beneath her cheekbones carved by rage and hurt.

The door opened wider and Jennifer edged into the bathroom. "Okay, you're right," she said, looking at Ashley in the mirror. "I did want to hide after those men attacked us in Mexico. But so did you when you found Brad and that woman together. You hid at Patsy's house."

The tip of Jennifer's nose was red and wisps of her blonde hair had stuck to her cheeks with static electricity. "You can't make it on your own any better than I can, Ash. No one can. We all need help."

Looking from herself to her friend and back again, Ashley realized how much alike they were. Young. Confused. Afraid.

But Jennifer did possess one trait Ashley had only observed . . . something she had never been able to find in her own life. Jennifer could look beyond herself. Though she had struggled, she always returned to her faith. That was where she found her strength.

Ashley looked inward. She relied on her own willpower. She believed only in herself. She trusted no one, not even God, to save her. Like Yappy the night Brad brought him home, Ashley had always felt empty, hungry. Now she had been abandoned like a dog in a cardboard box. Deserted. Discarded.

But even when Jennifer was sad and bewildered, Ashley reflected, she was filled with the certainty that God loved her. Jennifer never felt alone. She knew her Master. She was owned.

"Are you sure you don't want some help, sweetpea?" Patsy set one hand on her hip and eyed the young redhead. Ashley had been living with her for more than a month, and the thought of her moving to a lonely apartment did not sit well. "That sofa is going to be heavy. You can't move it all by yourself. Why don't you let me come along?"

The meeting of the TLC had just ended, and as the members filed out of Just As I Am, Ashley had approached Patsy with a request. Would she ask Pete if he'd be willing to loan his truck for the rest of the afternoon?

"I know he'll say yes," Patsy assured Ashley. "But, honey, you won't be able to lug that stuff on your own. I'll be glad to give you a hand."

"You're working here until six," the younger woman pointed out. She glanced down at Patsy's stiletto heels. With a grin, she rolled her eyes. "Besides, I wouldn't want you to sprain your ankle again. And by the way — you're not supposed to wear shoes like that for at least six weeks. Doctor's orders."

"Oh, phooey on him. I don't have any pretty low-heeled work shoes. I can't imagine what the man was thinking when he said that. I'm barely over five feet tall. I've always worn shoes that give me a little boost."

"I know what the doctor was thinking. Pete told me after your last appointment. If you don't quit wearing those high heels, you're going to have bunions, hammertoes, or corns."

"Stop changing the subject on me, Ashley." Patsy did not want to discuss her feet, especially in the salon where pedicures were part of her stock in trade. She always kept her customers' focus on pretty toenails and soft heels. Who wanted to think about bunions?

"You go next door and ask Pete yourself,"

she continued. "He'll be happy to let you borrow his truck. Is Brad going to be there to help out?"

"He'd better not show up. I sent him a text message and told him I needed the house to myself for a few hours. He said he'd be at Charlie Moore's until eight this evening. I plan to use my dad's dolly to roll the sofa outside. I'll rig up some kind of a ramp and drag it onto the truck bed."

"Have you looked outside? It is raining, girl. And we're supposed to have a freeze tonight. I expect it to start sleeting before I leave the salon."

"Then I'll bring a tarp. I'm only taking the sofa and chairs. Plus the table. It belonged to my grandma, and it's mine. I sent Brad an e-mail saying I would make the payments for the living room furniture. He's got the refrigerator and the truck to deal with. We're splitting the house payment until the place sells."

Patsy felt the blood drain from her cheeks. This was what she had been dreading from the moment she opened her door to find Ashley on the porch that Christmas Eve night. This young marriage — not even a year old — was about to die.

Lowering her voice, she asked the awful question. "Do you already have the papers?"

Ashley patted her purse. "Right in here."

She had decorated the large tote bag's surface with small beads left over from her Christmas supply. Everyone in the salon had admired it that afternoon. Miranda Finley declared it would be a hit with the boutique owner who had placed the big bead order. Of course, Miranda didn't know what Patsy had begun to fret over. Ashley had not created a single bead since the night her world crashed in.

"Did you sign the documents?" Patsy asked.

"Of course. I'm planning to leave them in the kitchen after I finish moving my stuff. My new address is on the front page, so he can mail them to me."

"Oh, dear. Well, nuts. I am going to miss you so much, sugar."

Fussing with the wisps of auburn hair that she had woven into her own blonde do a few days before, Patsy studied her feet. Bunions and hammertoes were nothing compared to divorce. Divorce was huge and permanent, and it changed a person's whole life forever.

She wasn't at all sure that Brad and Ashley were ready to take this step. Especially now. Patsy knew the kids' first anniversary was the next day. What a Valentine that would be for Brad — divorce papers. Surely Ashley could wait a while longer. What if she lived to regret her decision? They had made no effort to repair the relationship. At least . . . Ashley had done nothing.

"All right, I know I'm not supposed to talk about this." Patsy glanced across the room as though her fiancé might be staring at her through the dividing wall. "It's a private matter, and they don't talk about it, and besides, you know how I feel about gossip. But I simply have to tell you something."

She took a deep breath, closed her eyes, and spilled the beans. "Brad has been going to Alcoholics Anonymous meetings."

Ashley's eyes widened. "No way. You're joking."

"I swear. Hope to die, stick a needle in my eye." Patsy knew the man she loved would want to wring her neck if he found out she had told this all-important secret. Still, her hope outweighed the risk.

"Pete accidentally mentioned it to me the other day." She dropped her voice to a whisper. "He said Brad was looking at colleges, and I asked when they'd had that conversation. Pete blurted out, 'AA,' and then he made me promise not to tell. Don't you dare say a word. I just felt I had to bring it up, because you're going on your merry way without giving that husband of yours a second thought."

"So? He sure wasn't thinking about me on Christmas Eve."

"But Brad is changing, Ashley. He's been going to the men's Bible study and AA. I saw him at church last Sunday too. He came with that guy he works for."

"Bill Walters?"

"Yes, he's a regular. Tomorrow's your anniversary, Ashley. You ought to at least talk to Brad."

Adjusting the strings of beads around her neck, Ashley looked out the window. "I want out before tomorrow. I have to move my furniture, Patsy. I'm sorry."

As Ashley turned away, Patsy couldn't help but catch her arm and swing her around.

"Now you listen to me, young lady," Patsy said, hearing her own mother's tone. "What Brad did was wrong. Wrong, wrong, wrong. But what you're doing is not right either. Don't you *dare* let pride and selfishness get in the way of God's best plan for your life."

Ashley took a step toward Patsy and pointed her index finger. The words hissed out. "God does not know I exist."

Before either could speak again, Ashley turned and headed for the door. Passing

Patsy's five thirty manicure, she stepped out into the icy rain.

"Did you notice I didn't mention Reenor once during the TLC meeting?" Cody asked, stepping to Patsy's side. "I did good social skills. Brenda says I'm learning, and I am."

"Cody Goss," Patsy said, giving his shoulder a squeeze, "follow that girl. Tell Pete that I said you had to go along and help Ashley move her furniture or he was not to let her borrow his pickup."

Cody gaped. "Patsy. You're being bossy again."

"Yes, I am. Now go!"

Without a backward glance, Cody stuffed a cupcake into his mouth and took off across the salon.

His windshield wipers unable to keep up with the blowing sleet, Brad squinted at the darkened roadway ahead. Why was he always unprepared? After clearing the frost that morning, he had gone back into the house, forgetting to throw his ice scraper into the car. It was probably lying somewhere on the deck, covered with frozen rain.

As he watched for oncoming traffic, Brad reflected on the way everything in life seemed to have sneaked up on him. He had never expected to be a good athlete. His parents hadn't had time to take him to Little League games or soccer practice. The ability to throw a football took him by surprise. And quarterback? He had worked hard for the position, but he'd never expected to earn it.

Same thing with his grades. He had merely been trying to stay on the team. Yet he had ended up with that 4.0 GPA — useless though it was.

Failure to get a college scholarship had taken him by surprise too. So had the offer of a construction job from one of the high school team's supporters. How had the man even known Brad needed work?

Ashley had been the biggest bombshell of all. Brad never planned to fall in love. He didn't want marriage and all its trappings. Not for a long, long time — if ever. And then he had seen that cape of long red hair and those big brown eyes. A jolt of adrenaline unlike anything he'd known on the football field had shot through him the moment Ashley turned her head.

How had it happened? Why?

Trying to keep the car from sliding into a ditch, Brad headed for the little house at the base of the long, gentle slope. He couldn't see the lake in the distance. His headlights barely penetrated the swirling gusts of white sleet.

And now his wipers stuck. Frozen to the glass. He turned them off and glided into the driveway. Barely in time, he spotted a large black truck parked in his usual spot. He stepped on the brake pedal. His car slid smoothly up to the other vehicle's bumper, coming to rest with a kiss of rubber on rubber.

The front door of his house flew open. A running figure skidded toward him, arms flailing. Cody Goss fell against the car with a loud thud. The muffled sound of his voice in the wind made the words unintelligible.

Brad waved Cody back and pushed his way out. The ice on the outside of his car cracked and splintered as the door swung wide. Shivering, Cody had wrapped his arms around himself. He hopped up and down from one foot to the other.

"Hey, Brad! Thank goodness you're here because this is an ice storm! I have to go to Mr. Moore's house now. I'm scared of storms. All kinds."

Brad opened his mouth to respond, but Cody had more to say. In the pale light from the porch lamp, his lips were blue.

"Ashley and I already put the two chairs and the table in Pete's truck and covered them up. But we couldn't get the couch. It's a sleeper sofa, and Ashley's end is too heavy. She said, 'Don't you dare leave me alone like this, Cody Goss.' She said she had to get that truck unstuck before you got here because tomorrow's your anniversary, but we tried and we can't unstick it. The wheels spun way down in the mud and you should put some gravel on your driveway. Anyway, now you're here, so okay, I have to go!"

"Cody?" Ashley's thin silhouette appeared in the doorway. "Come back here! I told you not to leave! Who's — ?"

Apparently recognizing Brad's car, she turned back into the house and slammed the door.

"Bye!" Cody ran off into the night, his feet sliding out from under him with every step.

Brad jammed his hands into his pockets. So Ashley was still here. Inside what once had been their home.

Lifting his head, he let the tiny pellets of sleet pummel his cheeks and forehead and eyelids. He couldn't do this. He could not do it. He wasn't ready to see her again in private. Not yet.

When he had passed Larry's a few minutes ago, the lights had been on. Maybe he could back his car out of the driveway and . . .

Words of calm filtered in through the alarm bells going off inside Brad's head. *God, grant me the serenity to accept the things I cannot change.*

Courage.

Wisdom.

Dear Lord, he prayed. *Wisdom. Please give me the wisdom to know what to do.*

Squaring his shoulders, he crossed the ten feet from the driveway to the porch, crunched across the thin sheet of ice that covered the cedar planks, and pushed open the front door.

The living room was empty.

Maybe she had crawled out a back window.

With the door bolted tightly behind him, Brad took off his denim jacket. In the warm room, ice melted from the tread of his work boots and formed a pair of puddles on the tile floor.

Ashley had turned up the heat, he noted. That was just like her, wasn't it? Never mind that he could barely afford to pay their bills; she thought only of her own comfort.

Serenity.

Flexing his shoulders, Brad offered up another prayer. Charlie had talked to him about God's peace. Tranquility amid the storm. Calm in the face of the unthinkable.

Brad took a step into the room and looked across at the kitchen. The refrigerator was still there. At least she hadn't loaded *that* onto the truck.

Why had Pete let Ashley borrow his truck? Brad felt as though the man he'd considered his friend was choosing sides, agreeing to participate in the final destruction of the marriage.

Did Pete and Patsy support only Ashley in this mess? Had Pete's help with AA been nothing more than an act of obligation toward a man in trouble? Or was it merely a duty performed at Charlie's request?

As Brad crossed to the counter, where he had left a half-eaten bag of white bread and a jar of peanut butter, he squeezed his hands into fists and then relaxed them again. He glanced into the bedroom. The overhead light was off. Could she be hiding in there? Was Ashley actually afraid of him?

He thought back to their shouting, his kicking down the front door, his accusations against her. Maybe he had not only betrayed but also frightened her.

"Ashley?" His voice came out too high, like a teenager's warble. He blew out a breath. "Hey, Ashley, I'm not here to bother you. It's eight thirty. You said you'd be gone

361

by now, so I came home. Do you want me to leave again?"

"Yes!" The word came from the laundry room just off to the side of the kitchen. The bifold doors were slatted, and now he saw the light was on behind them, casting bars of gold across the kitchen floor.

"I think my car is stuck," he told her. "It slid in behind Pete's truck. The driveway's frozen. I guess I could walk over to Charlie's house. Do you want me to do that?"

"Yes!"

Brad thought about the icy road he would have to climb. Charlie, Cody, and Boofer didn't sound like ideal companions. But how could he refuse Ashley's request? Look what he had done to her.

"I'll go, but . . ." He took another step toward the kitchen. "Are you going to be okay here? Cody said the pickup is stuck. You won't be able to leave tonight. Not unless someone comes for you."

A terrible thought suddenly tore into Brad's brain. What if another man had already captured Ashley's heart? Brad hadn't found it difficult. She had been so eager to love him, eager to give herself away. With his betrayal fresh in her mind, she would be vulnerable. Easy prey for some guy who might take a fancy to her. Maybe

Jay, that manager at the country club.

"Is someone coming for you?" Again he sounded weak, plaintive. He cleared his throat. "I could call Patsy if you don't want to spend the —"

"No! Stop! Come back here, you bad dog!"

The laundry door banged open and a ball of fur with floppy ears and gangly legs bounded toward him.

"Yappy?" Brad bent down and caught the pup in his arms. "You've grown! I can't believe how big you are. Whoa, look at those feet!"

His eyes flooding, he rubbed the dog behind the ears and buried his nose in the soft brown fur. "I've missed you, buddy. How've you been? Aw, yeah, you remember me, don't you? Sure you do."

The damp pink tongue licked Brad's cheeks, and tiny sharp teeth nipped at his earlobe. "Hey now. Is that any way to behave? You be a good boy."

Brad hunkered down and set the dog on the floor. Yappy was beside himself with joy, wagging his tail so hard he nearly knocked his own back legs out from under him. He danced around Brad, leaping to press a cold, wet nose under his master's chin.

"Brooo!" Backing up, Yappy crouched in

363

the sign that he wanted to play. *"Wow! Wow-wow!"*

Brad reached out and ruffled the pup's ears. He was wondering where he had left the little rubber ball they used to play with. And then a shadow crossed the dog.

"You said you were leaving." Ashley stood over him, her arms crossed. She wore a skinny T-shirt, faded jeans, ropes of beads around her neck and both wrists. Her long hair was pulled back in a braid.

"Yeah." He stood. Yappy began to circle him, diving at the laces on his work boots. Nabbing one, he growled and pulled at it, oblivious to the two humans who towered over him.

Their eyes met. "Hey, Ash. You look good."

She turned her head to one side, her chin high. "So go. I have work to do."

"There's some dog food in the pantry. I kept it."

"Fine."

"I don't have much you can eat here." He felt her icy rejection, a wall between them. "There's bread and peanut butter on the counter. Milk in the fridge. Cereal. Maybe a couple cans of soup. It won't last long."

"I'm not *staying*." She faced him again, her brown eyes flashing.

"Is someone picking you up? Who?"

"None of your beeswax. Isn't that what you always say when someone is butting into your life?"

"Okay. No problem." He held up his hands in surrender. "I know what you think of me, Ashley, but I do care about what happens to you. If you have trouble —"

"You have no idea what I think of you!"

He recoiled. "Well . . . I'm pretty sure you hate me. I'm trying to change, but I was a real jerk to you, Ash. I know I was."

"You're still a jerk. And don't tell me you're thinking of yourself as some kind of a good guy now. I know you too well to believe you could ever change that much."

Her words bit into him, but he knew he deserved every drop of poison from her lips.

"You're right. I haven't changed much. I'm still the same man you married a year ago. Only . . . I'm ashamed of what I did to you. Embarrassed."

"Good. You should be."

"After you moved out, I started to see myself in a different light. I didn't like the guy in the mirror. I didn't want to be the man I was becoming."

"Don't bother giving me this baloney, Brad. Number one, I don't believe you. Number two, I don't care."

"So I apologized. To God."

"God?" She set her hands on her hips. "Oh, now that's a good one. Just what is that supposed to mean?"

"It means I'm sorry. I'm working to turn my life around, to become a better man. I want to earn your trust again. Ashley, I want to win back your heart."

"Well, good luck with that." Swinging around, she headed back toward the kitchen. Her voice quavered with emotion. "Come on, Yappy. Let's find my purse and call my dad."

Relief washed through Brad like summer rain. Her dad. Not Jay. Not some other guy she had hooked up with.

Brad didn't know why he felt so happy at this, but he did. Clearly Ashley was finished with him. It wouldn't be long before another man did discover the beauty and joy she had radiated when they first met. Still, for right now . . . in these moments . . . she was tied to no one else. In some small way, she was still his.

"Okay, where is it?" Her thick braid had fallen over her shoulder, and now she flipped it back. A familiar motion Brad had seen a thousand times. The puppy had let go of the shoelace and skittered into the kitchen with Ashley. Sniffling, she was searching high and low. "Where did I put my purse, Yap?"

Brad looked around. Immediately he spotted the beaded bag lying on the floor beyond the edge of the sofa.

"I need my purse!" Eyes red and watery, Ashley looked directly at him through the kitchen doorway. "I thought I laid it down out here."

Brad knew he couldn't lie. No lying allowed. Not anymore. But how could he just hand it over to her and let her walk away?

"You're always losing things," he said finally. "Remember the time we found your car keys buried in that potted plant?"

She paused. For a moment, he thought he saw a tight grin begin to emerge.

"The dog did that," she snapped. "And speaking of plants, what is the deal with the Christmas tree?"

Brad cast his eyes in the direction of the slender pine he had stripped of its bark and needles. In his lonely evenings, he had decided to remake the tree just as he was remaking himself. He had clipped each branch to a length of four inches. Then he had sanded and polished the trunk. On the shortened limbs, he had carefully rehung all of Ashley's beaded ornaments.

"When I first saw the tree, I loved what

you had done for us." He sat down on the sofa, trying not to look toward the missing purse. "The beads especially. They catch the light in the mornings before I go to work. The stars you made . . . they're amazing."

Ashley left the kitchen and entered the living room again. "You hate my beads, Brad Hanes. Don't try to suck up to me. I know how you act when you want something."

Pausing, she seemed to realize the significance of her words. Then she lifted a glittering snowflake. "Anyway, no matter what you're after, you won't get it. I have my own place and my own money. It's all spelled out in the papers."

He stiffened. "What papers?"

"The papers in my purse. For the divorce."

"We haven't talked about a divorce."

"We don't need to talk about it." Her voice was hard again, her face impassive. "You already showed me exactly how you feel about our marriage. Remember? That memory is a lot more significant than the one where we found my keys in a potted plant. I got the message loud and clear, and now you have my reply."

"Ashley, I'm sorry." He stood. "Please —"

"Shut up!" She came at him, finger pointed. "You shut up! Don't ever tell me you're sorry again. You can't be sorry enough to fix this. A hundred million *sorry*s won't undo what you did. I will never forget and I will never forgive. It's too late, Brad."

"I know I can't undo it. Nothing I say will ever erase your memory. But will you at least listen to me?"

"Why? What's the point?" She flung herself toward the bedroom. "Where is my purse? If Cody moved it, I'll kill him."

Brad followed. He flipped on the light, an excruciating glare above their bed. "Mr. Moore told me that if you and I don't forgive each other, the bitterness will eat us up. He said I have to admit my sin to you, and I am. I confess it right here. I . . . I committed adultery."

For a moment, he couldn't speak. When the words came again, they were forced out through a throat tight with anguish. "I'm trying to figure out how to forgive myself, because I know what I did was so wrong. I know I hurt you, and I hurt myself, and I . . . I know I've destroyed our marriage. But, Ashley, please don't leave this house without forgiving me. Please."

She stood opposite him across the king-size mattress they had bought. "Why should

I forgive you?" she spat. "So you can feel better? I would never give you that satisfaction. I hate you! I hate what you did to me. I hate what you did to . . . to us. You ruined it. You ruined everything."

Her face began to crumple. "Leave me alone! Get out of this house, Brad. I mean it! I'll call the police."

"Forgive me so the bitterness inside you will go away," he pleaded. "I know I killed your love. I know I ruined our marriage. But I don't want to have ruined *you*. I can't stand the thought of you living the rest of your life with this wound inside, Ashley. I can't live with myself if —"

"Fine," she cut in. "If that will shut you up, fine. I forgive you."

At that moment, ice on a power line at the edge of Deepwater Cove snapped the cable from its supporting pole. The furnace shut down. The water well stopped pumping. And the lights went out.

CHAPTER SEVENTEEN

Ashley froze in the utter blackness. As always in the dark, she felt like a child again — alone, lost, uncertain where to turn. The urge to cry out for help rose inside her, but she stifled it.

No. She wouldn't say a word. In moments, the power would return. It always did.

Glancing toward the window, she could see no light through the curtains. No moon. No streetlamp. Nothing.

Where was Brad? Moments ago, he had been standing at a distance from her — a king-size mattress away. She had felt safe. But now, in the stillness, she saw and heard nothing. He might be anywhere. He might be very close.

She shut her eyes.

Something brushed against her leg, and she gasped.

"Ashley?" Across the room, Brad's voice was deep. "Are you all right?"

"Wow! Barooo!"

Yappy. Letting out a breath, Ashley bent down and felt for the puppy's soft head. "Come here, boy. It's all right."

Gathering the dog in her arms, she sat on the edge of the bed. *Wait,* she told herself. *Just wait in silence. Don't say another word.*

The lights would come back on soon, and then Brad would leave. If he didn't go, she would call the police to force him out of her life. First, though, she had to find her purse to get at her phone. Where could she have left it, and what would she tell the police when they arrived? *This man committed adultery. He broke my heart.* They wouldn't take a person to jail for that.

But one of them had to go. Ashley and Brad couldn't stay in this house together. This was the night before Valentine's Day. Tomorrow would be their first anniversary. She had to get away from him.

Laying her cheek on Yappy's warm head, she tried not to cry. It was bad enough to see the man she had loved so desperately. But to hear his apologies all over again. To listen to his confession. To know he was trying to change himself. Somehow it was too much to bear.

Ashley wanted her anger. Forgiveness would soften her, and then she would hurt even more. If she forgave Brad, how could she move on? Rage and hurt had propelled her to find an apartment, to quit her job, to hire Jennifer. She needed the fury that had kept her going through the long weeks of separation.

"Do you know if we have any candles in the house?"

Brad again.

She wouldn't answer his question, Ashley decided. It was the perfect example of why she despised him so much. How long had they lived in this house? Nearly a year — and he'd never once noticed the candles she had clustered in each room. Sometimes she put fresh wildflowers around them. Other times, she displayed the candles with framed photos of herself and Brad. This past fall, she had surrounded them with small pine-cones and berries. She regularly lit them to freshen the air and provide a welcoming atmosphere.

But Brad would walk in the house, sniff the enticing aromas, and ask what she was cooking for dinner.

They're candles, you dummy, she had wanted to say. *Can't you see anything?*

"Ash?"

His voice again. It used to make her shiver.

"Hey, Ashley, could you just answer me

about the candles?"

"No," she told him.

"All right, but if I can't see, I'm going to stand here all night."

"The power will come back on. Just wait."

She could hear him let out a breath of frustration. Good. Maybe Brad would snap out of this repentance stunt he was trying to pull and turn back into himself. He would order her to answer him about the candles. He would stomp around and mutter, and then he would yell at her.

She waited.

"So, Ashley, how've you been?"

His large shape materialized beside her in the darkness, his weight sinking into the mattress. His hand brushed hers as he reached for the dog.

"Get up, Brad," she snarled, pushing at him. "Get away from me."

It was like trying to move a block of concrete. He didn't budge. She scooted along the bed toward the pillow. They were on *his* side, she realized, and suddenly she could smell the scent of the man on the sheets and blankets. Yappy bounded off her lap and began snuffling around the pillows.

"I wanted to tell you something," Brad said. "I quit drinking."

Knowing this already, Ashley refused to

respond. He was still too close, but she couldn't find the bedroom door in the darkness without stumbling over his big feet or his knees.

"Mr. Moore played a part in it." His voice was low. "There was no way I could deny that alcohol had been part of our problem, not to him. He wouldn't let me get away with anything. Finally I stopped denying what it had done to me. Staying dry has been harder than I expected. I go to AA meetings with Pete Roberts."

"That's nice. Now move."

"I go right after work, when I would have headed for Larry's. The people in my group help. We're all in the same boat. Even Pete, and he hasn't had a drop in years."

Ashley put her hand back to brace herself and accidentally touched Brad's pillow. It was soft, and for a moment, she ran her palm across its cotton surface.

AA meetings. Maybe Brad was serious.

But she couldn't let herself care. She *didn't* care. She pulled back from the pillow and knotted her fingers together in her lap.

He spoke again. "Mr. Moore and I have been doing a little painting over at his house. He wanted to change the walls to white because the purple was making him miss his wife so much he couldn't take it.

We talk a lot. I've got to hand it to Mr. Moore. For an old guy, he understands me better than you might think."

For the first time in months, Ashley heard a gentleness in Brad's voice. Long ago, he had talked to her this way. Loving. Kind. Respectful.

"Now I can understand why you were so upset when Mrs. Moore died," he went on. "I know a lot more about her from hanging out with Mr. Moore. Plus . . . well, he's become a good friend to me now. If he died, I would feel really bad. He's a little out of touch, but he's still pretty feisty."

He paused, and Ashley could hear the hint of a smile in his voice.

"Feisty?" she asked. "What's that supposed to mean?"

"I think he kind of has a little thing for Bitty Sondheim. You know they went to California together over Christmas."

"Bitty, the wrap lady?" Ashley was stunned. "But what about his wife? How can he have any feelings for Bitty Sondheim? The Moores were married all those years. They loved each other. That's terrible! What would Mrs. Moore think if she knew?"

"Hold on, Ashley." Brad shifted on the bed. "Bitty's just a friend. She encourages Mr. Moore, that's all. They're remodeling her restaurant, and I think he's having fun. No one will ever take Mrs. Moore's place in his heart. It's good for him to find some happiness, though."

Ashley couldn't agree. Charlie Moore should mourn Esther for the rest of his life. Certainly *she* would never get over the loss of her friend.

"There's a man for you," she muttered. "Out with the old, in with the new."

"Aw, you know Mr. Moore is a good guy." Somehow in the utter blackness of the night, his finger found her rib. "Come on, Ash. Stop taking it so hard."

"Don't you dare touch me!" She slapped his hand away and moved farther down the bed. "I thought you were going. Why don't you get out of here?"

"I'm not leaving you here alone in the dark. The furnace has shut down, and it's already getting cold in this room. Our well pump is off too, so there won't be any water."

"I don't need water. I'm not staying. Once I find my purse, I'm calling my dad."

Brad fell silent. Ashley hugged herself. It *was* getting chilly. She knew the leaky old windows would let in enough air to make the place a refrigerator in no time. The last thing she had expected to be doing on this night was sitting on the bed talking to Brad. That definitely was *not* in the plan.

This event was supposed to have gone quickly. She would breeze in, move the furniture, and beat a hurried retreat before Valentine's Day — with all it had meant to her — could begin. But Pete and Cody had delayed her by having a discussion about Patsy. At the house, the living room chairs had been almost too heavy to maneuver. She'd forgotten that the old oak table wouldn't fit through the door. So she and Cody had dismantled it, a nightmare of legs and hidden leaves and mysterious joinery. Then they had tried to lift the sofa.

"I've gone to church a few times too."

Brad's voice from the darkness startled her all over again. Why hadn't the power come back on? This was ridiculous. It always returned right away. Surely the electric co-op had backup generators.

"Pastor Andrew is a good guy. At first, I didn't think I would like him. He's so scrawny, and he has that big Adam's apple. He looks kind of weird. Turns out he's smart. He knows the Bible better than Cody."

Ashley leaned back against Brad's pillow and closed her eyes. To keep from listening to him, she tried to picture her future apartment. Jennifer would help her clean the place and get the business organized. They would set out the beads in cups. While on one of her many shopping ventures, Miranda Finley had purchased a tray to spread the beads on. It would be easier to thread a necklace.

"Anyway, bottom line — you probably won't believe me, and maybe you'll think it sounds dumb, but I'm a Christian now."

Brad's announcement lifted the hair on Ashley's arms. He'd said that as a child he hated church. Organized religion was not for him.

"It happened the day I found your ring under the Christmas tree," he continued. "I . . . well, basically I just apologized to God, and He forgave me."

"How do you know that?" she scoffed.

"Forgiveness is what He does. I didn't learn much in church, but I learned that. Praying isn't what I thought either. The way the men in the Bible study group do it, they're just talking to God. Mr. Moore says he prays pretty much all the time. No matter what he's doing, he's weighing it out with God. Asking for help. Confessing. He gave me a Bible. It belonged to Mrs. Moore."

"It did?" Ashley hadn't intended to speak

again. But this was all too much. Brad kneeling on the floor? Praying? Reading Mrs. Moore's Bible?

"Yeah, I guess she had quite a few. This one is purple." He chuckled. "You'd probably be more comfortable carrying it around. But I don't give a flip what people say about me anymore. I used to want approval. It was like I needed people to compliment me and tell me what a great job I was doing. I ate that up. It was part of what I loved about you. You loved me. So I loved you back."

Unable to respond, Ashley picked up Brad's pillow. Hugging it tightly, she pressed her face into it. He could *not* hear her crying. She would never allow that.

"I'm still the same Brad Hanes," he went on. "You're right about that. People stay who they are. But I'm way different, too, Ash."

"Yeah, right." She could hear her own disbelief muffled in the softness of Brad's pillow.

"I know you don't believe me," he said gently. "And I can't blame you. I'm sure you don't trust me."

"No, I don't," she said. "I never will, either. No matter what you do, I can't trust you. You broke your vow, Brad. We can't ever go back to where we were before."

He was silent for a moment, as if her rejection was finally sinking in. But when he spoke again, it was to dispute her. "We can't go back, but Mr. Moore told me that it's possible to start over. I think we could."

Patsy's message of encouragement rose inside Ashley. She squelched it. "Sorry, but I don't believe that. What's broken is broken."

"Let me try to repair the break, Ashley." Brad's words held a note of confidence she hadn't heard before. "I want to try to win back my wife. I want your trust . . . and I want your love."

"No way," she murmured. It sounded as ludicrous as Patsy gluing together the shards of her broken teacups.

"I've been thinking this over for a long time. And if you'll let me, I will make you a new wedding vow tonight. I will promise never to drink again. I'll never even set foot inside a bar. I swear I'll be faithful to you as long as I live."

Ashley frowned. What nonsense. It was much too late for Brad to make such empty promises.

But he wasn't done. "And I have an idea about how it could work too. To prove I'm keeping my promises this time, I'll turn my life into an open book. You can check on me any time you want. Scan my cell phone to see who I've called. Take my checkbook and credit cards. Go through my wallet. Look into our bank accounts. Whatever you need to do to be sure of me, Ash, just do it. I want you to. I won't get mad."

"Oh, Brad." She shook her head, unwilling to believe he could be so honest with her after what he had done.

"Listen to me, Ashley," he went on. "I won't go anywhere without telling you. I'll never leave a place unless I've called to let you know where I'm headed. I won't get upset if you drive by to check on me and make sure I've told you the truth. You can ask my friends about me. Ask Bill Walters or Pete or Mr. Moore. Ask anyone."

Ashley struggled to hold back her tears.

This offer was impossible. Surely Brad didn't mean it. He was too cool, too confident, too self-assured to humble himself so much. Yet he was speaking this vow. He was offering concrete ways for her to find out whether he was trustworthy.

"Please believe me," he said, laying his hand alongside hers at the edge of the bed. "I know it's going to take a long time to rebuild what I broke. I don't expect you to suddenly trust me. But give me a chance to prove myself. Let this be the beginning of a new start for us."

Ashley felt tired all of a sudden. Everything came rushing out in a flood of tears that dampened the pillow. It was as though the hurt and anger had been holding her together, and then Brad had pulled the plug. She poured her sobs into the fabric, hoping it muffled the sound.

Brad mustn't be allowed to hear. He mustn't know how much she wanted to believe him. How dare she allow herself one smidgen of faith in such a man? She was too afraid. Too scared he would hurt her again.

She had to get out of the house. Pete's pickup was stuck, but she could walk. She would leave Yappy with Brad and go to Patsy's house. No doubt Patsy would take her in again.

But this time Ashley's friend wouldn't be so sympathetic. Brad's message would make sense to Patsy. Worse, Patsy would believe him.

Patsy, Pete, and Mr. Moore were good people, but Ashley had seen the behavior of others who claimed to be godly and paraded their faith around. Then they showed up at the country club with their snide remarks, their racist jokes, their affairs. Ashley rarely took people at face value. Why should she take Brad that way now?

"The last thing I want to tell you," he said, "is that I love you, Ashley. I do. I remember how it was when we first met . . . and I know we really did love each other . . . and things were good."

He stopped speaking. She could hear him swallowing, trying to control his emotions, and she could hardly believe it. It was impossible that Brad Hanes would cry. He never cried. The only emotions the man had ever shown were lust, anger, and drunken exuberance.

But sorrow? Pleading? An offer of total openness? This was not the person she had married.

"Even if I decided to try trusting you again," she said, "how can I forgive you, Brad? I'll never forget what you did to me on Christmas Eve."

His arm touched hers as he lifted his hand to wipe at his face. "I know you won't forget. But surely you can hear my apologies. You can't deny that I'm sorry. I hate what I did to you, and I've sworn never to do anything like that again. Why can't you forgive me?"

"Maybe I can in my head. I even said the words a few minutes ago. But in my heart?

My heart would be lying if I said I forgave you. What you did hurt too much. Every time I remember it, I feel the same pain. How am I supposed to get rid of that?"

"I don't know. It's been hard for me to get past the pain I've caused you too. I don't have all the answers. And I probably don't even have the right to ask you this. I just know how much I love you and how much I want us to try again. Please, Ashley, will you give me another chance?"

The word *no* screamed inside her head. *No, no, no!* She would never give Brad another chance. Why should she? He was a cheater and a liar. Surely he was lying even now, telling her these things and begging her to put away the blame.

"Brrrp. Brrrp." Yappy's snores sounded loud in the dark bedroom.

Ashley lifted her face from the pillow and drew in a deep breath. The air had grown much colder. The electricity had not come back on, and the longer it stayed off, the more certain she became that the night would continue without it. Sleet was still pelting the windows, and suddenly she heard a loud bang. The sound of gunfire.

Tensing, she instinctively leaned toward Brad. "What was that?"

"A branch," he said. "It broke under the

weight of the ice."

"I don't like this. I want to be somewhere else."

"But God put you here."

"Oh, enough with all this God stuff, Brad. You sound weird. You sound like . . . like Mrs. Moore."

Without warning, she burst into tears again, weeping for the losses that were too much to bear. Her innocence. Her belief in fairy tales. Her friendship with Mrs. Moore. And finally her husband. She had lost her marriage, and it would never come back. Despite what Brad said, despite the hope Patsy held, none of these losses could be undone.

"Ashley." Brad moved toward her in the dark. He touched her arm and then her shoulder. "I'm sorry about Mrs. Moore."

His fingers slipped into the tangle of her braid. He cupped her head, drawing her close. As she wept, he pressed her cheek to his chest and wrapped his arms around her.

"I love you, Ashley," he whispered as the night filled with the rapid-fire crack of frozen limbs breaking from trees. "I love you so much."

Buried under bedding, Ashley lay on the sofa with Yappy snoring softly beside her.

The candles she had gathered on the coffee table had burned down to puddles of colored wax. As Brad studied them in the light of dawn, he was reminded of his wife's brightly hued beads. At some point in the night when he had been unable to sleep, he had watched the wax drip and realized he had been jealous.

Jealous of beads.

Inanimate objects had compelled him to curse and boil with anger at his wife. He had truly believed she loved her beads more than she loved him. What a fool. He'd acted like a kid, envious and resentful of another youngster's toys. Maybe he *was* a kid. Ashley, too. Maybe their youth and immaturity had something to do with all the problems. Charlie Moore certainly believed Brad was as irresponsible as a child and had berated him for it.

On this day, with one year of marriage behind them, Brad knew he could do nothing but pray that Ashley would forgive him. A hesitant reunion between them had begun the night before when the trees started to shatter. Still wary, Ashley had allowed Brad to lead her into their living room. In the dark silence, they ate some slices of bread with peanut butter. Then, her breath trembling and her hands cold, Ashley let him cover her and the dog with blankets and their heavy comforter.

Sitting on the floor beside her, Brad had dozed on and off. He had fitful dreams, waking every time another branch broke outside. As the room lightened, he could hardly stand the apprehension. What would happen when Ashley awoke? Would she leap out of bed and head for the door? Or would she stay and forgive him?

As he pondered, Yappy suddenly lifted his head and yawned. Ashley's eyes, swollen from crying, fluttered open. Brown and deep, they lingered on Brad's face.

Then she jerked the comforter over her head. "Oh no — not you!"

"Ashley." He touched her arm. "It's okay."

"Is the power back on?" she asked from under the bedding.

"I have a bad feeling it's going to be down for a while. I'm worried our pipes are frozen."

She emerged again, her hair curling around her face like wisps of cedar shavings. Eyes closed and an expression of pain written on her face, she spoke.

"I want to make it clear that I don't believe you, Brad. The things you said last night are not true. The drinking and the religious stuff and the changes. Maybe right now you're different, but it won't last."

"One day at a time," he murmured, reaching up to touch a tendril. "That's what we say in AA meetings. It's in the Bible, too. Jesus told people not to worry about tomorrow. He said God keeps His eyes on the sparrows, and He gave the lilies their colors. If He cares so much for them, we can be sure He'll watch over us, too."

"Here we are freezing to death, and you're babbling like Cody."

"Cody's smarter than I'll ever be. Plus, he knows the Bible up one side and down the other, and he cares about people. On top of that, he tries to have good social skills."

"Now *there* you could learn something."

"Hey!" He gave her a squeeze. Unable to help himself, he kissed the smooth plane of her forehead. "Nah, you're right. I'm a dolt. At least Cody makes an effort."

Her lips, pressed tightly together, were trembling. "Don't," she whispered. "Don't be nice, Brad."

"C'mon, Ash, it's our anniversary. Say you'll let me try. I have a lot to learn. I know sometimes I'll still do the wrong thing. But you can trust me to be faithful, to love you, and to spend the rest of my life with you. I'm never going to be perfect, but I have changed."

"How do you know? How can I be sure? If you ever cheated on me again —"

"I will not do that, Ashley." He leaned one shoulder against the sofa. A branch popped outside, but he kept his focus on his wife. "I can make promises all day long, but at some point, you're just going to have to decide to have faith."

She stroked Yappy's downy head. "I don't know. It's hard not to think about the past. I remember it all the time, and I'm still angry. Really angry."

For a moment, Brad couldn't think how to respond. Of course she was furious, and how could he ever diminish her rage? At the thought of living under Ashley's constant wrath, he felt a curl of despair well through his chest.

"Mr. Moore told me a husband has to learn to listen to his wife," Brad offered. "I want to know about your beads, Ash. I'd like to start supporting your dream instead of discouraging it. Dreams — like your dad's ideas — they aren't such bad things."

Her eyes grew thoughtful. "I heard you were looking into college."

"I've already enrolled for a block class at the community college in March. Basic composition. Turns out Bill Walters goes to LAMB Chapel. We were talking after church last Sunday, and I mentioned my old dream of teaching math and coaching football. Bill offered to pay for my classes — except in the summer when he needs me on the job. He said if I do well, he'll carry me the whole way until I get the degree. Crazy, huh?"

Her silence said more than words.

Brad puffed a breath of warm air into his hands and then rubbed them together. "Listen, Ashley, I want to give this marriage everything I've got. We're different, sure, but I think we can balance each other. What do you say? Can we try again?"

He waited, feeling much as he had near the end of a tight football game. Could he pull it off? Would he throw the ball into the receiver's arms? Would there be a perfect catch, a touchdown that saved the game for the home team?

"I'll have to think about it." Her voice quaked like that of a little girl on the edge of tears. "I didn't expect —"

A boom that shook the floor silenced Ashley. She glanced toward the window and then caught his shoulders. "Brad! It's Miranda Finley's house. A tree fell on it. The whole roof looks caved in . . . and . . . oh, Brad, I think it's on fire!"

CHAPTER EIGHTEEN

"Boots, boots!" Brad scrambled around the living room in search of his footwear. Yappy had leaped off the sofa and was racing around in circles, barking like a maniac. Brad found a boot and began pulling it on. "Your purse is there. Right by the couch. Call 911, Ash!"

"Here's your other boot!" She tossed it toward him as she lunged for her beaded bag.

Deftly catching the boot, Brad reached for the dog. "Keep Yap inside, okay? You stay here too, Ash. Pray no one's in there."

"I can't find my phone!" Even as she spoke, Ashley's hand closed around the chilled metal. She drew it from her bag and flipped it open. "It's dead. It must be the battery. I bet it froze."

"Try to find my phone. It might be in the bedroom. Yappy, stop grabbing my laces!"

"Come here, Yap!" She snatched up the

puppy and stood to look out the window. No doubt now — the small house next door was aflame. Smoke billowed through an attic vent as well as the crushed roofline. "Hurry, Brad. What if Mrs. Finley's hurt? There's no water! How are we going to get her out?"

"I'll use the chain saw." Throwing open the door, he tore out of the house, Yappy at his heels.

"Yappy! No! Come back." As Ashley struggled into her own boots, the chain saw hiccupped several times. She realized Brad was already pulling the starter cord. Running toward the entryway, she heard the high-pitched whine of the saw coming to life. *Thank God!*

But the moment Ashley stepped onto the icy deck, her feet went out from under her. Breathless and lying flat on her back, she couldn't move. She tried to suck down a gulp of frigid air as Brad raced toward the flower of flame shooting out through the crumpled roof. Yappy was halfway across the patch of crystalline grass between the two houses when a gasp inflated her lungs.

"Yap!" she wheezed. Curling to her knees, Ashley tried again. "Yappy, come here! Come *now!*"

The puppy skidded to a halt and looked

back at her.

"Come, Yappy!"

As she slapped her thighs and called to him, the pup bounded in a circle and scampered back toward her. When he reached the deck, Ashley slid on her knees to the edge and scooped him up.

"Good doggy!" she said. As she hugged the puppy, she scanned the burning house. The huge oak tree in Miranda's backyard had snapped in two. Its frozen branches reached upward, as though gnarled white fingers were grasping for the roof.

"You're going inside," she told the pup. She pushed Yappy through the front door and shut it, closing him inside.

In an effort to warm up her phone, she rubbed it against her leg. How dare the thing just up and die when she needed it most? This was insane. Not a single button worked. And why wasn't anyone else in the neighborhood racing outside to help Brad? Hadn't they heard the tree break too? Did they expect Brad to do it all?

Images of a chain saw gnawing through fresh timber surfaced in Ashley's brain. What if Brad got hurt? In his hurry, he might forget to be careful. He could be bleeding even now.

Straightening, Ashley gripped the deck

railing and slid her way down the icy steps. Her ears rang as frost nipped at them. She could hear the chain saw in the distance and behind it the sound of a woman screaming.

"Mrs. Finley!"

Scrambling, falling, righting herself again, Ashley made her way across the grass toward the house. As she ran, she pressed the buttons on her cell phone. "Work, you dumb thing! Work!"

And suddenly it did. The numbers appeared on the screen — *9-1-1.* She held it to one stinging ear.

A woman's calm voice answered. "Emergency, how can I help you?"

"A tree fell through Mrs. Finley's roof, and the house is on fire. Send an ambulance and a fire truck!"

"What is the address, ma'am?"

"It's Miranda Finley's house. I don't know the number." Ashley paused, gasping for air, feeling as though each breath turned to ice crystals in her lungs. She focused on the black mailbox by the road-side. "Okay, I've got it. It's 4312 Shadyside Lane. Did I say Deepwater Cove already? That's where we are. Send a fire engine out here with water. Everything's frozen. Mrs. Finley's wall is burning, and her roof collapsed. And my husband has gone over there with a chain saw. He could get hurt!"

"Please stay on the line with me, ma'am," the dispatcher said. "I'm contacting emergency services. One moment."

Ashley tried to hold the phone to her ear as her feet slipped and skidded toward the burning house. "Brad!" she shouted. "Brad, are you okay?"

A piercing scream split the air. Miranda again! Ashley grabbed the porch post and heaved herself onto her neighbor's deck. She had to help. First, she needed to find Brad. He couldn't get hurt. He couldn't die. Not yet. They weren't finished. There was more to say, more to do.

Black smoke wafted past Ashley, and she bent over, coughing. Her fingers had gone numb. Her teeth wouldn't stop chattering. She had forgotten gloves, a hat, her scarf. Skating along the deck, she paused to peer through a window.

Inside the house, she could see the silhouette of a man — coal black against a picture window behind him. He wielded the chain saw on the ice-encased tree branches surrounding him, lowering it to let the revolving teeth bite through timber, then raising it and mechanically bending to cut again.

Smoke poured from the house. The roof

and back wall were mostly gone. The bank of windows facing the lake reflected a bright orange flame that danced through the curtains and licked up the wallboard and studs.

"Ma'am, are you still there?" The dispatcher's voice startled her. "Emergency vehicles are en route to 4312 Shadyside Lane. Ma'am, is that near Tranquility?"

"Yes — Deepwater Cove is right down the road from Tranquility. Did I tell you my husband is inside the house? He could die in there! I gotta go!"

Unable to bear the tension any longer, Ashley folded her phone and shoved it into her pocket. She pulled her way around the deck to Miranda Finley's front door. It hung on the frame by a single hinge.

"Brad!" she shouted into the engulfing smoke. "Brad, are you okay?"

"Ashley?" The chain saw squealed down to a low sputter. Brad's deep voice called over it, "Get away from this house, Ash! Go find Derek Finley. Tell him his mom's trapped, but I'm nearly there."

Ashley stepped through the door onto the carpet. At once, she could see the scope of the devastation. The huge treetop had snapped from its trunk, slammed into the roof, and filled the living room, imprisoning

Miranda inside her own home. The fire now blazed out of control. Could Brad even stay conscious with so much smoke?

Ashley shivered. What if a burning branch or roof beam fell on her husband? What if the fire reached the propane tank not far outside the back door? Again, Miranda cried out for help.

"Brad, I'm scared for you!" Ashley shouted. "I don't want you to die!"

Suddenly he emerged through the smoky cloud. Chain saw in one hand, he caught her close with the other. "Ashley, I love you," he said as he urged her out the door again. "Please stay away from this place."

"I called 911," she choked out. "Help is coming."

Face coated in soot, Brad waited an instant, his bright blue eyes fastened on her, and then he vanished into the house again. As though suspended in midair like a puppet, Ashley froze on the icy deck, unable to move. Then the chain saw roared to life again, and heat poured back into her veins.

Grabbing the phone from her pocket, she scanned her saved numbers. Kim and Derek Finley weren't among them, so she dialed the Hansens. Jennifer answered. Picking her way across the road toward the Finleys' house, Ashley told her friend the situation.

Ashley pictured Brad's face, his intense eyes, his pleading voice. He loved her. He had done everything he knew how to do. He wanted to win her back.

Tears blurring her vision, Ashley slid down the sidewalk to the Finleys' front steps. She had just lifted her fist to hammer on their door when it flew open. Derek barged through, nearly knocking her over. Struggling for balance, she felt his hand grip her arm.

"Did you see my mother?" he asked, his face pale. "Where is she?"

"She's alive but trapped. Brad has his chain saw. There's a lot of smoke. He needs help, Derek."

"Can you stay here with Kim? I'm worried about her, and the twins are freaking out about their grandma. I need you to do this, Ashley."

"Okay, but hurry." She caught his coat sleeve as he started away. "Derek, it's not just your mom in that house. It's my husband!"

"Brad's a smart man, Ashley. He'll be fine."

"You make sure he's all right. Promise me!"

"I will."

As Derek sprinted off toward the road,

Ashley stepped into the house. From the fireplace, Luke and Lydia ran at her with all the pent-up energy two eleven-year-olds could possess. But Kim was two steps ahead of them.

"Ashley!" she cried. "Thank God you're safe. Come over to the fire and warm up. What on earth is happening?"

Before Ashley could move, Kim ordered her twins to run next door, check on Opal Jones, and then come straight home. After the power went out the night before, Kim told Ashley, the widow had flatly rejected any offer to leave. She wouldn't hear of intruding on the Finleys or consider going to a motel. In fact, Opal wouldn't hear at all.

"She refused to put in her hearing aid," Kim explained as she edged down onto a pile of cushions near the hearth. Despite the layered sweaters Kim wore, Ashley could easily discern the mound of her belly. The second set of Finley twins seemed as determined to make their presence felt as the first.

"Derek argued with Opal until he was blue in the face," Kim continued. "She told him she had waited out many an ice storm in her ninety-five years, and she wasn't about to let this one dislodge her. It's been

400

a while since I've seen Derek so frustrated. I'll bet he checked on her every half hour through the night."

Ashley held her hands out toward the crackling blaze on the metal grate, but as her fingers warmed, all she could think of was Brad's soot-streaked face. The fire trucks and ambulance seemed to be taking forever to get to Deepwater Cove, and she knew that even the main roads must still be icy.

"Derek's mother was nearly as bad as Mrs. Jones," Kim said. "We called her, of course. Miranda insisted she was perfectly fine at home. Now look at what her stubbornness has done. Oh, I hope she's all right."

Ashley glanced at Kim. "I'm scared for Brad, breathing so much smoke. Branches are all around him. It's like he's tangled up in that tree. Anything could happen . . . and I . . . oh, Kim, I've been way more stubborn than Mrs. Jones or Derek's mother. I didn't want to listen to Brad. All those weeks when he called and e-mailed and sent messages through my parents — I was too angry to even speak to him. I deleted every message without even reading it. Last night when we got stuck in the house together, he kept telling me how much he loved me . . . and I just pushed him away. I've been so mad at Brad. I hated him . . . but now I'm afraid I might lose him. I don't know what to think."

"Hey now." Kim smiled as she gently squeezed Ashley's hand. "Take it easy. It'll be all right. Derek and Brad both know what they're doing. I'm sure they'll be fine. You'll still have a chance to work things out with Brad."

"That's the crazy part. I'm not even sure I *want* to work things out with Brad. I've been so . . . so . . . angry and hurt and . . ." She swallowed hard. She didn't want to start blubbering in front of Kim.

"I understand how you feel. Maybe better than you realize. I don't know if you know this, but just a few months ago I was sure that marrying Derek was the biggest mistake I'd ever made." Kim gave a wry smile. "Or maybe the second biggest, after my first marriage. I know the problems in my first marriage were even worse because I still had so much growing up to do."

Ashley nodded. "Brad's immaturity definitely contributed to our marriage falling apart."

"Only Brad's?"

"What's that supposed to mean?"

"Do you think the whole problem is Brad's fault? I know he was unfaithful, and

I can't even imagine how that must make you feel. But I know from my own experience that anytime there's trouble in a marriage, *both* people contributed."

Blinking at the tears that flooded her eyes, Ashley gazed into the fire. "Patsy said the same thing. She said I was wrong to hang on to my evening shift at the country club even though I got better tips. I didn't want to accept that. But I guess she was right."

"Now you're on the right track." Kim squeezed her hand.

"I wasn't at home for my husband. Even when our schedules did cross, I was usually over at the Hansens' house, working on my beads. Brad was drinking so much that I stopped wanting to be with him."

"I know what that's like. You both start pulling back in little ways, and before long, you've pretty much checked out of the marriage."

"I didn't mean to." Ashley brushed the heel of her hand under her eye and it came away damp. "At first, I loved Brad so much. But he did stupid things. Like he bought that truck on credit, and then he wrecked it. But he's done some really wonderful things, too. He fixed up our house with Mr. Moore's help. He built a bridge for you and Derek. He led the parade to honor Mrs.

Moore right before she . . . she died. And also . . . he used his savings to buy my engagement ring. I loved it so much."

Bending over in pain at the memory of Brad's loving gesture, Ashley covered her face with her hands. "Oh, Kim, I know it wasn't all his fault. We both did stupid things."

Awash in the torment of her own guilt, Ashley felt her heart flood with fear. "I have to make sure Brad's okay," she said, rising from the hearth and heading across the room to the front window. For a moment, all she could see was a spiderweb of frost coating the glass. Then she heard the sirens.

"Finally!" she called, turning back toward Kim. "The fire trucks are coming."

"What's happening at Miranda's house?"

"I can't see it. The Hansens' place is in the way."

"Run down to our bedroom at the end of the hall. Derek told me he keeps an eye on his mom's shenanigans through that window."

Ashley glanced at Kim, who waved her off. "Don't worry about me. This is my second set of twins. Everything's normal. It's just Derek — he's driving me nuts fretting over every little thing."

Hurrying down the hallway, Ashley passed

framed photographs of the Finley family. Images of Luke and Lydia seemed to run on forever. Then she burst into the master bedroom. Pushing back the curtains, she studied the scene through the window.

The plume of flame in the sky had been replaced by smoke. Ashley spotted the red fire trucks with their lights still flashing but their sirens off. An ambulance waited near the deck. Firemen in their heavy gear were climbing ladders propped against the front of the house. Water shot through hoses into the air. From a safe distance, Charlie Moore and Cody stood watching the unfolding drama. And then she saw Brad.

Carrying a limp Miranda Finley in his arms, he emerged through the front door of her ruined house. Before Ashley could assess the situation, EMTs surrounded him. They lowered Miranda to the deck. Someone lifted an IV bag overhead. And Brad vanished into the crowd.

Fearing he had gone inside again, Ashley ran back to the living room. "Brad carried Mrs. Finley out," she called. "I saw him on the deck."

"Is she all right?"

"I'm not sure. The ambulance is there."

"Did you see Derek?"

Ashley shook her head. "People are

swarming the place. I saw Mr. Moore and Cody. Maybe Patsy, too. It looked like Steve Hansen was talking to Cody."

"Please go find my husband, and then call me right away." Kim rattled off her cell number while Ashley entered it into her own phone. "And make sure Luke and Lydia don't go near that house. Check on Opal Jones, too. Oh, I hope the kids didn't leave her and run off to see the fire."

"Are you sure I should leave, Kim? Derek wanted me to stay with you."

"Go — *please!* Go to your husband. Just make sure Derek's okay, and find out about Miranda."

Ashley dropped the phone back into her pocket. "I'll call you as soon as I know anything."

A firefighter carrying a water hose pushed past him as Brad descended from Miranda Finley's deck into her yard. Ice-coated grass crunched underfoot. Chain saw in hand, Brad stepped into the road and then turned around to survey the house he had just exited. He could hardly believe it was the same place that had stood next door only hours earlier. Shattered glass and torn shingles lay scattered across the lawn. There was no roofline. Skeletal tree branches protruded from what had been the living room. Water used to douse the flame already formed icicles in the frigid air.

"You all right, buddy?"

Brad looked to find Charlie Moore standing beside him. Bundled in a heavy overcoat and a black-and-red checkered woodsman's cap, the older man was frowning. "You don't look good, Brad. Better let a medic take a listen to those lungs."

"I'm fine." Brad coughed out the words.

Charlie's left eyebrow lifted. "Never listen, do you?"

"I've listened to you more than I do most people, Mr. Moore. But I'm okay. I just need to catch my breath. It was cold in there. And hot, too. Weird, huh?"

"That was quite a blaze."

Brad set the chain saw on the sidewalk. "When I got to Mrs. Finley, she said she'd left candles burning all night. She got pinned under a limb and watched her living room drapes catch fire. We did the candle thing too — Ashley and me. By this morning, they had melted and gone out."

"Wait — Ashley stayed with you? Really?"

Brad nodded. Rubbing his scratchy eyes, he tried to recall how that miracle had happened. Immobilized by weather and darkness, Ashley had remained inside their home. Somehow — by the grace of God — she had actually listened to him.

"Well, she couldn't get out," he admitted. "Pete's truck is stuck in our —"

"Brad!"

At the familiar voice, he turned. All arms and legs, Ashley skidded down the street and fell into his arms. "Oh, thank goodness you didn't die. Are you hurt? Did you get cut? Or burned? Are you all right?"

"I'm fine." Hardly able to believe that the slender redhead was clinging to him, Brad glanced at Charlie Moore in surprise. "Yeah, Ash. I'm good."

She lifted her face to his, her brown eyes aglow. "Brad, you saved Mrs. Finley!"

"Sure. I mean, I cut some branches."

"You saved her life! And you're okay!" Ashley was blinking back tears. "I'm so glad."

"Mrs. Finley's going to be fine too. She might have a broken arm, but that's no big deal."

"Not for *you*, maybe. You're tough."

Smiling down at her, Brad noted that Charlie had sidled off to rescue a fireman from Cody. "Are *you* okay, Ashley?" He brushed away a tear from her cheek, and his fingertips left two streaks of soot on her pale skin. "What's the matter, honey?"

Before she could respond, the ambulance siren went off, splitting the chilled air with its wail. As the vehicle pulled away from the curb, a sudden roar went up from the watching crowd. Brad glanced over to see sparks spurt from the top of a utility pole. A loud hum was followed by the blink of the Hansen family's porch light. Evidently the electrical co-op had just restored power to Deepwater Cove.

But Brad was far more interested in the woman in his embrace. This was *Ashley.* She had her arms around him and her face pressed against his chest, and she was crying. And suddenly he realized her tears had nothing to do with fear of the fire or worry about Miranda Finley.

She was sobbing over *him.*

He swallowed. "Ash?"

"Brad, I have to say something to you right now," she choked out. "It's about us. About me. I did bad things in our marriage too."

Fear shot through him like an arrow. "You did? Was it that guy at your job? Jay?"

"Customer services Jay?" She frowned. "He's my dad's age. He has six kids and a bunch of grandkids and . . . what — you thought I *liked* Jay? No!" Ashley shook her head in disbelief. "I'm trying to tell you that

409

I know I played a part in our problems. I was selfish about my beads and my job. I was mad at you and worried about our debt. I didn't trust you, so I pulled away and then I got all caught up in myself. I was wrong, and I'm sorry. I'm sorry that I didn't say I was sorry. I was too angry. But now I really mean it. I'm sorry."

Brad couldn't hold back a grin. "Wow, Ash. That's quite an apology."

"I'm serious!" She swatted his shoulder. Then she looked into his eyes and her face suddenly crumpled as she began crying again. "Oh, Brad, this has all been so awful! I didn't want to admit my part. But I can't keep denying the truth. And . . . and now I don't know what to do. I'm still mad and hurt, and I'm scared, too. I want to believe you've changed. I wish I could trust you. Today is our anniversary. If we could fix things, that would be wonderf-f-f—"

"Hey now." He pulled her closer. "Let's give this to God, Ash. I don't want to live the rest of my life wading around in the pain of the past. I want to focus on today. And the future."

"Me, too."

Brad felt the first wave of real hope surge up inside him. "You do?"

"I think so."

"You mean you're willing to give our marriage another shot?"

"Yeah." Her voice wavered on the brink of tears.

"You don't sound sure."

"I'm not. It's going to be hard. I don't have very much faith."

"I'll do my best to live up to however much faith you can put in me. I believe we can make it, Ashley. Just walk beside me. Stay with me until it gets better. Will you do that?"

Sniffling deeply, she looked up at him. "I will," she whispered.

"Oh, Ash, you are the most beautiful girl in the world." He studied her tear-streaked face and tangled hair. "Could I . . . would you mind . . . is it okay if I kiss you?"

Trembling in his arms, she nodded. Gently, he brushed his mouth across her lips. Eyes closed, he breathed in the scent of his wife's sweetness, the familiar fragrance that drifted from her skin and hair.

"Kissing you feels like a prayer," he murmured.

"Don't let go of me, Brad. Don't stop holding me ever again. It's crazy, but I still love you."

"I love you, Ashley. Happy anniversary to

us. I can't wait to start our new life together."

As he spoke the words, Brad opened his
eyes. In the distance, he saw Charlie Moore
standing beside Patsy Pringle. They were
both smiling.

CHAPTER NINETEEN

Ashley walked beside Jennifer to the front door. They had worked on a big bead order all day, and both were exhausted. With a brief hug of farewell, they agreed on a time to meet the next morning.

As the weeks had passed following the ice storm, a season of warmth had slowly slipped into Deepwater Cove. Bright blue skies and sunny days greened up the grass, urged daffodils and tulips to pop out of the ground, and swelled leaf buds. Cardinals and robins hunted for nesting twigs as they sang out in search of mates. Forsythias unfurled yellow blossoms as squirrels played chase among the redbud branches. And to everyone's delight, the pink and white dogwoods began to bloom.

Ashley was shutting the door just as Brad's car pulled into the carport. Her stomach instantly knotted. She was still committed to trying to salvage their marriage. But despite her willingness to forgive, her fears, hurt, and even some anger lingered.

From the window, she watched him gather sacks of groceries. Ashley had taken him up on his offer to be an open book. She *did* check on her husband. If he said he was going to an AA meeting, she called Pete Roberts to make sure he was there. Once he went to the post office to mail several packets of necklaces for her, and she followed him in secret. She regularly drove by Larry's Lake Lounge and scanned the parking lot. He had never once lied.

But that was only a short period of honesty. It was important, but Ashley needed a lifetime. Her forgiveness could not remove the consequences of Brad's wrongdoing — and he knew it.

For her part, she had set out to address the issues that had divided them. Because she no longer worked at the country club, her new schedule meant the couple had plenty of time together. Her bead business continued to thrive, and Brad suggested she churn the profits back into the little company. But Ashley wanted to reduce their debt, and so they had sat at their dining room table for many hours talking, planning, and paying bills. Now that their new room addition had become her workshop, she made sure she was home to greet him when he got in from the construction site.

"Hey, Ash." A grin tilting one corner of his mouth, Brad stepped into the house. Before she could respond, he swept a cluster of red roses from behind his back. It was the fourth bouquet that week.

"Oh, they're beautiful." She mustered a smile and kissed his cheek. "They smell wonderful."

"Not as good as you." Carrying the groceries into the kitchen, he tracked the usual trail of dirt through the living room. Thank goodness the man had taken up vacuuming. He set the bags on the counter. "So how's the bead queen tonight?"

"The queen is happy," she reported. "I think I can mail all the bracelets by Monday afternoon."

For a moment, he looked concerned. "Are you planning to work this weekend?"

"No. We're nearly done."

"Good, because I have a plan. Don't even ask. Not telling."

Ashley had to laugh. Brad was trying so hard to win her heart that he was about to wear himself out. He regularly vacuumed floors, did laundry, and helped scrub the bathroom. When he had blurted out a sarcastic comment about her cooking one evening, he apologized so profusely that she finally had to kiss him into silence.

That part of their marriage was going to need some time to fully heal. Ashley still loved her husband's touch, and many times each day he would take her into his arms. Brad seemed to understand how much it meant to her to be held, and every time he hugged or kissed her or even played with her hair, she felt a little more of the ache slip away. She had faith that with enough time and gentleness from Brad, she could eventually let go of her pain and experience the joy of rekindled desire.

"Oh, come on," she said, setting a hand on her hip. "Tell me what you're planning. Saturday is the Dogwood Festival, you know. Mrs. Finley is going to sell my beads and wants me to be there."

He feigned hurt. "Do you think I would forget something like the Dogwood Festival? I helped Mr. Moore build the sets for his photo shoots. Hey, what smells so good?"

"It's chili." She shook off memories of his former attitude. "But this is not how we made it at the snack shop. Mrs. Moore gave me this recipe and . . ."

Brad folded her into his arms and kissed her lips. "I'll love it. Especially because you

416

got it from her."

Ashley lingered, enjoying the strength of his embrace and running her fingers over the muscles in his arms. And then — without warning — she thought of Yvonne Ratcliff. Her hands had touched Brad's body too. Ashley pushed away from him, turning to take bowls and plates down from the kitchen cabinet.

That afternoon, following the regular TLC meeting, she had stayed late, talking with Patsy and some of the other women. Patsy believed Ashley's doubts were the old devil poking at her, trying to steer her off course. Brenda and Kim agreed. They said that in marriage, some pain never quite went away. But both acknowledged they had hurt their husbands, too. Blame went both ways. And in time, healing would ease the sting.

It helped a lot to have the support of women she respected, Ashley acknowledged as she ladled chili into the bowls and set them on the table. Brad attended the men's Bible study in Pete's shop, and he said how much it meant to hear the others discuss struggles similar to his.

"Mack's going down the tubes," Brad commented as he pulled his chair away from the table. "I talked to Bill Walters about him at work today, but we don't know what to do. I think he might be getting into drugs."

Ashley sat down and reached for a napkin. "Are you serious? What makes you say that?"

"He's missed a lot of work. It might be hangovers, but I heard him talking the other day. Sounded like he was revved up on something."

"I hope not."

He tilted his head. "I thought you hated Mack."

"I didn't like it that he was your best friend, but —"

"Not anymore. That's the past." Brad frowned for a moment. "I'm sorry to cut you off. I just don't like talking about all that happened. I feel sick when I think about it. You know — sick inside."

"I know."

Their eyes met, and she read the sorrow on his face. She reached across the table and took his hand. "I love you, Brad."

He let out a breath. "I love you, too, Ash."

Squeezing his fingers, she smiled. "Are you going to pray?"

As he bowed his head and began talking to God, Ashley lifted up her own silent offering of thanks. Praying was yet another thing that had begun to alter their lives. To Ashley's surprise, she discovered she was beginning to trust the changes in her husband. Brad was in the midst of a battle, but he wasn't alone in the war. Not only did he have the friendship and support of the men of Deepwater Cove, he had God.

Ashley's heart had begun to soften toward religion. Though she had seen enough unpleasant things about so-called Christians to make her wary, her eyes had been opened in a new way. Jesus, she began to understand, brought a genuine difference into people's lives. Patsy and Jennifer had been telling her that, but with Brad, she actually *saw* it. Her husband wanted to be a new and better man — and he was slowly but surely transforming right in front of her.

Not only did Brad's new life touch Ashley, but her memories of Mrs. Moore's life began to take on even more significance. Her old purple Bible was filled with underlining and notes. Things she had thought important and worth remembering. Now Ashley saw their value too. She realized this strong trust in God was the thing she had loved most about her friend. Not the cooking and the laughing they had done. Not the bead sorting. Not the deep conversations or the encouragement. It was Mrs. Moore's faith that made her so special. If such a woman wanted to live her life for

Jesus, then Ashley felt she might want to do the same. But not for Esther's memory — for her own present and future.

"Amen," Brad finished, lifting his head.

Ashley echoed his affirmation. "Amen."

CHAPTER TWENTY

"You know what they say about Missouri," Cody told Ashley as they stood outside Bless Your Hearth on a warm, sunny Saturday afternoon in April. "If you don't like the weather . . . uh, too bad."

She laughed. "If you don't like the weather, stick around, because it'll change."

"Okay." He scratched his head. "I don't get it."

Cody rarely understood humor in the way others did, so this was nothing new to Ashley. She patted his shoulder. "Hey, what's this I hear about you and Jennifer? Is it true?"

They were sipping punch as they waited in line outside a large white tent in the parking lot of Tranquility's strip of little shops. For two weeks, Bless Your Hearth's big spring celebration had been announced in the *Lake Sun* and the *Westside Star.* Pink posters dotted the windows of every store in the area. Tired of the harsh winter, people had turned out in droves to shop the sales and listen to Color of Mercy singing their gospel and patriotic music on a platform decorated with streamers. Those who so desired could have Pastor Andrew pray for a blessing on their baby or renew their wedding vows.

With evident trepidation, Brad had asked Ashley if she would be willing to stand with him and pledge their vows again in public. To her own surprise, she agreed and suddenly understood that it was what she wanted to do more than anything else in the world.

This had been the first part of Brad's big anniversary plan, and Ashley was delighted.

"It's true," Cody announced proudly. He looked from Ashley to Brad, who had his arm around his wife's shoulders. "You're not the only one going to college. Jennifer is too, starting in the summer. She's going to become a master, and I will be her subject."

"Sounds serious," Brad said.

"Jennifer is already a bachelor, which is not what you call a lady unless you're talking about college. And now she's studying autism, and I am going to be her guinea pig. Which is a lot better than chicken livers."

"That's for sure, dude." Brad punched Cody in the arm. "Good for you."

Ashley suspected her husband had no idea what Cody was talking about, but — as usual these days — Brad was working hard on his social skills. Along with everything else.

"Jennifer is going back to college for her master's degree," she explained to Brad as Cody set off toward the table where Miranda Finley was selling Ashley's beads.

Brad brushed a curl of hair from Ashley's cheek. "Jennifer's still going to be working with you, though, isn't she?"

Ashley reflected for a moment on the spare room that Mr. Moore and Brad had added onto the Haneses' house. Maybe one day it would become a nursery, but for now . . .

"Yesterday as she was leaving, Jen let me know that she's decided to help autistic adults," Ashley told her husband. Though they were in the last group to renew vows, she didn't mind. She had worn Brad's favorite dress and a set of necklaces she'd made especially for the occasion, and she was enjoying the compliments of friends and neighbors — not to mention Brad's obvious appreciation. Though Ashley had often thought of herself as gangly and unattractive in the past, his constant admiration was beginning to sink in.

"Autism," Brad said. "That's what Cody has."

Ashley returned to the subject at hand. "It seems that way. Jen's going to start classes at Missouri State University this summer, so she'll know more soon. They agreed to let her develop strategies that can help improve the quality of life for people like Cody who missed out on an early diagnosis and intervention in school. He's going to be her main subject of study."

"First she says she's going to be a missionary; then she's part of your bead business. Now she's going to work with autistic people? I thought Jen of all people would know exactly what God wanted from her. He didn't change His mind, did He?"

Ashley shook her head. Despite the fact that it was a Saturday afternoon, Brad had dressed in a white shirt, a pair of indigo jeans, and a suit coat borrowed from Charlie Moore. He had made reservations for dinner at an expensive restaurant in Osage Beach, and he told Ashley he wanted the evening to be memorable for both of them. With his dark hair and bright blue eyes, Brad was, without a doubt, the handsomest man at the gathering.

Unable to resist, Ashley stood on tiptoe and kissed his cheek.

"God doesn't change His mind," she whispered in his ear. "He knows everything. But Jen says God has plans we can't even begin to guess."

"Hmm. I guess that's true."

"Of course it is. She says God put her at the training center to teach her how to use language and how to handle life when it went in a direction she didn't expect — like what happened to her in Mexico. Now she has a better idea of how it might feel to be autistic — scared, misunderstood, unable to communicate well, even taunted or attacked. She said autistic people feel like aliens in our world, and that's how she felt when she left America. So, this was God's plan the whole time."

"Wow." He touched her hair again. Then he whispered, "You know, I'm doing my best to listen to you, girl, but it's hard when you look so darn hot."

Blushing, Ashley glanced away and realized they had come to the head of the line. "Hey, it's our turn."

They stepped into the tent with a group of four other couples. When they spotted the candles and the small altar, they saw that Pastor Andrew was all business. He stood on a low platform as someone played a flute to one side. When the couples had gathered, he cleared his throat.

"The union of man and woman was ordained by God," he began. "God said that for this cause a man should leave his parents and cling to his wife. Jesus, too, confirmed the blessing of marriage by performing his first miracle at a wedding. Now, in obedience to the Lord, please turn to each other, hold hands, and repeat your vows after me."

When Ashley looked into Brad's face, she saw that his eyes had filled with tears. His large hands held hers tightly as he spoke words of commitment. When he promised before God to be faithful to her for the rest of his life, Ashley couldn't hold back her own emotion. While tears trickled down her cheeks, he slipped his hand into the pocket of his jacket and took out her diamond engagement ring. As he fitted it onto the third finger of her left hand, she murmured her vows.

"And now, husbands, you may kiss your wives," Pastor Andrew intoned. "Ladies, give 'em a big one!"

Laughing, Brad and Ashley wrapped their arms around each other and kissed until the minister finally cleared his throat. Taking her husband's hand, Ashley hurried them across the tent to the white lattice arbor where Mr. Moore took their picture.

"This one is going to hang by the front door," Ashley said. "So we don't forget."

"Forget? I'm never going to forget this day!"

Ashley caught her breath in a gasp as Brad scooped her up off her feet and spun her around in circles. When he carried her out of the tent, a roar of cheering and applause arose. At first, Ashley thought it must be for her and Brad. Though their problems were hardly a secret, could the entire community know what they'd been through and how grateful they were to be starting anew?

But when Brad set her down, she spotted a billow of white lace, organza, silk, netting, and petticoats emerging from the front door of Just As I Am. As one, the crowd turned toward Rods-N-Ends, where a dapper gentleman in a top hat and tails had just stepped through the front door.

"Oh, my stars!" Patsy's shriek came from behind the lacy pouf. "Someone hang on to my veil! This breeze is about to knock me off my feet."

Ashley laughed in surprised delight as Patsy hurried toward the white tent. Her ample figure was enhanced by every imaginable doodad that could adorn a wedding gown — seed pearls, satin ribbon, cutwork lace, and bows galore. She tottered through the crowd on six-inch heels, waving her bouquet of white lilies, baby's breath, and tendrils of ivy.

"Surprise, everyone! Surprise!" she called out. "Pete and I decided to get married today so you could all be here. Where is that man? Don't tell me he decided to back out."

She halted midway through the crowd and then squealed in delight. "Pete Roberts, is that you?"

"It's me, baby doll! Let's get hitched; what do you say?"

"You bet!" She turned to the gathering of people. "Come on, folks. Let's go inside. There's room for everyone, and you have to see this. It's going to be the start of something wonderful!"

DISCUSSION QUESTIONS

The principles and strategies illustrated in this novel are taken from *The Four Seasons of Marriage* by Gary Chapman. In this book, Dr. Chapman discusses marriage as a journey back and forth through different "seasons."

- **Springtime** in marriage is a time of new beginnings, new patterns of life, new ways of listening, and new ways of loving.
- **Summer** couples share deep commitment, satisfaction, and security in each other's love.
- **Fall** brings a sense of unwanted change, and nagging emptiness appears.
- **Winter** means difficulty. Marriage is harder in this season of cold silence and bitter winds.

1. In *Winter Turns to Spring,* which season of the year is it in Deepwater Cove, Missouri? Which season are Brad and Ashley Hanes experiencing in their marriage? How can you tell?

2. During the Bible study starting on p. 77, the men discuss their marriages and other relationships. Which season are Brenda and Steve Hansen in? Which season are Kim and Derek Finley in? How is Charlie feeling about Esther? What does he think of Bitty?

3. Have you ever had a mentor to help you learn a skill or in some other way? Who is Brad's mentor? Who is Ashley's mentor? How has each of these mentors influenced the young couple? Can you think of anyone you could mentor?

4. Strategy 1 in *The Four Seasons of Marriage* challenges couples to deal with past failures. Failure alone will not destroy a marriage, but unconfessed and unforgiven failure will. Couples are urged to identify past failures, to confess and repent, and finally to forgive. How has Brad failed Ashley? How does Ashley fail Brad? When does each of them identify their failure?

When does each confess it? When do they forgive each other? How do Brad and Ashley deal with disappointments and failures at the start of the story? How do they handle them later in the book?

5. Strategy 2 in *The Four Seasons of Marriage* reminds couples of the importance of choosing a winning attitude. Dr. Chapman claims that a negative, critical attitude pushes you toward the coldness of winter, whereas a positive attitude, which looks for the best in your spouse and affirms it, leads to the warmth of spring and summer. At the beginning of the book, what evidence do you see that Brad and Ashley have allowed their attitudes to become negative and critical? What helps Brad begin to notice Ashley's desirable qualities? When does she begin to be able to see her husband's attractive attributes again?

6. Strategy 3 in *The Four Seasons of Marriage* encourages couples to discover and speak each other's primary love language. The five love languages are (1) words of affirmation, (2) acts of service, (3) receiving gifts, (4) physical touch, and (5) quality time. What is Brad's love language?

How does he express it? What is Ashley's love language? How does she express it? (See pages 27, 30, 108, 123, 222, and 416.)

7. Strategy 5 in *The Four Seasons of Marriage* urges couples to discover the joy of helping each other succeed. Practical ways to do that include (1) offering encouraging words, (2) taking supportive action, (3) providing emotional support, and (4) expressing respect for your spouse. What are Ashley's dreams and goals? In what ways does Brad learn how to help her succeed? What are Brad's goals? What are some ways Ashley learns to help him succeed?

8. Strategy 6 in *The Four Seasons of Marriage* encourages couples to learn to maximize their differences. In God's plan, differences are designed to be complementary, not to cause conflicts. Practical ways to maximize differences include (1) identifying your differences, (2) looking for assets in your differences, (3) learning from your differences, (4) replacing condemnation with affirmation, and (5) discovering a plan for maximizing your differences. In this novel, what are some of the differ-

ences between Brad and Ashley in personality? in desires? in their needs? By the end of the book, what steps have they begun to take to learn how to make the most of the other's uniqueness?

9. If you could tell the end of each character's personal story, what would you say about Patsy and Pete? Brenda and Steve? Kim and Derek? Brad and Ashley? Charlie? Miranda? Cody? Jennifer? Bitty?

ABOUT THE AUTHORS

Catherine Palmer lives in Missouri with her husband, Tim, and sons, Geoffrey and Andrei. She is a graduate of Southwest Baptist University and holds a master's degree in English from Baylor University. Her first book was published in 1988. Since then she has published over forty novels and won numerous awards for her writing, including the Christy Award — the highest honor in Christian fiction — in 2001 for *A Touch of Betrayal.* In 2004, she was given the Career Achievement Award for Inspirational Romance by *Romantic Times BOOKreviews* magazine. More than 2 million copies of Catherine's novels are currently in print.

Dr. Gary Chapman is the author of *The Four Seasons of Marriage,* the perennial best seller *The Five Love Languages* (over 4 million copies sold), and numerous other marriage and family books. He is a senior associate pastor, an internationally known speaker, and the host of *A Love Language Minute,* a syndicated radio program heard on more than 200 stations across North America. He and his wife, Karolyn, live in North Carolina.

The employees of Thorndike Press hope you have enjoyed this Large Print book. All our Thorndike, Wheeler, and Kennebec Large Print titles are designed for easy reading, and all our books are made to last. Other Thorndike Press Large Print books are available at your library, through selected bookstores, or directly from us.

For information about titles, please call:
  (800) 223-1244

or visit our Web site at:
  http://gale.cengage.com/thorndike

To share your comments, please write:
  Publisher
  Thorndike Press
  295 Kennedy Memorial Drive
  Waterville, ME 04901